ONCE SHUNNED

BLAKE PIERCE

Blake Pierce is author of the bestselling RILEY PAGE mystery series, which includes fifteen books (and counting). Blake Pierce is also the author of the MACKENZIE WHITE mystery series, comprising nine books (and counting); of the AVERY BLACK mystery series, comprising six books; of the KERI LOCKE mystery series, comprising five books; of the MAKING OF RILEY PAIGE mystery series, comprising three books (and counting); of the KATE WISE mystery series, comprising four books (and counting); of the CHLOE FINE psychological suspense mystery, comprising three books (and counting); and of the JESSE HUNT psychological suspense thriller series, comprising three books (and counting).

ONCE GONE (a Riley Paige Mystery—Book #1), BEFORE HE KILLS (A Mackenzie White Mystery—Book 1), CAUSE TO KILL (An Avery Black Mystery—Book 1), A TRACE OF DEATH (A Keri Locke Mystery—Book 1), and WATCHING (The Making of Riley Paige—Book 1), are each available as a free download on Amazon!

An avid reader and lifelong fan of the mystery and thriller genres, Blake loves to hear from you, so please feel free to visit www.blakepierceauthor.com to learn more and stay in touch.

BOOKS BY BLAKE PIERCE

A JESSIE HUNT PSYCHOLOGICAL SUSPENSE SERIES
THE PERFECT WIFE (Book #1)
THE PERFECT BLOCK (Book #2)
THE PERFECT HOUSE (Book #3)
THE PERFECT SMILE (Book #4)

CHLOE FINE PSYCHOLOGICAL SUSPENSE SERIES
NEXT DOOR (Book #1)
A NEIGHBOR'S LIE (Book #2)
CUL DE SAC (Book #3)
SILENT NEIGHBOR (Book #4)

KATE WISE MYSTERY SERIES
IF SHE KNEW (Book #1)
IF SHE SAW (Book #2)
IF SHE RAN (Book #3)
IF SHE HID (Book #4)
IF SHE FLED (Book #5)

THE MAKING OF RILEY PAIGE SERIES
WATCHING (Book #1)
WAITING (Book #2)
LURING (Book #3)
TAKING (Book #4)

RILEY PAIGE MYSTERY SERIES
ONCE GONE (Book #1)
ONCE TAKEN (Book #2)
ONCE CRAVED (Book #3)
ONCE LURED (Book #4)
ONCE HUNTED (Book #5)
ONCE PINED (Book #6)
ONCE FORSAKEN (Book #7)
ONCE COLD (Book #8)
ONCE STALKED (Book #9)
ONCE LOST (Book #10)
ONCE BURIED (Book #11)
ONCE BOUND (Book #12)
ONCE TRAPPED (Book #13)
ONCE DORMANT (Book #14)
ONCE SHUNNED (Book #15)
ONCE MISSED (Book #16)

MACKENZIE WHITE MYSTERY SERIES
BEFORE HE KILLS (Book #1)
BEFORE HE SEES (Book #2)
BEFORE HE COVETS (Book #3)
BEFORE HE TAKES (Book #4)
BEFORE HE NEEDS (Book #5)
BEFORE HE FEELS (Book #6)
BEFORE HE SINS (Book #7)
BEFORE HE HUNTS (Book #8)
BEFORE HE PREYS (Book #9)
BEFORE HE LONGS (Book #10)

BEFORE HE LAPSES (Book #11)
BEFORE HE ENVIES (Book #12)

AVERY BLACK MYSTERY SERIES
CAUSE TO KILL (Book #1)
CAUSE TO RUN (Book #2)
CAUSE TO HIDE (Book #3)
CAUSE TO FEAR (Book #4)
CAUSE TO SAVE (Book #5)
CAUSE TO DREAD (Book #6)

KERI LOCKE MYSTERY SERIES
A TRACE OF DEATH (Book #1)
A TRACE OF MUDER (Book #2)
A TRACE OF VICE (Book #3)
A TRACE OF CRIME (Book #4)
A TRACE OF HOPE (Book #5)

ONCE SHUNNED

(A Riley Paige Mystery—Book 15)

BLAKE PIERCE

Copyright © 2019 by Blake Pierce. All rights reserved. Except as permitted under the U.S. Copyright Act of 1976, no part of this publication may be reproduced, distributed or transmitted in any form or by any means, or stored in a database or retrieval system, without the prior permission of the author. This ebook is licensed for your personal enjoyment only. This ebook may not be re-sold or given away to other people. If you would like to share this book with another person, please purchase an additional copy for each recipient. If you're reading this book and did not purchase it, or it was not purchased for your use only, then please return it and purchase your own copy. Thank you for respecting the hard work of this author. This is a work of fiction. Names, characters, businesses, organizations, places, events, and incidents either are the product of the author's imagination or are used fictionally. Any resemblance to actual persons, living or dead, is entirely coincidental. Jacket image Copyright sahachatz used under license from Shutterstock.com.

Table of Contents

Prologue ·xi
Chapter One · 1
Chapter Two · 6
Chapter Three · 13
Chapter Four · 17
Chapter Five · 23
Chapter Six · 30
Chapter Seven · 36
Chapter Eight · 42
Chapter Nine · 47
Chapter Ten · 58
Chapter Eleven · 64
Chapter Twelve · 69
Chapter Thirteen · 77
Chapter Fourteen · 84
Chapter Fifteen · 90
Chapter Sixteen · 96
Chapter Seventeen · 102
Chapter Eighteen · 109
Chapter Nineteen · 116
Chapter Twenty · 124
Chapter Twenty One · 131
Chapter Twenty Two · 138
Chapter Twenty Three · 150

Chapter Twenty Four · 155
Chapter Twenty Five · 164
Chapter Twenty Six · 172
Chapter Twenty Seven · 177
Chapter Twenty Eight · 184
Chapter Twenty Nine · 189
Chapter Thirty · 193
Chapter Thirty One · 200
Chapter Thirty Two · 205
Chapter Thirty Three · 212
Chapter Thirty Four · 218

Prologue

Robin's eyes snapped open.

She found herself lying wide awake in her bed. She thought at first she'd been awakened by a noise coming from somewhere in her little house.

Breaking glass?

But as she lay there listening for a moment, she heard nothing except the comforting rumble of the furnace in the basement.

Surely she'd just imagined the sound.

Nothing to worry about, she thought.

But as she turned on her side to try to get back to sleep, she felt a sudden sharp pain in her left leg.

This again, Robin thought with a sigh.

She switched on the lamp on the nightstand and pulled away the covers.

She no longer felt surprised to see that she had no left leg. She'd gotten used to that months ago. The leg had been amputated above the knee after her bones were crushed to a pulp in a terrible car accident last year.

But the pain was plenty real—a cluster of throbbing, cramping, and burning sensations.

She sat up in bed and stared at the stump under her nightgown. She'd suffered from phantom limb pain like this ever since the amputation, mostly at night when she was trying to sleep.

She looked at the clock on the nightstand and saw that it was four o'clock in the morning. She let out a groan of discouragement. She was often awakened by the pain at this hour or earlier, and she knew there was no chance of going back to sleep while this sensation was tormenting her.

She considered reaching under the bed for her mirror box, a therapy device that often helped her through episodes like this. It involved slipping the stump into the end of a long, prism-shaped box with a mirror on one side, so that her remaining leg cast a reflection. The mirror box created the illusion that she still had both of her legs. It was a weird but effective technique for diminishing or even getting rid of the phantom pain.

She'd watch the reflection while manipulating her remaining leg, clenching and unclenching the muscles in her feet, toes, and calves, as she tricked her brain into believing that she still had both legs. By imagining that she was controlling the missing leg, she could often work out the pain and cramping she felt there.

But it didn't always work. It required a level of meditative concentration that she couldn't always attain. And she knew from experience she had little chance of success just after waking up in the early morning hours.

I might as well get up and get some work done, she thought.

She briefly considered putting on the prosthetic leg that she kept beside her bed. That would mean stretching a nylon gel liner over her stump, pulling a couple of socks over the liner to compensate for the shrinkage of her stump, then fastening the prosthesis into place, putting her weight on it until she felt it pop fully into place.

It hardly seemed worth the trouble right now—especially if she got lucky and the pain faded on its own and she could go back to bed and get some more sleep.

Instead, she pulled on her bathrobe, reached for her elbow crutches, slipped her wrists through the cuffs and gripped the handgrips, then hobbled out of the bedroom into her kitchen.

A pile of papers awaited her there on the Formica-topped table.

She'd brought home a huge bundle of poems and short stories to read—submissions for *Sea Surge,* the literary magazine where she worked as the assistant editor. She'd read more than half of the pieces last night before she'd gone to bed, selecting just a few that might be worthy of publication while setting the many others aside for rejection.

Now she skimmed through a batch of five especially bad poems by a remarkably untalented writer, the sort of greeting-card verses that the magazine too often received. She laughed a little as she plopped the poems onto the rejection pile.

The next batch was altogether different, but also typical of the sort of thing she often had to wade through while sorting through submissions. These poems immediately struck her as dry, bloodless, obscure, and pretentious. As she tried to make some sense of them, her mind started wandering, and she found herself thinking about how she'd wound up living alone in this cheap but comfortable little rented house.

It was sad to remember how her marriage had broken up early this year. Shortly after the accident and the amputation, her husband, Duane, had been attentive, caring, and supportive. But as time went on, he'd become more and more distant until he'd pretty much stopped showing her any intimacy or affection.

Although Duane wouldn't admit it, Robin had realized that he simply didn't find her physically attractive anymore.

She sighed as she remembered how wildly in love they'd been during the first four years of their marriage.

Her throat tightened as she wondered whether she'd ever experience that kind of happiness again. But she knew she was still an attractive, charming, intelligent woman. Surely there was a wonderful man out there who could see her as a whole person, not merely as an amputee.

Still, the shallowness of Duane's love for her had been a blow to her self-confidence and to her faith in men in general. It was hard not to feel bitter toward her ex-husband. She reminded herself as she often did...

He did the best he could.

At least their divorce had been amicable and they still remained friends.

Her ears perked up at a familiar sound outside—the approaching garbage truck. She smiled as she looked forward to a little ritual she'd developed on such sleepless mornings.

She got up from the table, put on the crutches, hobbled over to the living room window, and opened the curtains.

The truck was pulling up in front of her own house now, and the huge robotic arm clamped onto her bin and lifted it and dumped its contents into the truck. And sure enough, walking alongside the truck was an odd young man.

As always, Robin found something endearingly earnest about him as he followed the truck on its way, gazing attentively in all directions as if keeping some sort of lookout.

She figured he must work for the town's sanitation department, although she wasn't sure just what his job could be. He didn't seem to have anything to do except walk along and make sure the big machine did its job and didn't drop any stray pieces of garbage.

As she always did when she saw him out there on the lighted street, she smiled, took an arm out of a cuff, and waved at him. He looked straight back at her, as he always did. She found it odd that he never waved back, just stood there with his arms at his sides returning her gaze.

But this time he did something he'd never done before.

He lifted his arm and pointed in her direction.

What's he pointing at? she wondered.

Then she felt a chill as she remembered the moment when she'd woken up…

I thought I heard a sound.

She'd thought it might be breaking glass.

And now she realized…

He's pointing at something behind me.

Before she could turn around and look, she felt a powerful hand seize her right shoulder.

Robin froze with fear.

She felt a sudden deep pain as something sharp plunged into her ear, and the world around her quickly dissolved.

In another moment she felt nothing at all.

Chapter One

The moment Riley plopped down on the sofa in the family room and kicked off her shoes, the doorbell rang. She groaned softly. She figured it was someone promoting a cause, wanting her to sign a petition or write a check or something like that.

Not what I need right now.

She'd just dropped off her daughters, April and Jilly, for their first day of school. She'd been looking forward to relaxing for a while.

Just then she heard Gabriela, her Guatemalan housekeeper, call out to her from the kitchen…

"*No te muevas, señora.* I'll get the door."

As she listened to Gabriela's footsteps heading for the front door, Riley leaned back and propped her feet up on the coffee table.

Then she heard Gabriela chattering cheerfully with the person at the door.

A visitor? Riley wondered.

Riley scrambled to put her shoes back on as she heard approaching footsteps.

When Gabriela escorted the visitor into the room, Riley was surprised and pleased to see who it was.

It was Blaine Hildreth, her handsome boyfriend.

Or is he my fiancé?

These days she didn't know for sure, and apparently neither did Blaine. A couple of weeks ago he had more or less proposed to her, then just last week he had said he wanted to take things slowly. She hadn't seen him for a few days now, and she hadn't expected him to show up this morning.

As Riley started to rise from the sofa, Blaine said, "Please, don't get up. I'll join you."

Blaine sat down beside her and relaxed against the elderly family room sofa. Riley grinned and kicked her shoes off again.

With a slight laugh, Blaine kicked his own shoes off, and they both propped their feet up on the coffee table.

Being so comfortable with him felt really nice to Riley, even if she wasn't quite sure where things stood in their relationship.

"How's your morning been?" Blaine asked.

"OK," Riley said. "I just dropped the girls off at school."

"Yeah, I just dropped off Crystal too."

As always, Riley could hear a note of affection whenever Blaine mentioned his sixteen-year-old daughter's name. She liked that about him.

Then with a laugh Blaine added, "She seemed pretty anxious for me to drive away once we got there. I guess she wanted me to get out of sight of her friends."

Riley laughed as well.

"It's the same with April," she said. "Kids seem to be embarrassed to have their parents around at that age. Well, starting tomorrow, mine will be taking a bus."

"Mine too."

Blaine put his hands behind his head and leaned back and heaved a deep sigh.

"Crystal will be driving soon," he said.

"So will April," Riley said. "I guess she can apply for her license in November. I'm not sure how I feel about that."

"Me neither. Especially since teaching Crystal to drive has made me a nervous wreck."

Riley felt a pang of guilt.

She said, "I'm afraid I haven't spent much time teaching April. Hardly any time, really. She's mostly had to make do with driver's training at school."

Blaine shrugged and said, "Do you want me to spend some time teaching her?"

Riley winced a little. She knew that Blaine managed to be more of a hands-on parent than she seemed capable of being. Her work with the BAU kept tugging her away from the usual mother-daughter routines, and she felt bad about that.

Still, it was kind of Blaine to offer to help out, and she knew she mustn't feel jealous if he spent more time with April than she could. After all, he might wind up being April's father before too long. It would be great for April and Jilly to have a dad who gave them real attention. That would be more than Riley's ex-husband, Ryan, had ever done.

"That would be nice," she said. "Thanks."

Gabriela came into the living room carrying a tray. The stout woman deftly steered her steps as Jilly's small, big-eared dog, Darby, and April's rapidly growing black-and-white kitten, Marbles, scampered around her feet. Then Gabriela set the tray down on the coffee table in front of them.

"I hope you both are in the mood for coffee and *champurradas*."

"*Champurradas!*" Blaine said with pleasure. "What a treat!"

As Gabriela poured two cups of coffee, Riley reached for one of the crisp, buttery cookies rolled in sesame seeds. The *champurradas* were freshly baked—and, of course, absolutely delicious.

Just as Gabriela turned to head back to the kitchen, Blaine said, "Gabriela, won't you join us?"

Gabriela smiled. *"Por supuesto. Gracias."*

She went to the kitchen to fetch another cup, then came back, poured herself some coffee, and sat in a chair near Riley and Blaine.

Blaine started chattering away with Gabriela, half in English and half in Spanish, asking her about her *champurrada* recipe. As a master chef and the owner of an upscale restaurant, Blaine was always interested in hearing Gabriela's culinary secrets. As usual, Gabriela coyly resisted saying much at first, but she finally gave him all the details about how to make the exquisite Guatemalan cookies.

Riley smiled and listened as Blaine and Gabriela went on to discuss other recipes. She enjoyed hearing them talk like this. She thought it was remarkable how at home the three of them were together.

Riley searched in her mind for the word to describe how things felt right here and now. Then it came to her.

Cozy.

Yes, that was it. Here she and Blaine were, lounging shoeless on the couch, feeling thoroughly cozy together.

Then Riley felt a bit wistful as she realized something.

One thing the situation was *not* was romantic.

At the moment, Blaine hardly seemed like the passionate lover she'd sometimes known him to be. Of course, those romantic moments had been few and far between. Even when they had spent two weeks in a nice beach house this summer, they'd slept in separate rooms on account of their children.

Riley wondered…

Is this how things will stay between us if we get married?

Riley stifled a sigh at the thought that they were already acting like an old married couple. Then she smiled as she considered…

Maybe there's nothing wrong with this.

After all, she was forty-one years old. Maybe it was time to put passionate romance behind her. Maybe it was time to settle down to coziness and comfort. And at the moment, that possibility really seemed OK.

Still, she wondered…

Is marriage really in the cards for Blaine and me?

She wished they could make a decision one way or the other.

Riley's thoughts were interrupted by her ringing cell phone.

Her heart sank a little as she saw that the call was from her longtime BAU partner, Bill Jeffreys. As fond as she was of Bill, she felt sure that this wasn't just a friendly call.

When she took the call, Bill said, "Riley, I just got a call from Chief Meredith. He wants to see you and me and Jenn Roston in his office immediately."

"What's going on?" Riley asked.

"There have been a couple of murders up in Connecticut. Meredith says it looks like a serial. I don't know any details myself just yet."

"I'll be right there," Riley said, ending the call.

She saw that both Blaine and Gabriela were looking at her with concern.

Blaine asked, "Is it a new murder case?"

"It looks like it," Riley said, putting her shoes back on. "I'll probably head up to Connecticut right away. I might be gone for a while."

Gabriela said, "*Ten cuidado,* Señora Riley."

Blaine nodded in agreement and said, "Yes, please be careful."

Riley kissed Blaine lightly and headed on out of the house. Her go-bag was already packed and ready in the car, so she didn't need to make any further preparations.

She felt a surge of anticipation. She knew that she was about to step out of a world of coziness and comfort into a much-too-familiar realm of darkness and evil. A world inhabited by monsters.

The story of my life, she thought with a bitter sigh.

Chapter Two

Riley felt a sharp tingle of urgency in the air when she walked into Special Agent in Charge Brent Meredith's office in the BAU building. The daunting, broad-framed Meredith was sitting at his desk. In front of him, Bill Jeffreys and Jenn Roston stood holding their go-bags.

Looks like this is going to be a short meeting, Riley thought.

She figured that she and her two partners would probably be flying out of Quantico within minutes, and she was glad to see that they'd all be working together again. During their most recent case in Mississippi, the three of them had broken even more rules than usual, and Meredith had made no secret of his displeasure with all of them. After that, she'd been afraid that Meredith might split them up.

"I'm glad all of you could get here so quickly," Meredith said in his gruff voice, swiveling slightly in his desk chair. "I just got a call from Rowan Sturman, Special Agent in Charge at the New Haven, Connecticut, FBI office. He wants our help. I take it all of you've heard about the recent death of Vincent Cranston."

Riley nodded, and so did her colleagues. She'd read in the newspapers that Vince Cranston, a youthful heir in the multibillionaire Cranston family, had died just last week under mysterious circumstances in New Haven.

Meredith continued, "Cranston had just started his first year at Yale, and his body was found early one morning on the Friendship Woods jogging trail. He'd just been out for a morning jog, and at first his death seemed to be from natural causes—a cerebral hemorrhage, it looked like."

Bill said, "I take it the medical examiner came to a different conclusion."

Meredith nodded. "Yeah, the authorities have kept it quiet so far. The ME found a small wound that ran through the victim's ear straight into his brain. He'd apparently been stabbed there with something sharp, straight, and narrow."

Jenn squinted at Meredith with surprise.

"An ice pick?" she asked.

"That's what it looked like," Meredith said.

Riley asked, "What was the motive?"

"Nobody has any idea," Meredith said. "Of course, you can't grow up in a wealthy family like the Cranstons and not acquire more than your share of enemies. It's part of your inheritance. It seemed like a good guess that the poor kid was the victim of a professional hit. Narrowing down a list of suspects looked like it was going to be a formidable task. But then…"

Meredith paused, drumming his fingers on his desk.

Then he said, "Just yesterday morning, another body was found. This time the victim was Robin Scoville, a young woman who worked for a literary magazine in Wilburton, Connecticut. She was found dead in her own living room—and at first, the cause of her death also looked like maybe a cerebral hemorrhage. But again, the ME's autopsy revealed a sharp wound through the ear and into the brain."

Riley's mind clicked away as she processed what she was hearing.

Two ice pick victims in one little state, over the course of just one week.

It hardly sounded coincidental.

Meredith continued, "Vincent Cranston and Robin Scoville were about as different as two people can get—one a wealthy heir in his freshman year in an Ivy League school, the other a young divorcée of markedly modest means."

Jenn asked, "So what's the connection?"

"Why would anyone want them both dead?" Bill added.

Meredith said, "That's just what Agent Sturman wants to know. It's already a nasty case—and it's liable to get a lot nastier if more people get killed this way. No connection of any kind has turned up, and it's hard to make sense out of this killer's behavior. Sturman feels like he and his New Haven FBI team are way out of their depth. So he called me and asked for help from the BAU. That's why I called you three."

Meredith stood up from his chair and growled…

"Meanwhile, you've got no time to lose. A company plane is ready and waiting for you on the landing strip. You'll fly to the Tweed–New Haven Regional Airport, and Sturman will meet you there. You'll get right to work. Needless to say, I want this solved quickly."

Meredith paused and leveled his intimidating stare at each of the agents.

"And this time, I want you to do everything by the book," he said. "No more shenanigans. I mean it."

Riley and her colleagues all sheepishly muttered, "No, sir."

Riley certainly meant it. She didn't want to face Meredith's anger again, and she was sure Bill and Jenn didn't either.

Meredith escorted them out of his office, and a few moments later they were walking across the tarmac toward the waiting plane.

As they walked, Jenn remarked, "Two ice pick murders, two apparently unrelated victims—maybe even random. Does that sound weird or what?"

"We ought to be used to weird by now," Riley said.

Jenn scoffed. "Yeah, *ought* to be. I don't know about you two, but I'm not there yet."

With a chuckle, Bill said, "Look at it this way. I hear the weather in Connecticut's lovely this time of year."

Jenn laughed as well and said, "It sure ought to be nicer than Mississippi."

Riley grimaced as she remembered the heavy, suffocating heat in the disagreeable coastal town of Rushville, Mississippi.

She felt sure that late summer weather in New England couldn't help but be an improvement.

Too bad we're probably not going to get much of a chance to enjoy it.

Once Shunned

❧ ❧ ❧

When the plane landed at the Tweed–New Haven Regional Airport, Special Agent in Charge Rowan Sturman greeted Riley and her colleagues on the tarmac. Riley had never met Sturman, but she knew him by reputation.

Sturman was in his early forties, about the same age as Riley and Bill. In his younger years he'd been considered a promising, up-and-coming agent who was expected to climb high in the ranks of the FBI. Instead, he'd contented himself with running the New Haven FBI office. Rumor had it that he simply hadn't wanted to move to D.C. headquarters or Quantico or anywhere else. His roots and family were planted firmly right here in Connecticut.

Of course, Riley figured, he might not have had an appetite for the political maneuvering that could play a role in those power centers.

She could relate to that possibility.

Riley liked being at the Behavioral Analysis Unit because investigating strange personalities drew on her unique abilities. But she hated the way the power plays of higher-ups sometimes interfered with investigations. She wondered how soon that sort of thing would kick in over the death of an heir to great wealth.

Riley immediately found Sturman to be warm and likeable. As he walked them to a waiting van, he spoke in a pleasant New England twang.

"I'm taking you straight to Wilburton, so you can get a look at where Robin Scoville's body was found. That's the fresher crime scene, and I've called the local police chief to meet us there. Later I'll show you where Vincent Cranston was killed. I sure hope you folks can figure out what's going on, because my team and I can't make any sense of it."

Riley, Bill, and Jenn sat together in the van as Sturman drove north. Jenn opened her laptop computer and started searching for information.

Sturman said to Riley and her colleagues, "I'm glad you're here. My team and I can only do so much with the skills and resources we've got on hand. We're trying everything we can think of, though. For one thing, we're contacting hardware stores throughout the region to get whatever information we can on recent ice pick purchases."

"That's a good idea," Riley said. "Any luck so far?"

"No, and I'm afraid it's kind of a long shot," Sturman said. "At this point we're not getting a lot of names, mostly only people who bought their ice picks with credit cards, or the storekeepers had some other record. Out of those names we're not sure what we might be looking for. We'll just have to keep at it and see."

Riley remarked, "Using an ice pick as a murder weapon seems kind of quaint to me."

She thought for a moment, then added, "On the other hand, what else is an ice pick useful for anymore?"

Jenn scowled as she scanned the information that was appearing on her screen.

She said, "Not much—at least not for a century or so. Back in the days before refrigerators, people kept their perishables in old-fashioned iceboxes."

Bill nodded and said, "Yeah, my great-grandmother told me about those. Every so often, the iceman would come to your house to deliver a block of ice to keep your icebox cool. You'd need an ice pick to break chips off the block of ice."

"That's right," Jenn said. "After iceboxes got replaced by refrigerators, ice picks got to be a popular weapon for Murder Incorporated. Bodies of murder victims sometimes had twenty or so ice pick wounds."

Bill scoffed and said, "Sounds like kind of a sloppy weapon for professional hit jobs."

"Yeah, but it was scary," Jenn said, still poring over the screen. "Nobody wanted to die that way, that was for sure. The threat of getting killed by an ice pick helped keep mobsters in line."

Jenn turned the screen around to share her information with Bill and Riley.

She said, "Besides, look here. Not all ice pick murders were messy and bloody. A mobster named Abe Reles was the most feared hit man of his time, and the ice pick was his weapon of choice. He'd stab his victims neatly through the ear—just like our murderer. He got so good at it that sometimes his hits didn't even look like murders."

"Don't tell me," Riley said. "They looked like the victims died from a cerebral hemorrhage."

"That's right," Jenn said.

Bill scratched his chin. "Do you think our killer got the idea from reading about Abe Reles? Like maybe his murders are some kind of homage to an old master?"

Jenn said, "Maybe, but maybe not. Ice picks are coming back in style with gangs. Lots of young thugs are doing each other in with ice picks these days. They're even used in muggings. Victims are threatened with an ice pick instead of a gun or a knife."

Bill chuckled grimly and said...

"Just the other day I went into a hardware store to buy some duct tape. I noticed a rack with brand new ice picks for sale—'professional quality,' the labels said, and 'high carbon steel.' I wondered at the time, just what does anybody use something like that for? And I still don't know. Surely not everybody who buys an ice pick has murder in mind."

"Women might carry them for self-defense, I guess," Riley said. "Although pepper spray is probably a better choice, if you ask me."

Jenn turned the screen toward herself again and said, "As you can imagine, there hasn't been much success passing laws to restrict ice pick sales or possession. But some hardware stores voluntarily ID ice pick buyers to make sure they're over twenty-one. And in Oakland, California, it's illegal to carry ice picks—the same as it's illegal to carry switchblades or similar stabbing weapons."

Riley's mind boggled at the thought of trying to regulate ice picks.

She wondered...

How many ice picks are there out there?

At the moment, she and her colleagues knew of at least one.

And it was being put to the worst possible use.

Agent Sturman soon drove the van into the little town of Wilburton. Riley was struck by the sheer quaintness of the residential district where Robin Scoville had lived—the lines of handsome clapboard houses with shuttered windows, fronted by row after row of picket fences. The neighborhood was old, possibly even historical. Even so, everything gleamed with paint so white that one might think it was still wet.

Riley realized that the people who lived here took great pride in their surroundings, preserving its past as if the neighborhood were a large outdoor museum. There weren't many cars on the streets, so it was easy for Riley to imagine the town in a bygone era, with horse-drawn buggies and carriages passing by.

Then it occurred to her…

An iceman used to make his regular rounds here.

She imagined the bulky cart carrying loads of ice, and the strong man who hauled the blocks to front doors with iron tongs. In those days, every housewife who had lived here owned an ice pick that she put to perfectly innocent use.

But the town had experienced a bitter loss of innocence the night before last.

Times have changed, Riley thought. *And not for the better.*

Chapter Three

Riley's nerves quickened as Agent Sturman parked the van in front of a little house in a well-kept neighborhood. This was where Robin Scoville had lived, and where she had died at the hands of a killer. Riley always felt this heightened alertness when she was about to visit a crime scene. Sometimes her unique ability to get into a twisted mind would kick in where the murder had taken place.

Would that happen here?

If so, she wasn't looking forward to it.

It was an ugly, unsettling part of her job, but she had to use it whenever she could.

As they got out of the van, she noticed that the house was the smallest in the neighborhood—a modest one-story bungalow with a compact yard. But like all the other properties on the block, this one was immaculately painted and maintained. It was a picturesque setting, marred only by the yellow police tape that barred the public from entering.

When Riley, Jenn, Bill, and Agent Sturman entered through the front gate, a tall, uniformed man stepped out of the house. Agent Sturman introduced him to Riley and her colleagues as Clark Brennan, Wilburton's police chief.

"Come on inside," Brennan said in an agreeable accent similar to Sturman's. "I'll show you where it happened."

They walked up a long wooden ramp that led to the porch.

Riley asked Brennan, "Was the victim able to move around independently?"

Brennan nodded and said, "Her neighbors say she didn't much need the ramp anymore. After the car accident last year, her left leg was amputated above the knee, but she was getting around really well on a prosthetic limb."

Brennan opened the front door, and they all entered the cozy, comfortable house. Riley noticed no further signs that anybody disabled had lived here—no special furniture or handholds, just a wheelchair tucked away in a corner. It seemed obvious that Robin Scoville had prided herself on living as normal a life as she possibly could.

A survivor, Riley thought with bitter irony.

The woman must have thought she'd endured the worst hardships life could throw at her. She'd surely had no idea of the grim fate that awaited her.

The small, tidy living room was furnished with inexpensive furniture that looked rather new. Riley doubted that Robin had lived in this house for very long. The place felt transitional somehow, and Riley thought she might know why.

Riley asked the police chief, "Was the victim divorced?"

Brennan looked a little surprised at the question.

"Why, yes," he said. "She and her husband broke up earlier this year."

It was just as Riley had suspected. This place seemed much like the little house where she and April had lived after her marriage to Ryan ended.

But Robin Scoville's challenge had been much greater than Riley's. She'd had to put both a divorce and a crippling accident behind her as she'd tried to start life anew.

A taped outline on the hardwood floor showed the position of the body. Brennan pointed to a small, dark stain on the floor.

"She'd bled from the ear just a little. Perfectly consistent with a cerebral hemorrhage. But because of the recent Cranston murder, the ME got suspicious right away. And sure enough, his autopsy showed that Robin was murdered in the same way as Cranston."

Riley thought…

The same method, but such different circumstances.

And she knew that any differences were likely to prove as important as similarities.

She asked Brennan, "Were there any signs of a struggle?"

"None at all," Brennan said.

Sturman added, "It looked like she was taken by surprise, attacked swiftly from behind."

Bill asked, "Was she wearing her leg prosthesis at the time of her death?"

"No," Brennan said. "She was using her elbow crutches to get around."

Riley knelt down and examined the position marked by the body tape. She had fallen right in front of the window. Robin had most likely been struck while she was looking out the window.

She asked Brennan, "What was the estimated time of death?"

Brennan said, "Around four in the morning."

Riley stood and looked through the window at the calm, pleasant street and wondered…

What was she looking at?

What had been going on in the neighborhood at such an hour that might have caught Robin's attention? And did it matter one way or the other? Did it have anything to do with her actual killing?

Riley asked, "How was her body found?"

Brenan said, "She didn't show up the next morning for her job as an editor at a local literary magazine. And she wouldn't answer her boss's phone calls. He found that to be strange and worrisome, not like her at all. He was worried that maybe she'd had some kind of an accident on account of her disability. So he sent an employee to her house to check on her. When she didn't answer the door, the employee went around behind the house and found that the back door had been broken into. He came on inside the house and found the body and called nine-one-one."

Riley stood there for a moment, still wondering what Robin might have been looking at outside.

Had something happened out there that awakened her and brought her to this spot?

Riley had no idea.

Anyway, what the victim had experienced just before her death was of markedly less interest to Riley than what had been going on in the mind of the killer. She hoped maybe she could get a hint of that while she was here.

"Show us where the killer broke in," Riley said.

Brennan and Sturman led Riley and her colleagues through the little house to a door that opened onto stairs to the basement. Near the top of the stairs was a landing from which another door opened onto the backyard.

Riley saw right away that the pane of glass nearest the dead bolt and the doorknob had been broken. The killer had obviously broken the glass and reached through the frame and unlocked and opened the door.

But Riley noticed something else that struck her as important.

Pieces of contact paper were stuck to the shards that remained in the frame.

Riley carefully touched a shard with some paper on it.

The killer had carefully placed the contact paper on the pane, hoping not to make too much noise, but also...

Maybe he didn't want to make too much of a mess.

Riley shivered at a sudden near-certainty.

He's fastidious.

He's a perfectionist.

It was the sort of sharp flash of intuitive insight she'd been hoping for.

How much more could she learn about the killer right here and now?

I've got to try, she thought.

Chapter Four

As Riley mentally prepared to reach into a killer's mind, her eyes met with Bill's for a moment. He was standing with their other colleagues, watching her. She saw Bill nod, obviously understanding that she wanted to be alone to do her work. Jenn smiled a little as she, too, seemed to pick up on Riley's intention.

Bill and Jenn turned and led Sturman and Brennan back into the house, shutting the basement door behind them.

Alone on the little landing, Riley looked again at the broken window. Then she walked outside, pushed the door shut, and stood in the well-kept little backyard. There was an alley just beyond the picket fence at the edge of the yard.

Riley wondered—had he approached from the alley?

Or had he slipped around from the front, between Robin's house and one of her neighbors' homes?

The alley, probably.

He might have parked a vehicle on a nearby side street, walked down the alley, and slipped quietly through the back gate. Then he'd crept through the narrow yard straight to the back door and...

And then?

Riley took a few long, slow breaths to ready herself. She carefully visualized how the backyard must have looked at that hour of morning. She could imagine the sound of crickets and could almost feel the pleasant, cool air of a September night. There would have been some glow from the streetlights but probably little light from the houses themselves.

How had the killer felt as he'd readied himself for his task?

Well prepared, Riley thought.

After all, he'd obviously picked out his victim in advance, and he would have known a few crucial things about her, including the fact that she was an amputee.

Riley looked again at the broken pane of glass. Now she could see that the contact paper had been cut almost exactly to the shape of the windowpane. That surely meant he'd stood right here and cut the paper to fit even in the dim light, probably with a pair of scissors.

Again that word flashed through Riley's mind...

Fastidious.

But more than that, he'd been calm and patient. Riley sensed that the killer had been utterly dispassionate—not the least bit angry or vengeful. Whether he'd known the victim personally or not, he'd harbored no feelings of animosity toward her. The killing had been cold-blooded in the fullest possible sense.

Almost clinical.

She made a fist and imitated the gentle but firm blow he must have used to break the glass. Before she reached through the broken pane, she suddenly sensed a spasm of discomfort.

Did he make more noise than he'd expected?

She remembered seeing a shard of glass lying on the floor inside the door. A piece had fallen despite the care he'd taken, causing a tinkling sound.

Had he hesitated?

Had he considered giving up on his plan and quietly slipping away the way he'd come?

If so, he'd quickly regained his resolve.

Riley gingerly reached through the pane and reopened the door and stepped onto the landing, slipping her shoes off as he surely had in order to move about quietly.

And then...

He'd heard a noise upstairs.

Sure enough, the woman had awakened at the sound, and he could hear clattering and thumping as she put on her elbow crutches and started moving through the house.

Riley thought maybe his hopes had sunk for a few moments.

Maybe he'd hoped to creep up on Robin as she lay in bed fast asleep, then drive the ice pick into her ear without her ever knowing he'd been there.

It wouldn't be like the earlier killing, when he'd murdered young Vincent Cranston while he'd been jogging outdoors. But Riley sensed that the killer had no interest in a consistent MO. All he wanted was to get the killings done as cleanly and efficiency as possible.

But now...

With the woman on the move upstairs, did he dare continue?

Or should he run away before she came back here and found him?

Riley sensed that he froze here on the landing for a moment, struggling with his indecision.

But then...

The woman didn't come to the back door. She moved on elsewhere in the little house. Maybe she hadn't heard the glass breaking after all. The killer might have breathed a little easier at the realization, but he still wavered. Did he dare attack the woman while she was up and around?

Why not? he may have wondered.

Disabled as she was, he'd surely be able to overpower her much more easily than he had his earlier victim.

Still, he didn't want to be sloppy or careless. A struggle might spoil everything.

But he reminded himself that this was urgent business. He was driven by some deep imperative that only he could understand.

He couldn't back out—not now. When would he get another chance like this?

He summoned up his will and decided to get on with it.

Following in what she imagined to be the killer's footsteps in her stocking feet, Riley climbed the steps up to the door that led to the kitchen. She turned the doorknob and tugged the door open...

Perfect!

The doorknob didn't squeak, and neither did the door hinges.

Feeling more and more connected to the killer by the moment, Riley crept on into the kitchen. Ignoring the fact that Bill, Jenn, Sturman, and Brennan were all standing nearby watching her, she looked all around. She knew that the scene had been untouched since the murder. So the same as right now, the kitchen table had been piled with stacks of paper that the woman had been reading.

But where was the woman?

Riley imagined looking through the killer's eyes, peering through the kitchen archway into the living room. Sure enough, she was standing right there, looking out the window, her attention entirely directed toward whatever she saw outside.

Riley imagined taking the ice pick in hand. Then she walked on across the hardwood floor, her shoeless feet stirring not so much as a whispering shuffle, until she stood right behind where Robin Scoville had been standing.

And then...

One swift, sharp, flawlessly aimed move was all it took.

The long point of the ice pick plunged effortlessly through the boneless passage through her ear into her brain, and the killer pulled the pick just as effortlessly out again, then watched his victim collapse to the floor.

And finally...

Riley felt sure that he was satisfied with his deed.

He was proud of himself for overcoming his uncertainties and going through with it.

But did he pause for a moment to admire his own handiwork?

Or had he slipped away immediately?

Riley's sense of the killer's mind dimmed now as she stood looking again at the taped outline on the floor.

There was a lot—too much—that she still didn't know.

But she felt sure of one thing.

She said aloud to her colleagues, who were now gathered around her...

"He's one cold son of a bitch."

Bill said, "Tell us more."

Riley thought for a moment, then said, "I can't be sure of anything yet. But I think it's personal for him—and yet it's *not* personal at the same time. I don't think he hated this woman. He may not have even known her name. But he had reasons for wanting her dead—important reasons, almost like killing her was some kind of…"

Riley paused, trying to think of the right word.

Then Jenn suggested, "Duty?"

Riley looked at her younger colleague and nodded.

"Yeah, that's exactly the feeling I get. A sense of obligation, almost."

Riley noticed now that Chief Brennan was staring at her with his mouth hanging open. She'd long since gotten used to people's surprise when they watched her going through this strange process of hers. And she knew she'd just looked pretty strange, walking trancelike through the house in her socks, pantomiming the moves of the killer.

Agent Sturman, by contrast, didn't look surprised at all. Of course, as a seasoned FBI agent, Sturman had surely at least heard of Riley's unique propensities, which were well-known throughout the Bureau.

Sure enough, Sturman nudged Brennan with his elbow and said, "I'll explain it later."

Bill had gone to the landing in back of the house. He now came back with Riley's shoes and handed them to her. As Riley sat down on a footstool and put them back on, doubts started to creep into her mind.

Did I get everything wrong?

She often felt swept with such uncertainties after these exercises.

After all, she wasn't a mind reader, and there wasn't anything magic or paranormal about the process she used. It was pure intuition, nothing more or less. She'd been wrong sometimes in the past, and she might be wrong now.

She got up from the footstool and wondered…

Did I miss something?

She looked toward the window and imagined the young woman standing there staring outside, oblivious to the danger that was creeping up behind her.

What was she looking at?

Riley had no idea.

But she knew she'd better find out.

Chapter Five

Riley stood looking out the window, trying to imagine what the street had looked like in the early morning hours, at the exact moment when someone had driven an ice pick into Robin Scoville's skull.

What was out there? she wondered.

What did Robin see just then?

The question nagged harder at Riley by the moment.

She said to Chief Brennan, "I didn't notice that this house has any security cameras. Does it?"

"No," Brennan said. "The owner didn't bother to install them in a small rental like this. Too bad, because maybe we'd have a video recording of what happened. Or better yet, cameras might have deterred the killer."

Followed by her colleagues, Riley walked out through the front door. She stood on the sidewalk looking up and down the street. Again she noticed that Robin's house was the smallest house in an upscale neighborhood.

She said to Brennan, "I assume you've interviewed all the neighbors."

"As many of them as we could," Brennan said. "Nobody was awake when it happened, so nobody noticed anything unusual."

She could see cameras on some of the front porches. In several yards, signs warned that these houses were protected by one or another security company.

"I see that some neighbors have security cameras for their own houses," Riley commented.

"Most of them do, I'm sure," Brennan said with a shrug. "But it doesn't look like any of them are going to do us any good."

Riley could see what Brennan meant. None of the cameras appeared to be directed toward Robin's house, so they couldn't have picked up anything concerning the break-in or the murder. And yet a Nest camera fastened to a porch post of the nearest house caught her interest.

Riley pointed to the house and said, "Have you talked to the people who live there?"

Brennan shook his head. "No, a retired couple named Copeland live there, but they haven't been at home for a week or so. The neighbors say they're vacationing in Europe. They're supposed to come back in a couple of weeks. So they definitely couldn't have seen what happened. And their camera isn't aimed at Robin's house either."

Not at the house, Riley thought. *But definitely at the street in front of the house.*

And what had happened on the street was exactly what Riley was curious about right now. Because the couple was gone for an extended time, maybe they'd left the surveillance system programmed to keep a continuous record of all that happened in their absence.

Riley said, "I want to see what, if anything, that camera picked up."

Agent Sturman replied, "We'll have to track down the Copelands and get their permission. To see the recording we'll need their password. Or we'll have to get a warrant and go after it through the company."

"Do it," Riley said. "Whatever we need. As quickly as you can."

Sturman nodded and stepped aside, taking out his cell phone to make a call.

Meanwhile, before Riley could decide what she and her colleagues should do next, Jenn spoke to Chief Brennan.

"You said Robin was divorced. What can you tell us about her ex?"

Brennan said, "His name's Duane Scoville, and he plays in a local rock band called the Epithets." The chief laughed a little and added, "I've heard them play. They're not bad, but it seems to me they'd better keep their day jobs."

Jenn asked, "Where does Duane live?"

Brennan pointed. "Just over on the east side of town."

Jenn said, "I take it you've interviewed him."

"Yeah, we don't think he's a viable suspect," Brennan said.

"Why not?" Jenn asked.

"Duane says he and the Epithets were playing a gig over in Crestone, Rhode Island, the night of Robin's murder. He says he and the band stayed the night, and he showed us a motel receipt. We don't have any reason not to believe him."

Riley saw that Jenn looked doubtful.

And with good reason, Riley thought.

It didn't sound like the local police had done a very thorough job of interviewing Duane Scoville, let alone eliminating him as a suspect. And even if Duane wasn't the murderer, he still might have important information to offer.

Jenn said, "I'd like to talk to him some more."

"OK, I'll give him a call," Brennan said, reaching for his cell phone.

"No, I'd rather not give him advance notice," Jenn said.

Riley knew that Jenn was right. If there was even the slightest chance that Duane was their killer, it was best to try to catch him off guard.

Riley said to Brennan, "Could you drive us to where he lives, see if we can find him at home?"

"Certainly," Brennan said.

Agent Sturman ended his phone call and rejoined them. "I've got an agent tracking down the Copelands," he said. "But I've got another case in progress, and I need to get back to headquarters."

"You'll let us know as soon as you get anything?" Bill asked.

"Absolutely," Sturman promised, and strode off toward his van.

Chief Brennan said, "My vehicle is over here. I can take you to Duane Scoville's place."

As Riley and her colleagues climbed into Brennan's police car, Riley noticed the determined expression on Jenn Roston's face. It felt good for Riley to see her young protégé looking so engaged. Riley glanced at Bill and could tell that he felt the same way.

She's really turning out to be a hell of an agent, Riley thought.

And the three of them together were becoming a remarkable team.

She decided she and Bill should let Jenn take the lead in interviewing Duane Scoville. It might give her a chance to shine, Riley figured.

And she definitely deserves that.

During the short drive across town, Jenn Roston found herself remembering Riley's actions back at Robin Scoville's house, and the conclusion she'd drawn about the killer...

"*He's one cold son of a bitch.*"

Jenn didn't doubt that Riley was right. She'd seen Riley get into a killer's mind a number of times now, but it never ceased to amaze her.

How does she do it?

No one in the BAU seemed to know, except maybe for Riley's one-time mentor, a retired agent named Jake Crivaro who now lived in Florida. Riley herself didn't seem to be able to explain the process or even what it felt like.

It seemed to be nothing more or less than pure gut instinct.

Jenn couldn't help but envy Riley for that.

Of course, Jenn had her own share of strengths. She was smart, resourceful, tough, ambitious...

And nothing if not self-confident, she thought with a smile.

Right now she was pleased that Riley had agreed with her about the need to interview Duane Scoville. Jenn felt anxious to make meaningful contributions to solving this case. She regretted some of her own behavior during the previous case she'd worked on with Riley and Bill—the case of the so-called "Carpenter," who'd killed his victims with a swift hammer blow to the head.

A bitter remark Jenn had made in response to Riley's criticism kept echoing through her mind...

"I suppose this is where you accuse me of not being objective."

It had been a cheap shot—especially since Jenn knew perfectly well that Riley had had good reason to doubt her objectivity. As an African-American agent, Jenn had been on the receiving end of some pretty overt racism while they'd been working in Mississippi. She hadn't taken it well, and she had to admit it had affected her judgment.

She hoped she could make up for all that now.

She hoped she could make up for a lot of things.

She looked forward to a day when, at long last, she could put her troubled past behind her.

As Chief Brennan drove, darker memories began to crowd into Jenn's mind—the dysfunctional parents who'd abandoned her when she'd been a child, then her years under the care of a brilliant but sinister foster parent who called herself "Aunt Cora." Aunt Cora had trained Jenn and her other foster children to become master criminals in her own criminal network.

Jenn had been alone among Aunt Cora's pupils in escaping from her clutches, hoping to make a different and better life for herself. She'd become a decorated cop in Los Angeles, then had made phenomenal scores at the FBI Academy before becoming a full-fledged BAU agent.

Even so, she hadn't been able shake off Aunt Cora completely. The woman had been in touch with her earlier this year, trying to pull her back into her sphere of influence, even trying to make Jenn beholden to her by helping out on an FBI case.

Jenn hadn't heard anything from Aunt Cora for a few weeks now. Had her one-time mentor given up on her for good?

Jenn could only dare to hope.

Meanwhile, Jenn's gratitude toward Riley knew no bounds. Riley was the only person who knew the truth about Jenn's past. More than that, Riley sympathized. After all, Riley herself had once been entangled with a criminal mastermind, the brilliant escaped convict Shane Hatcher.

Jenn knew more than anybody else did about Riley's secret, just as Riley knew all about hers. It was one of the reasons Jenn felt such a close bond with her new mentor—a bond based on mutual understanding and respect. Because of that bond, Jenn wanted to live up to Riley's high expectations of her.

Jenn's thoughts were interrupted by the sound of Brennan's voice as he turned a corner.

"We're almost there."

Jenn was surprised to see a huge change in the surrounding community. Gone were all the dignified, gleaming white houses with their flawlessly straight picket fences. They passed down a street littered with modest-sized businesses that included vegan restaurants, organic food stores, and a thrift store.

Then they continued into a neighborhood filled with smaller houses, somewhat shabby but nevertheless rather charming. Pedestrians were a varied lot, from young bohemian types of diverse races to old hippie types who looked like they'd lived here since the sixties.

Jenn felt immediately more comfortable here than she had in the homogenized, ultra-white, upper-class area they'd just left. Still, this was a small neighborhood, and Jenn guessed that it was getting rapidly smaller.

Gentrification is closing in, she thought a bit sadly.

Brennan parked in front an old brick apartment building. He led Jenn and her colleagues up to the front door. There, Riley gave Jenn a look that told her she was to take the lead now.

Jenn glanced at Bill, who nodded at her to go ahead.

She gulped with anticipation, then rang the buzzer for Duane Scoville's apartment.

No one answered at first. Jenn wondered if maybe he wasn't home. Then she rang again and heard a grumbling voice over the speaker.

"Who is it?"

The voice crackled for only a couple of seconds. But Jenn thought she heard music in the background.

Jenn called back, "We're from the FBI. We'd like to talk to you."

"What about?"

Jenn felt a bit taken aback by the question. And this time she was sure she heard music.

She said, "Um ... about your ex-wife's murder."

"I talked to the cops about that already. I was out of town when it happened."

There was another snippet of music, and this time it sounded familiar to Jenn—almost eerily so.

Brennan interjected, "This is Police Chief Brennan. I talked with you earlier. The agents would still like to ask a few more questions."

A silence fell, then the buzzer rang and the door clicked. Jenn opened the door and she and her colleagues walked inside.

She thought...

It doesn't sound like we're exactly welcome.

Jenn wondered why not.

She decided she was going to find out.

Chapter Six

Jenn followed Chief Brennan into the building and up the stairwell to the second floor. Riley and Bill followed behind as they walked down the hall toward Duane Scoville's apartment.

Jenn's ears perked up as she heard the sound wafting from some nearby room.

That music again.

This time she was sure she'd heard it before, but it had been a long time ago, and she wasn't sure where or when. It was a classical piece—something slow, soft, and incredibly sad.

They arrived at Scoville's apartment, and Chief Brennan rapped on the door.

A voice called out, "Come in."

As she and her colleagues walked inside, Jenn was startled by the appearance of the apartment. The place was a mess, all scattered with beer cans and food wrappers.

About ten guitars were in view, some of them on stands, others in open cases, still others lying about in the open. Some were acoustic, some electric. There were also amplifiers, speakers, and miscellaneous electronic equipment scattered about.

Duane Scoville himself sat in a battered beanbag chair. He had long hair and a beard and wore jeans, a tie-dye shirt, a peace symbol on a cord around his neck, and round-framed "granny glasses."

Jenn had to suppress a giggle. Scoville looked like he was in his twenties, but he was trying his best to look like a sixties-style hippie. The room's decor included beads, cheap tapestries, faux-Persian throw rugs, lighted candles, and general disorderliness. Some of the posters on the wall were psychedelic images, others promoting rock music groups and performers that had been popular long before Jenn's time.

There was a strong odor in the air—of incense and...

Something else, Jenn realized.

Duane Scoville sat staring blearily into space as if no one had arrived. He was obviously quite stoned, although Jenn saw no signs of drugs anywhere.

Chief Brennan said to him, "Duane, these are FBI Agents Paige, Jeffreys, and Roston. Like I just said, they've got a few more questions for you."

Duane said nothing, and he didn't offer his visitors a place to sit in the crowded little room.

Jenn felt perplexed as she remembered how immaculately neat the victim's little home had been. She could hardly believe Robin Scoville had ever known this man, much less been married to him.

And then there was the music...

Instead of the Doors or Jefferson Airplane or Jimi Hendrix or something else more appropriate to these surroundings, Duane was listening to soft Baroque chamber music with a haunting woodwind solo like a high-pitched, mournful birdsong.

Suddenly recognizing the piece, Jenn said to Duane, "That's Vivaldi, isn't it? The slow movement of a piccolo concerto."

Still without looking at Jenn or her companions, Duane asked, "How did you know?"

Jenn felt jolted by the question. She remembered vividly where she'd heard the music before.

It had been back in Aunt Cora's foster home, where she'd grown up.

Aunt Cora had always kept classical music playing in the background when she'd been teaching her kids how to be master criminals.

Jenn shivered a little. She found it eerie and unsettling to hear this melancholy melody again after so many years. It brought back strange, disturbing memories of days Jenn had tried hard to put behind her.

But she knew she mustn't let it distract her.

Keep your head in the game, Jenn told herself sternly.

Instead of answering Duane's question, she said...

"You don't strike me as a Vivaldi kind of guy, Duane."

Duane finally looked at her and met her gaze.

He said in a dull voice, "Why not?"

Jenn didn't reply. From studying at the academy and her experiences working with Riley and Bill, she knew she'd accomplished a little something just by getting him to look at her. Now they had at least a tentative connection. Jenn decided to wait and let Duane speak next.

But he said nothing right away.

The slow, sad movement came to an end and a sparkling fast movement started.

Duane clicked his player so the same slow movement began to play again.

Finally he said, "Robin really liked this piece. It was her favorite movement. She couldn't get enough of it."

Then with a trace of a sneer he added...

"I hope they play it at her funeral."

Jenn was chilled by a telltale note of anger and bitterness in his voice. She wondered—what was behind those dark emotions?

She glanced at Bill and Riley. They gave her slight nods, silently encouraging her to keep following her instincts.

She took a step closer to Duane and asked, "Are you going to Robin's funeral?"

Duane said, "No, I don't even know when or where it's going to be. Over in Missouri, I guess. That's where Robin grew up, where her family still lives. St. Louis, Missouri. I don't guess I'll be invited."

Then with a barely audible chuckle he added, "And I don't guess I'd be welcome if I did go."

"Why not?" Jenn asked.

Duane shrugged. "Why do you think? Her folks don't like me very much."

"Why don't they like you?"

Duane abruptly switched off the music. His face twisted a little with what appeared to be disgust.

Then he said spoke directly to the three agents. "Look, let's get right to the point, OK? You folks want to know if I killed her. I didn't. I went through all this earlier with Chief Brennan here. It's like I told him, I was over in Rhode Island, playing a gig with my band. We stayed the night."

He reached into his hip pocket and pulled out a piece of paper and offered it to Jenn.

"Do I need to show this again?" he said. "It's our motel bill."

Jenn crossed her arms and let him hold the paper in his hand.

Whatever was written there, she doubted she'd find it convincing. It might only mean that some members of the band had stayed there that night.

She said, "Can your bandmates vouch that you were with them all night?"

He didn't reply. But he did look uncomfortable with the question. Jenn's suspicions were thoroughly piqued now.

She said to him, "Could you tell us how to get in touch with them?"

"I guess," Duane said. "But I'd rather not."

"Why not?"

"We weren't on the best of terms. They'd just kicked me out of the group. They might not exactly cooperate."

Jenn began to pace a little.

"It might be a good idea for *you* to cooperate," she said.

Duane said, "Yeah? Is that what a lawyer would tell me? Do I need a lawyer?"

Jenn didn't reply right away. But as she walked past a closed living room closet, she noticed that Duane sat up uneasily. She looked at the door and walked closer to it, then turned and noticed that Duane's anxiety seemed to be mounting.

She said, "I don't know, Duane. *Do* you need a lawyer?"

Duane settled back down and tried to appear relaxed again.

He said, "Look, I'd really like for you guys to leave now. This is kind of a tough time for me, you know? You're not making it any easier. And I've got rights. I'm pretty sure I don't have to answer your questions."

Jenn stood there looking back and forth between Duane and the closet. She felt really close to finding out whatever it was Duane didn't want her to know.

She reached over and touched the closet doorknob, and Duane winced sharply.

Jenn saw Riley shaking her head sharply, silently warning her not to open the closet.

Of course, Jenn didn't need a warning. She knew better than to open the closet without a warrant. Her move was only a bluff, an attempt to get more of a reaction out of the man who lived here.

And she was definitely succeeding.

Duane lifted a hand toward the closet and said in a shaky voice…

"Don't do that. I've got rights."

Jenn smiled at him, but she didn't move away from the closet door.

She was about to ask the retrograde musician to come to the police station to answer more questions when Riley said, "Thanks for your time, Mr. Scoville. We'll leave now."

Jenn's smile disappeared.

She felt dumfounded. But she saw that Riley, Bill, and the police chief were all headed for the door.

Obediently, Jenn followed them out of the room.

As they headed back down the hallway and down the stairs, Riley said to Jenn…

"What did you think you were doing back there? You can't go poking around like that without a warrant."

Jenn said, "I know that, Riley. I wasn't going to *open* the closet."

Riley said, "Well, I'm glad to hear that."

"Aren't we going to take him in for questioning?" Jenn asked.

"No," Riley said.

"Why not?"

Riley sighed and said, "I'm hungry. Let's go get something to eat. We can talk about it then."

The discussion went on hold as Chief Brennan drove them to a nearby fast food place. Jenn and her colleagues ordered their generic burgers and sat down at a table together.

Then Riley said to Jenn, "Now tell me your thoughts about Duane Scoville."

Jenn sensed that Riley was about to give her a little question-and-answer lesson in police work.

Don't get defensive, Jenn told herself sternly. After all, she was probably going to learn something, whether she liked it or not.

She thought about Riley's question

What are my thoughts about Duane Scoville?

She thought back to the interview and replayed bits of it in her mind.

She remembered his sneer when he'd mentioned that the Vivaldi piece had been Robin's favorite...

"I hope they play it at her funeral."

Why would a rocker like him even be listening to Vivaldi, apparently the same movement over and over again?

Except maybe to gloat.

Then she remembered his look of disgust when he'd switched the music off.

Self-disgust.

Jenn could think of one good reason for him to feel that way.

"I think he's guilty," Jenn said.

Riley smiled a little and said, "I think so too."

CHAPTER SEVEN

Riley could see the shock in Jenn's face at what she'd just said. The younger agent's mouth hung open for a moment.

Jenn took a quick glance at Bill and Captain Brennan, who were listening attentively, then stared back at Riley.

Riley suppressed a smile and waited for Jenn to say something.

Finally Jenn asked, "You think he's guilty too? Guilty of murder?"

"I didn't say that," Riley said.

"Then what do you mean?"

Riley saw that Bill was now grinning broadly and Brennan just looked mystified. But she didn't want to say exactly what she meant, at least not outright. She wanted to draw her young protégé out with questions. After all, Jenn still had some things to learn about thinking like a BAU agent. And maybe Riley could coax Jenn into seeing things Riley's way regarding Duane Scoville.

Riley asked, "What were your first impressions when you walked into the apartment?"

Jenn squinted in thought. "Well, it was weird. I mean, the music was weird enough, for a rock musician. But the way the place looked... Robin's little house wasn't anything like that. Everything there was so neat. And conservative."

"Hard to believe they were ever married, huh?" Riley said.

Jenn shrugged a little and said, "Not happily, anyway."

Riley smiled a little.

"It's not so hard for *me* to believe," Riley said. "I've got some idea what it's like to get married when you're young and stupid. It's pretty much the story of my life. Robin and Duane were probably crazy in love and happy for a while. Their marriage might not have even lasted long enough for them to realize how little they really had in common."

Jenn sputtered, "But—but he acted so..."

Riley said, "Guilty. Yes, I know. He had his reasons. Why do you think their marriage broke up? Aside from those differences that would probably have broken them up eventually anyhow?"

Jenn stared down at her untouched hamburger, obviously trying to think of an answer.

Riley said, "Well, it's not too hard to figure out. What do you know about Robin's recent past?"

Jenn said, "She was in a car accident last year, and she lost a leg and..."

Riley could see a light coming on in Jenn's eyes.

"Oh my God," Jenn said. "Duane couldn't deal with it. He'd married a gorgeous young woman, married her *because* she was beautiful, but suddenly she was...well, mutilated. He just didn't find her attractive anymore."

Riley nodded. "In short, he was a shallow little prick."

Jenn nodded slowly and said, "And he knows it, too. That he was a prick, I mean. He felt guilty about it as soon as he dumped her. But now that she's dead..."

Jenn paused for a moment, then continued.

"He keeps thinking, if only he'd been a better husband, a better *human being*, Robin would still be alive today. And he might well be right. So his guilt is eating him up right now."

Jenn shook her head and added, "Small wonder he acted the way he did. But...what about the closet? Why did he get so nervous when I acted like I was going to open it?"

Riley chuckled and said, "You'd be nervous, too, if you had two FBI agents and a police chief in your room, and you had a bong hidden in your closet."

Jenn rolled her eyes. "Of course. I should have known."

Riley didn't say anything. The truth was...

We don't really know anything.

For all Riley really knew, Duane Scoville might have killed his wife after all. Maybe killing her was a desperate attempt to put his shame at abandoning her behind him—an attempt that had failed miserably.

Riley didn't think that was likely to be the case, but she couldn't be sure. They really had nothing to go on so far and she was just keeping Jenn from jumping to rash conclusions. And she was glad that Jenn wasn't getting angry and defensive like she had when they'd been in Mississippi.

At that moment, Chief Brennan's cell phone rang. He took the call, then quickly cupped the phone with his hand to tell Riley and her colleagues…

"This is Agent Sturman on the phone. He says his people got in touch with the Copelands in Europe. They said their camera was set up to record continuously, and to save everything it recorded during their absence. Sturman says they understand the urgency of the situation, and they've given us a permission to look at their security feed. They've also turned over all the information we need to view it."

Riley saw Bill's face light up.

"That means we won't have to go scrambling after a warrant, then deal with the security company," he said.

Riley, too, was excited. She asked, "How do we access the feed?"

Jenn suggested, "From what I know about these systems, we ought to be able to connect online, from any computer or even cell phone."

"I'll find out," Chief Brennan said.

He spoke again with Sturman on the phone and jotted down some notes. Then he ended the call and showed the group his notes.

He said, "Sturman gave me a link, a sign-in name, and a password. We should be able to check it out right here and now."

Riley looked at Jenn, who obviously understood these systems better than she or Bill. She said to Jenn, "Go ahead, see what you can do."

Chief Brennan handed his notes to Jenn, who took her laptop out of her bag and opened it up on the table. It took just a few seconds for her to make the connection. Everybody at the table crowded around the laptop so they could see the image on the screen.

The picture wasn't at all sharp or clear. But it was exactly what Riley had expected, based on the position of the camera.

She pointed and said, "Look, this is the street right in front of the Copeland house. Although you can't see it, Robin Scoville's house is out of frame, right across the street."

"So what are we looking for?" Chief Brennan asked.

Riley stifled a sigh.

That's a good question, she thought.

She thought back to her attempt to connect with the killer's mind back at Robin Scoville's house. She remembered imagining how the killer found Robin staring out her front window, then creeping up behind her and taking her by surprise.

Robin had been looking at something outside. Riley was sure of it.

She said to the others, "We're looking for anything going on in the very early hours of that morning. We're not likely to see the actual killer out on the street, but we could get lucky. It seemed that Robin was looking out her front window when she was attacked. Maybe we can get a clue what she saw out there. I don't know what it might be. I hope we know it if we see it ourselves."

Then she said to Chief Brennan, "You said the time of Robin's death was around four a.m., right?"

Brennan shrugged. "That's the approximation the medical examiner gave us," he replied.

"It's something we can work with," Riley said. "Jenn, start the footage at, say, three thirty. Run it fast until we see something interesting."

Jenn fast-forwarded through the footage. At first, the street was empty. Then a car drove by without stopping. A few minutes later, another car went by and the street was empty again.

Then Jenn stopped the feed.

"What's that?" she exclaimed, pointing at something large and bulky that had come into view.

Looking at the still frame, Chief Brennan said, "It's just a garbage truck. Nothing sinister about that."

Maybe not, Riley thought.

Even so, she said to Jenn, "Back it up and run it slowly."

Jennifer backed up the feed to just before the garbage truck appeared. Then she ran it frame by frame. The truck was the kind with mechanical arms that automatically picked up garbage bins. Although the camera did not show Robin's house, it did show the machine picking up the bin on her curb and dumping it into the truck.

But Riley saw something much more important than that.

She pointed at the screen and said, "There's a man right there."

Riley's companions peered more closely at the screen as Jenn continued to run through the footage frame by frame. Sure enough, a man was walking alongside the truck. The low-resolution image didn't show him at all clearly. He appeared as little more than a fuzzy silhouette.

When the truck finished dumping Robin's bin, it began to drive on to the next house. But the man just stood there.

Riley realized with a tingle...

He's staring at Robin's house.

Then Riley gasped and said to Jenn...

"Stop on that frame!"

Jenn stopped the feed, stared at the image, and asked...

"What's he doing now?"

The shadowy figure seemed to have raised one arm.

"Almost looks like he's aiming a gun," Brennan said. "But the victim wasn't shot."

"It looks to me like he's pointing at something," Bill said.

"Pointing at the victim?" Jenn asked. "Threatening her?"

Riley said, "Keep running it slowly."

Jenn ran the footage frame by frame by frame. Riley and her colleagues could see the man standing there for a moment, arm raised, staring in the direction of the victim's house. Then he lowered his arm and hurried out of the frame.

Riley said to Jenn, "Run the whole thing again."

Jenn backed up the footage to where the truck was coming into view, than ran it slowly. Again, Riley and her colleagues saw the truck stop to pick up Robin's garbage bin. Again, they saw a man walking alongside the truck. They saw the truck start to pull out of view, then the man standing, gesturing, and finally leaving the scene.

"Who was that guy?" Chief Brennan asked in an amazed voice.

"What was he doing?" Jenn added.

And where did he go? Riley wondered.

Chapter Eight

Riley sighed in discouragement. There simply was nothing more to see.

She and her colleagues had been staring hard at the screen as Jenn ran the security camera footage several times. But the camera wasn't well focused for that distance from the house it was set up to protect. The man walking alongside the truck remained an indistinct blur.

They'd found no clue to suggest why he'd suddenly walked out of the frame, or where he'd gone. He had never come back into view.

Riley said, "We've got to find out who that man is. He and the truck driver seem to be the only signs of life on that street at that time."

"This guy was on the move at the approximate time of the murder," Jenn added. "We could be sitting here watching the killer."

"The truck appears to have continued on its way without him," Bill said. "We can't be sure they were even supposed to be together."

"I think I know how to find some answers," Chief Brennan said. He pulled out his cell phone. "I've got a direct number for Roger Link, the director of Public Works here in Wilburton."

Brennan punched in a number, then put the call on speakerphone so Riley and her colleagues could hear.

When Brennan got the director on the line, he said, "Roger, this is Clark Brennan."

The voice replied cheerfully, "Hey, how're you doing, Clark?"

Brennan scratched his chin and said, "Well, I'm hoping you can help me with a problem. I'm sure you know about the murder that happened the night before last."

"Yeah. Awful thing."

Brennan said, "Some FBI agents and I have been looking at a security feed, and we see that a waste collection truck went by the victim's house at about the time of the murder. There was a guy on foot alongside that truck, and he acted a little oddly."

Riley could hear the director gasp.

He said, "Surely you don't suspect any of our sanitation guys."

Brennan said, "Honestly, Roger, we don't know what the hell to think. But we need to know who was working that particular route that night."

"Our guys usually work alone," the director replied. "Now that we're using these robotic arm pickup vehicles, they don't even interact with people on their routes anymore. Generally speaking, things are better this way."

Brennan told him Robin Scoville's address.

"OK, I'll see what I can find out," the director said.

Riley and her colleagues heard clattering on a keyboard. Then the director spoke again.

"I may have found out something for you. This is a little unusual. The driver on that route's name is Dick Abbott. That night he did have someone kind of working with him, a young guy named Wesley Mannis. It seems that Wesley lives at Wilburton House, an IDD facility."

Jenn asked, "IDD?"

"Intellectual and developmental disabilities," the director said.

Chief Brennan squinted and asked, "So does that mean he's retarded or physically handicapped or …?"

"I wouldn't know," the director said. "But the facility and the city run a program together for live-in IDD residents. The city hires the residents for jobs outside the facility, helping them transition into regular lives. This Wesley Mannis was part of that program, and his job was sort of a made-up one, something that wouldn't be too demanding. Really, he just walked alongside the truck and made sure no garbage got dropped. Not much of a job, but it gave him something to do until..."

The director paused. Riley had to bite her tongue to keep from asking...

"*Until what?*"

After another clatter of keys, the director said, "Two days ago the driver filed a report that Wesley disappeared sometime during that morning's shift. We're required to do that when these workers don't show up or wander off."

"That was the morning Robin Scoville was murdered," Jenn said.

"Can you pinpoint the time?" Brennan asked.

"No," the director replied. "This doesn't say exactly when, where, or why Wesley skipped out. Apparently Wesley just walked away somewhere along the route and the driver didn't miss him right away. The Public Works Department alerted Wilburton House that one of their residents had walked off on a job and... well, that's all the report says."

Riley asked, "Nothing about whether Wesley eventually turned up at Wilburton House?"

"No, I guess you'll have to find that out from the staff there."

"We'll do that, thanks," Chief Brennan said.

He ended the call and looked back and forth at Riley and her two colleagues.

"What do you think?" he asked the three agents. "Maybe this Wesley Mannis is our killer?"

Riley had no idea, and judging from their silence, she was sure neither Jenn nor Bill did either.

"If he is," Jenn finally said tentatively, "we've got him."

"Now wouldn't that be nice and easy?" Bill muttered.

But the possibility didn't quite add up to Riley. Had the same resident from the same facility gone to New Haven a week ago and killed Vincent Cranston during his morning jog on the Friendship Woods trail? Riley found that hard to believe.

She said to Brennan, "We need to check in with Wilburton House."

Brennan nodded and punched another number on his cell phone.

When he got the facility's female receptionist on the line, he said, "Police Chief Clark Brennan here. I've got three FBI agents listening in on this call. We need to know—do you have a live-in resident there named Wesley Mannis?"

"Yes."

"Is he in the facility right now?"

"I'll check." After a brief pause, the receptionist said, "Yes, he's in his room."

Apparently unsure what to ask next, Brennan looked appealingly at Riley and her colleagues.

Riley said to the receptionist, "We need to know about Wesley Mannis's activities two days ago, during the very early morning hours."

A short silence fell.

Then the receptionist said, "I'm sorry, and I hope you understand, but I'm not very comfortable sharing information about a patient over the phone like this. Could you come and talk to someone on the staff in person?"

"We'll be right there," Chief Brennan said.

Brennan drove Riley and her colleagues across town to Wilburton House. As Brennan parked his car, Riley was impressed by the size of the facility, which looked like a tastefully designed small mansion.

As they all went inside, they were immediately greeted by a tall, willowy, smiling woman dressed in cheerful pastel colors.

She stepped toward the police chief and shook his hand and said, "You must be Clark Brennan. I don't believe we've met. I'm Dr. Amy Rhind, and I'm the director of the facility."

Riley, Bill, and Jenn produced their badges and introduced themselves to her. Dr. Rhind invited them to sit down in the comfortable lobby.

She said, "I understand that you're here about one of our residents, Wesley Mannis."

Her brow knitted with worry and she added, "I'm glad you're here. Perhaps you can help us understand what has happened to him. I'm afraid it's something of a mystery."

That word jolted Riley a little.

A mystery.

She'd been hoping for answers, not questions.

She heard Bill groan softly.

A mystery?

This might not be so nice and easy after all.

Chapter Nine

Riley was beginning to feel worried. They had come here looking for a solution, not for another mystery. She couldn't imagine what Dr. Rhind had meant just now when she'd said...

"Perhaps you can help us understand what has happened to him."

Hadn't the receptionist just told Riley and her colleagues on the phone that Wesley Mannis was in his room?

Riley asked, "Are you saying that Wesley is missing?"

Dr. Rhind shook her head. "No, he's here, but..." She fell silent for a moment and said, "Could you please explain why *you're* here?"

Chief Brennan said, "Dr. Rhind, we understand that Wesley is part of a program your facility has worked out with the city. He's been working with a sanitation driver during an early morning shift. Is that right?"

"That's right," Dr. Rhind said.

Brennan continued, "Well, we caught him on a security video. He was right outside the home of a woman who was murdered that night. Then he disappeared from view."

Dr. Rhind's eyes widened.

She said, "Oh, no. Surely you don't suspect that Wesley..."

Her voice trailed off and she glanced about uneasily.

Trying to sound reassuring, Riley said, "We don't know what to think, Dr. Rhind. We just need to talk with Wesley."

Dr. Rhind said, "I'm not sure whether it *is* possible. You see, Wesley is severely autistic. And like many autistic people, he has serious problems with social and language skills. He was making great progress for a while, and the work program seemed to be doing him a world of good, really drawing him out of his shell."

With a sigh, Dr. Rhind added, "Then the night before last, the Public Works Department called to report that he'd gone missing. We were terribly worried, but he did show up here a couple of hours later. He apparently walked all the way back from wherever he'd been. But…"

She squeezed her hands together worriedly and continued. "He's had some kind of terrible setback. He was getting along so well, but now he's returned to being completely uncommunicative. We had no idea why, although we seldom do know why with our autistic residents. Their progress is often touch and go, and we have to deal with our share of disappointments. But from what you're saying, maybe his setback had something to do with…"

Dr. Rhind looked deeply troubled now.

She added, "I really can't believe that Wesley would ever hurt anybody. He's not at all prone to violence."

Jenn said, "We have no reason to think otherwise, Dr. Rhind."

Bill added, "But we do need to talk with him if it's at all possible."

Dr. Rhind thought quietly for a moment.

Then she said, "His mother is with him in his room. She's been trying to help him through this setback. Let's go see how she's doing."

As Dr. Rhind led Riley and her four companions into the facility, Riley was surprised by her surroundings. She remembered all too well the last time she'd been to any kind of a care facility. It had been back in Mississippi when she, Bill, and Jenn had interviewed a man suffering from dementia.

That had been a home for the elderly, and the place had made Riley distinctly uneasy. It had all felt fake somehow, and more like a funeral home than someplace where living people were actually cared for.

But this place was entirely different.

For one thing, the people in the hallways were of all different ages, ranging from children to the elderly. And many of faces the were happy faces. Several residents waved and smiled at Riley and her companions.

Wait—are they residents or staff? Riley wondered.

No one seemed to be wearing uniforms of any kind, so Riley couldn't be sure she could tell residents from staff members.

They passed by a comfortable sitting room where people sat around talking and playing board games and eating snacks, and a classroom where a small group of students took notes and listened attentively to their instructor.

As they continued on past spacious apartment-style rooms, Riley said to Dr. Rhind…

"I'm impressed. This seems more like a combination school and dormitory than a…"

Riley stopped herself from finishing her sentence, but Dr. Rhind smiled broadly.

"Don't be afraid to say it," she said to Riley. "You mean a mental institution."

Riley nodded, blushing a little.

Dr. Rhind said, "We try not to treat our residents like…well, patients. Instead, we treat them as individuals, with their own problems, hopes, changes, challenges, abilities, limitations, and needs. We try to foster a feeling of family for residents and staff alike. This leads to positive networking and relationships that might last a lifetime, even after some of them leave here to live in the outside world. Our 'alumni' often come back to help others, to teach them valuable life skills and other lessons that they've learned. Above all else, we try to foster independence."

With a sigh she added, "We'd had such hopes for Wesley. He'd seemed to be doing so well."

Dr. Rhind stopped and knocked on a door to one of the rooms.

Riley heard a woman's voice say, "Come in."

Riley and her three companions followed Dr. Rhind into the large, pleasant studio apartment. A middle-aged woman and a young man were seated at a table near a fully equipped kitchen area.

The woman was watching the young man with a wistful, caring expression. The young man's attention was focused on an object spinning on top of a little stand on the table.

A toy gyroscope, Riley realized.

She'd had one herself when she was a little girl.

Wesley Mannis's focus on the gyroscope seemed to pass beyond mere fascination. He seemed positively rapt, almost hypnotized. He didn't even blink as the upright spinning object slowed, then leaned, then finally dropped off its stand onto the tabletop.

Without a word, Wesley threaded a piece of string into a hole in the gyroscope's axis, meticulously turned the axis until the string was wound neatly around it, and pulled the string to send the wheel spinning again.

Then he set the gyroscope back on the stand and watched again as it whirled and hummed.

Dr. Rhind quietly asked the woman. "Has there been any change?"

The woman shook her head and said, "At least he hasn't had any more meltdowns. He's been stimming like this ever since you were last here."

That word caught Riley's attention...

Stimming.

She'd heard it used in reference to people with autism, but she wasn't quite sure what it meant. In a hushed voice Dr. Rhind introduced Riley and her companions to Wesley's mother, Gemma Mannis.

But Dr. Rhind hesitated, as if groping for a way to explain a visit from the Chief of Police and three FBI agents.

With good reason, Riley thought.

The woman already had more than enough to worry about without being told that her son just might be a murder suspect.

Instead, Riley said to Gemma, as casually as she could...

"We just want to ask him some questions about the night before last, when he went missing for a little while."

Gemma squinted curiously at Riley, then at Riley's colleagues.

It wasn't much of an explanation, and Riley knew it. She hoped Gemma wasn't going to start asking questions. But to Riley's relief, the woman simply nodded. Riley guessed that she didn't simply want to hear the whole truth right now.

Whatever "the truth" turns out to be.

Riley thought that Gemma Mannis was about her own age, although the years hadn't been kind to her. Her eyes were hollow and worried-looking, and her face was deeply lined with anxiety. Riley also noticed that she wasn't wearing a wedding ring, although there was a very slight telltale indentation on her finger where a ring used to be.

Divorced, Riley thought. It seemed likely that many years of raising a disabled son had taken their toll, both on Gemma's emotional well-being and her relationships.

Riley wondered whether Gemma's husband might have been like Duane Scoville, too shallow and selfish to follow through on the "for better or worse" part of his wedding vows. If so, Gemma may have had to persevere mostly on her own.

Riley couldn't begin to imagine the burdens she must have carried.

As for Gemma's son Wesley, Riley found him to be a baffling presence.

He seemed to be in his early twenties, though he had his mother's hollow, anxious eyes. His features were long and thin, and he had a slight stubble on his chin. Riley wondered...

Can he shave himself?

The apartment was equipped for someone with fairly good life skills, so perhaps he could. But he probably hadn't shaved since whatever had happened a couple of nights ago.

Riley and her colleagues remained standing while Dr. Rhind sat down beside Wesley.

Dr. Rhind said to him quietly, "Wesley, you have visitors."

Winding the gyroscope string again, Wesley said in a stiff voice...

"I can see that."

"They'd like to talk to you," Dr. Rhind said.

"I don't want to talk to them."

"Why not?"

"I don't want to talk to anybody."

He pulled the string and set the gyroscope spinning on the stand again.

Since their arrival, Riley hadn't seen his eyes budge once from the gyroscope.

Even more unsettling, Wesley Mannis was simply a blank to her.

Not only did Riley's powers of empathy help her get into criminals' minds, it also helped her communicate with victims and witnesses. She'd often been able to draw people out, sometimes in spite of themselves.

But she could sense nothing about this intense young man.

Dr. Rhind spoke again. "Wesley, we know something happened to you the night before last. We need for you to tell us about it."

"There's nothing to tell," Wesley said. "I want you to go away. Except Mom. I want the rest of you to go away."

"Wesley—" Dr. Rhind began.

"I mean it," Wesley said, his voice shaking now. "Go away."

"OK," Dr. Rhind said.

Then she led Riley and her companions out into the hallway.

"I'd been hoping he might have improved a little," Dr. Rhind said. "But he hasn't. I'm really worried that this setback might be irreversible."

Chief Brennan looked puzzled. He said, "Surely he isn't going to say anything as long as he's playing with that toy. Can't you just tell him to stop? Can't you just tell him to look at us?"

Dr. Rhind sighed. "One of our newer staff members made that mistake a little while ago—politely asked him to stop stimming and to make eye contact with her. He had a terrible meltdown. Believe me, we don't want that to happen again if we can possibly help it."

"Stimming?" Riley asked.

"Self-stimulatory behavior," Dr. Rhind explained. "People with developmental disabilities often stim as a way of coping with overstimulation from the outside world, the terrifying onslaught of sensory input. That's what he's doing with the gyroscope. It's his personal favorite way of stimming. Believe me, it's very benign in comparison to some of the stimming I've seen in patients, which can include head-banging and other forms of self-harm."

"So you can't get him to stop?" Chief Brennan said.

"We wouldn't want to," Dr. Rhind said. "Right now, he feels like he really needs it. And we need to respect that feeling—that's part of our philosophy here at Wilburton House. As for making eye contact…"

Dr. Rhind shrugged slightly and continued, "Wesley is averse to eye contact, even when he's doing well. Just trying to make that kind of personal connection overloads him, sends him into a meltdown. That's common with autistic people. And we don't believe in trying to force the issue."

Riley's heart sank at what she was hearing, and she could see that Chief Brennan was about to protest. Riley silenced him with a shake of her head.

She asked the doctor, "So are you saying we've got no way to reach him?"

"Not right now," Dr. Rhind said. "We're looking into every possibility, but we can't rush it." She pressed her lips together and added firmly, "We won't rush it. I'll be sure to let you know if there's any change."

It was clear to Riley that there was nothing more to be done right now. She and her team would just be in the way if they hung around. But before they left Wilburton House, she asked Dr. Rhind to check on Wesley's whereabouts on the morning of Vincent Cranston's murder down in New Haven. According to the records, Wesley had checked back into the facility after his garbage shift and had spent that whole day right where he was supposed to be.

It was evening by the time they left the building. In spite of their success at accessing the security camera recording and tracking down Wesley Mannis, they had made no actual progress on the case. As Riley tried to think what to do next, she became aware that Bill was watching her.

He said, "We should regroup, discuss what we have, and get some sleep."

Riley nodded, but it felt like a defeat.

Chief Brennan drove the three agents to a charming little Colonial-era hotel called the Ramsey Inn. As he dropped them off, he said that he'd send a car over later for them to use for as long as they were in Connecticut.

After Riley, Jenn, and Bill got settled into their rooms, they all went downstairs to the restaurant. The place was cozy, with large paintings hung on dark antique wood paneling. The menu was pricier than their usual fare, since they usually tried not to charge too much to the FBI. But they decided to indulge themselves in some excellent-looking seafood dishes.

While they waited for their orders, Jenn was looking preoccupied.

"What's on your mind?" Riley asked her.

After a moment, the young agent muttered, "I've got a bad feeling about Wesley Mannis."

Bill scoffed and said, "Surely you don't think he's our killer."

Jenn shrugged and said, "Well, he apparently didn't kill Vincent Cranston down in Newport. But Robin Scoville? That's another story. The way he disappeared on that night at that time strikes me as very weird."

Riley squinted skeptically. Bill looked doubtful as well.

Bill said, "He didn't strike me as aggressive."

"Maybe not," Jenn said. "But I lived around an autistic kid … where I grew up."

Riley knew, of course, that Jenn meant Aunt Cora's foster home.

Jenn continued, "He was a brilliant kid, a real savant. But his meltdowns were terrible. We couldn't control him, and he hurt some of us pretty badly. He really could have killed somebody. And Dr. Rhind said that Wesley does have meltdowns."

Riley could well imagine Aunt Cora taking in an autistic kid with extraordinary abilities. She'd find him useful for her insidious purposes, but what might have finally become of a kid like that?

At least Jenn escaped that woman's clutches, Riley thought.

Jenn added, "I don't think we should count Wesley out as a suspect."

Bill shook his head. "Isn't it kind of a coincidence, two killings so close together in time, both of them in Connecticut, both with the same unusual murder weapon, carried out by two completely unrelated perpetrators?"

Jenn nodded toward Riley and said, "A coincidence, maybe, Bill. But Riley taught me that coincidences are a fact of life in investigative work. We can't dismiss a possibility just because it seems coincidental."

Riley shrugged silently. It was true that she had taught this lesson to Jenn. Riley's own mentor, Jake Crivaro, had taught her the same thing many years ago. For all any of them really knew, Jenn might well be right.

If we only knew.

Over dinner, they discussed their plans for tomorrow. There seemed to be nothing left for them to do in Wilburton, at least for how.

Riley said, "We might as well head back down to New Haven in the morning, have a look at the trail where Vincent Cranston was killed."

Bill nodded and took out his cell phone and tapped in a number. He said, "I'll message Agent Sturman right now and arrange to meet him."

After the excellent dinner and dessert, they all returned to their rooms. Hoping to relax and get a good start tomorrow, Riley took a hot shower and went straight to bed.

But she was still thinking about Jenn's words...

"I don't think we should count Wesley out as a suspect."

Riley knew that Jenn was right, of course, about coincidences. And since ice picks were coming back in style as murder weapons, maybe it wasn't as much a coincidence as it seemed.

And yet...

She pictured that strange young man staring at a spinning gyroscope. Did he become violent when he had a meltdown?

Back in Robin Scoville's house, Riley had sensed that the killer was cold, calculated, and efficient. Couldn't those be the characteristics of someone with autism?

Riley had no idea.

Her thoughts drifted to Gemma, Wesley's mother.

The poor woman.

Riley felt grateful to be raising two healthy teenagers, neither of them with developmental problems. True, both April and Jilly presented their own sorts of parental challenges, sometimes including more than their share of adolescent rebellion.

But nothing like Wesley.

Riley picked up her phone and sent text messages to both her daughters.

"Missing you," she wrote to April.

"Proud of you," she wrote to Jilly.

Then Riley hesitated. Shouldn't she also text Blaine something personal, maybe even something sexy? But she felt too tired to think up something clever. Finally she just entered the words, "Hope to see you soon."

Now, sleep started closing in around Riley.

Even so, an image stayed vividly with her.

It was that spinning gyroscope.

The gyroscope kept coming and going through Riley's dreams all night. It was whirling close to her, becoming larger and larger...

Then her cell phone rang.

Riley's eyes snapped open.

The early morning sun was lighting up her window.

She reached over to her phone and looked at it. She didn't recognize the number, but she took the call.

A man's voice said, "Hello, am I speaking to Special Agent Riley Paige of the FBI?"

"Yes," Riley said.

"My name is Bayle," the man said. "Kevin Bayle. I don't imagine you've heard of me."

Feeling puzzled now, Riley said, "No, I'm afraid I haven't."

"Well, *I've* heard of *you*. In fact, I know quite a bit about you. And I'm anxious to meet you in person. Today, if possible."

Riley felt a prickle of irritation at the man's rather flat, almost sinister voice.

A stalker? she wondered.

He was certainly starting to sound like one.

Anyway, meeting him today was certainly out of the question. Agent Sturman was expecting Riley and her colleagues in New Haven in a little while, and they had important work to do there.

"I'm afraid that's impossible," Riley said. Her brain clicked away as she tried to think about what to say to him if he insisted or wanted to meet her at another time. She felt sure she wanted nothing to do with him.

The man said, "That's a pity. I would have thought you'd be interested in learning more about Wesley Mannis."

Riley felt a jolt of surprise.

Who is this guy? she wondered.

Chapter Ten

Feeling groggy and disoriented, Riley struggled to make sense of the early-morning phone call.

"How did you get this number?" she demanded.

"Oh," the man said, sounding a little surprised himself. "I guess I didn't say, did I? Dr. Amy Rhind told me how to get in touch with you. In fact, she's rather expecting you and your colleagues to come over to Wilburton House right now. I'm here. We can talk more then."

Without another word, the man ended the call.

She was about to phone Dr. Rhind to say that the agents had other plans for the morning and couldn't meet with whoever this Bayle person was.

But Riley realized she was intrigued as well as annoyed.

The man had said "I'm here" as though that should be good news.

She looked at her watch and saw that she and her colleagues weren't due in New Haven for a little while. Whatever might be going on, there was still time to check it out. Riley got on her cell phone and called Bill and Jenn to wake them up.

Bill and Jenn hadn't asked a lot of questions when Riley grumpily insisted on heading over to Wilburton House without stopping for breakfast.

"This guy better deliver on his promise," she muttered as she drove them to the meeting that Kevin Bayle had requested.

When they walked into the lobby, they found Dr. Rhind eagerly awaiting them.

"Oh, I'm so glad you could make it!" she said. "Dr. Bayle said he'd gotten in touch with you, Agent Paige."

Riley exchanged startled glances with Bill and Jenn.

"*Dr.* Bayle?" she said. The man hadn't identified himself as a professional.

"Why, yes," Dr. Rhind said. "He's a therapist from Bridgeport, a specialist in severe cases like Wesley's. I called him yesterday. He's quite brilliant, and much in demand, and he's extremely picky about his cases. When I first got him on the phone, he didn't seem interested in coming here. But then..."

Dr. Rhind tilted her head at Riley and added, "As soon as I mentioned your name, Agent Paige, he was suddenly eager to come. He said he was anxious to meet you. He wouldn't tell me why."

Riley just stood there, speechless. She heard Bill chuckle.

Then Dr. Rhind said brightly, "Come on, he's expecting you."

Riley and her colleagues followed Dr. Rhind through the facility to Wesley's room. The scene was much as it had been yesterday. Wesley was playing with the gyroscope, and his mother was sitting at the table beside him.

But now, a tall man in a corduroy jacket was standing nearby. Riley thought he was in his early thirties, despite his prematurely graying hair. And he struck her as startlingly handsome.

Dr. Rhind introduced him as Dr. Kevin Bayle. As Riley and her colleagues produced their badges and introduced themselves, Dr. Bayle peered intently at Riley. She found his gaze to be more than a little unsettling.

He stood there with his arms crossed, not offering to shake hands with her.

"I'm very pleased to meet you at last, Agent Paige," he said in a crisp, oddly efficient-sounding voice. "We'll have much to talk about together, I'm sure. Meanwhile, though, we've got work to do. Let's get right down to it."

Dr. Bayle walked over to the table, and Gemma Mannis got up to let him have her seat. Then, without saying a word, Dr. Bayle sat and watched Wesley play with the gyroscope.

While she waited for something to happen, Riley glanced around Wesley's little studio apartment. At one side of the room was a strange object that hadn't been there yesterday. It was a wooden frame shaped something like a coffin that was open on each end. The bottoms and sides were covered with mattress-like padding.

Noticing Riley's curiosity, Dr. Rhind murmured to her, "We call that a 'squeeze machine.' Dr. Bayle said we should have one ready in case we needed it."

Riley wondered...

A "squeeze machine"?

She couldn't imagine what it might be used for.

Then Dr. Bayle spoke to Wesley almost in a whisper...

"I love gyroscopes."

"I do too," Wesley said, pulling the string to make the gyroscope spin anew.

Dr. Bayle then said, "May I try something?"

Still not looking at Dr. Bayle, Wesley made no protest as the therapist picked up the string and wrapped each end around his forefingers. Then he slipped the string under the spinning gyroscope and lifted it up so it balanced on the string like a tightrope walker.

As he maneuvered the gyroscope, Dr. Bayle continued to speak in an almost hypnotic voice.

"Amazing, isn't it? Almost like magic. Look how I can make it lean from side to side. Almost like it's defying gravity. But it's not defying gravity, not really."

The gyroscope slowed and fell off the string, wobbling around on the table until it came to a stop. This time Dr. Bayle threaded the string through the axis and wound it back up.

"Do you know how a gyroscope works, Wesley?" he asked.

Wesley shook his head almost imperceptibly.

"It's simple physics," Dr. Bayle said, sending the gyroscope spinning again. "It has to do with the conservation of angular momentum..."

His voice now gentle and purring, Dr. Bayle explained how the gyroscope worked and pointed out its parts, then went on to talk about the practical uses for gyroscopes, especially in navigational systems.

Riley realized she was finding the little lecture fascinating. Again, she remembered playing with her own gyroscope when she was a little girl.

But somehow, she remembered it as being more than just play.

The spinning wheels had been very important to her, although she couldn't remember just how or why.

Suddenly, Dr. Bayle looked directly at Riley and held her gaze for a moment.

Almost like he's reading my thoughts, she thought with a chill.

To Riley's relief, Dr. Bayle quickly turned his attention back to Wesley and continued his lecture.

Pretty soon Riley was startled to realize...

Wesley's looking at him!

In fact, the two men were actually making eye contact.

The gyroscope lay motionless on the table now as Dr. Bayle said...

"I hear you have a job working on a garbage pickup route."

Wesley nodded.

Dr. Bayle said, "Well, when I was younger, I had a job as a dishwasher. So I guess you could say that I've had experience working with garbage too."

His voice remained flat, as if he didn't mean this as a joke.

Then he said, "Tell me a little about your route, Wesley."

"What do you want to know?" Wesley asked.

"Anything you want to tell me. What sorts of things do you see when you're working?"

Wesley's face crinkled in thought.

Then he said, "Most of my route is along Victoria Street, and I see a lot of things at different addresses. At one0forty, they've got a broken gate. There's a swing on the porch at two twenty, and another at two-forty-five. The people who live at three-fifty-two leave their garage door open all night, I don't know why..."

Wesley's words began to pour out faster and faster as he kept describing countless odd details that he'd noticed on Victoria Street. He seemed almost frantic to say as much as he could. After a couple of minutes, the flood of words slowed and came to a halt—much like the gyroscope had.

Then Dr. Bayle said...

"What about four-sixty-five Victoria Street?"

Riley felt a stir of anticipation. She knew that was Robin Scoville's address.

Wesley went suddenly pale, and his mouth hung open.

"I don't know," he said.

"Are you sure?" Dr. Bayle said.

Wesley face twisted violently, and he barked out...

"I'm not a peeper."

"Nobody said you were," Dr. Bayle said.

"I'm not a peeper," Wesley repeated.

Dr. Bayle watched and listened silently as Wesley kept repeating those words over and over again, more loudly and violently every time...

"I'm not a peeper... I'm not a peeper... I'm not a peeper..."

Wesley began to shake all over as if he had a terrible fever or was going into a deep state of shock. Finally he collapsed onto the floor and curled up in a fetal position, sobbing uncontrollably.

Dr. Bayle rose from his chair and knelt down beside Wesley, offering him his hand.

"Come with me, Wesley," Dr. Bayle said.

"No-o-o-o!" Wesley wailed with despair.

Dr. Bayle calmly took hold of Wesley's hand and said again...

"Come with me."

He coaxed Wesley into a crouch, then helped him crawl across the floor to the strange object that Dr. Rhind had called a "squeeze machine."

He guided Wesley into the padded structure.

To Riley's surprise, the agitated patient simply lay on his back amid the padding and folded his arms across his chest.

Then Dr. Bayle pulled a lever, and the two sides closed in around Wesley, holding him firmly but gently.

Wesley's sobbing ebbed away. Instead, he made sighing, cooing sounds of relief.

Riley turned to Dr. Rhind and asked quietly, "What just happened?"

Dr. Rhind smiled slightly and said, "Some autistic people suffer from a paradoxical sort of a problem. They desperately need physical security, an embrace or a hug—and yet they can't tolerate human contact. Ironic, isn't it? Well, this is a sort of hugging mechanism that gives those patients exactly the kind of comfort they need. As you can see, it works extremely well with Wesley."

Looking at Bill and Jenn, Riley could see that they were as startled and shaken as she felt,

Jenn said, "This looks like a really bad setback."

Dr. Bayle put his hands on his hips and gazed down at Wesley, who seemed to be becoming calmer.

"Not necessarily," Dr. Bayle said. "This just means I can't stop now. It means the rest of you must leave Wesley and me alone."

With a sharp look at Gemma Mannis, he added, "That includes you."

Looking as if she was about to burst into tears, Gemma fled the room.

Riley was about to insist on staying when Bill touched her on the arm. "We've got to get down to New Haven."

Riley nodded reluctantly. But as Dr. Rhind was leading Jenn and Bill out of the room, Riley locked gazes with Dr. Bayle again.

Riley felt a deep shiver at that stare.

She wondered as she turned and followed the others out the door—what was it about that man that disturbed her so…?

And why does he seem to be so interested in me*?*

Chapter Eleven

As Bill drove their borrowed car south to New Haven, Riley felt her emotions still reeling from the shocking scene they'd just witnessed. The image of the tortured young man crawling his way to solace in that odd padded box kept replaying in her mind.

She sensed that both Bill and Jenn had been struck by that encounter too. After a few minutes on the road, she felt that it was time to get some of their feelings out in the open.

She said to Jenn, "What do you think about Wesley Mannis now?"

Jenn paused for a moment, then said…

"I'm still not ready to count him out as a suspect."

Jenn paused again, then added…

"For both murders, not just Robin Scoville."

Riley was startled. Just yesterday, Jenn had agreed that it was unlikely that Wesley had killed Vincent Cranston in New Haven. What had changed her mind?

"Why do you think that, Jenn?" Riley asked.

Jenn shrugged, then said, "Well, I had a bad feeling about him yesterday. And what just happened made me even more concerned. He seems to me to be a very erratic personality."

Bill said, "But we know that Wesley was in the facility when Cranston was killed."

"Do we, really?" Jenn said. "It's just a short trip from Wilburton to New Haven. And it's not like he was locked in the place. He could have gotten out if he wanted to. Maybe if he worked with a partner…"

"You're reaching, Jenn," Bill said with a shake of his head.

"Am I? That autistic kid I knew back where I grew up—his meltdowns looked a lot like that, and he could be really threatening. He had no empathy, and he manipulated people, fooled them into thinking he was more disabled than he was. He was highly organized, obsessive, and even cunning."

Riley felt a chill as she imagined how Aunt Cora would have exploited such a kid—someone who would follow her every order without letting any moral feelings get in the way.

Riley said, "And Wesley reminds you of him?"

"A lot," Jenn said.

The three of them fell silent. Try as she might, Riley couldn't buy into Jenn's suspicions. She was sure that Bill was right and Jenn was reaching, thrashing about blindly as she searched for a plausible hypothesis.

And that's not a bad thing, Riley thought.

Riley knew that at least one of them needed to be thinking far outside the box right now, and it might as well be Jenn. They needed to entertain even the most farfetched possibilities until they got more solid clues than they had just yet. But it was important that they didn't latch onto any of those ideas just yet.

It was only a twenty-minute drive to the park in New Haven called Friendship Woods. When Bill pulled up to the park's front entrance, Riley and her colleagues found Agent Rowan Sturman standing beside his car waiting for them.

As he led them along the jogging trail toward where Vincent Cranston was killed, Sturman said...

"We're still doing the best we can to keep it quiet that Cranston was murdered. God knows, we don't want to have to deal with a lot of media hysteria."

Bill asked, "Does anybody in his family know?"

Sturman said, "Yeah, his uncle, Niles Cranston, the family patriarch. As you can imagine, he's really been leaning on us to solve the case. And with his money, he could make a lot of trouble for us if we don't wrap it up soon. By the way, he's expecting us to pay him a visit today, and we probably had better do that as soon as we're finished here. It would really help if we could report some actual progress."

As they walked along, nothing about the green and peaceful setting gave Riley any notion about what had happened. Lean, fit, and stylishly dressed joggers trotted by at various rates of speed, some chatting companionably together, others more focused on their workout.

Riley looked all around and saw countless places where someone might have lurked, lying in wait in the brush alongside the wending path. Doubtless Agent Sturman and his team had combed the whole area looking for clues. So Riley wondered—what could she hope to find that hadn't been found already?

Agent Sturman brought the group to a stop in a place where the path took a sharp curve. He pointed to the ground.

"Vincent's body was found right here," he said.

He handed Riley a folder with some crime scene photos of the body. Riley glanced back and forth between the photos and the actual scene, trying to visualize exactly how the body had fallen on the path.

As she did so, she noticed something about the expression on the dead man's face. His eyes were open, and his lips were shaped into what almost seemed like a smile—or maybe a smirk.

She wasn't sure why that struck her as odd, except that facial muscles tended to go slack soon after someone died.

It probably doesn't mean anything, she thought.

What mattered right now was whether she could get any sense of the killer. It might not be easy a full week after the murder, with no physical clues to be found, and with passing joggers eyeing her and her colleagues curiously.

First she wondered—had the victim and the killer known each other?

She asked Agent Sturman, "Would anyone have expected to encounter Vincent here?"

Sturman shrugged. "Maybe. Vincent hadn't been in New Haven very long. He was just starting his freshman year at Yale. But from what I've been told, these morning jogs were already part of his routine. He'd been hoping to become a marathon runner."

Why an athlete and then an amputee? Riley wondered. *How is this killer choosing his victims?*

Bill observed, "If this was his routine, any number of people could have known he'd be here."

Riley nodded in agreement. As she looked around at the setting, she began to feel one thing about the killer...

He didn't conceal himself.

He hadn't ambushed Vincent from the brush. He hadn't felt any need for that. Instead, he'd met Vincent right out in the open.

That also seemed like a contradiction. The killer had sneaked into Robin Scoville's house and apparently *had* ambushed her.

Riley walked a short distance in the opposite direction from where Vincent had come. Then she retraced her steps, imagining that she was the killer preparing for his encounter with Vincent. She ignored the sound of Agent Sturman's cell phone ringing, and how he stepped away from the group to take the call.

She felt just a flicker of connection with the killer, but then it was gone. She couldn't even tell whether he had known Vincent or not. But as she approached the spot where the victim had fallen, she got a brief image that stopped her in her tracks.

For an instant, it was as though Vincent Cranston's eyes were staring into hers.

Then the vision was gone too, and she felt nothing at all about the scene of the murder. But now Riley was sure of one important thing about Vincent and his killer.

They looked directly at each other.

They made eye contact.

She gasped a little and said to Bill and Jenn...

"Wesley Mannis didn't kill this man."

"How do you know?" Jenn asked.

Riley was about to explain that Wesley making eye contact with Dr. Bayle had been very unusual and a sign of progress in his therapy. Under ordinary circumstances, Wesley just wouldn't be capable of staring directly into another person's eyes.

But then she heard Agent Sturman's voice.

"I've got some news. And you're not going to like it."

Riley turned and saw Sturman holding his cell phone.

"There's been another ice pick murder," Sturman said.

Chapter Twelve

Riley and her colleagues exchanged grim glances. Sturman had just announced the worst possible news they could hear right now.

Another ice pick murder!

Another person dead.

She knew that she, Bill, and Jenn were all thinking the same thing. This meant that their investigation was desperately behind.

How many more deaths might follow before they solved this case?

Sturman said, "We've got to go right now. We've got to get there before the tide comes in."

The tide? Riley wondered.

As they headed back along the path toward the park's front entrance, Sturman explained, "That was the state medical examiner, Alex Kinkaid. Another body was found over on the Wickenburg Reef. He and his team are at the crime scene now."

Bill said, "Is the body still there?"

Their pace quickened as Sturman replied, "Yes, and I told him not to move it. But we don't have much time. When the tide gets too high, Kinkaid and his team will have to take the body away whether we're there yet or not. That's all I know myself. I didn't have time to ask questions."

Riley and her colleagues got into their borrowed car and followed along behind Sturman's vehicle.

As Bill drove, Jenn called Wilburton House to check on Wesley Mannis's whereabouts. When she ended the call she said, "The staff says Wesley's still in his room recovering from his meltdown."

Then with a sigh Jenn added, "I guess that's puts an end to my suspicions about him. I feel stupid for bringing it up. Next time I get a crazy hypothesis like that, I'll keep my mouth shut."

Riley said, "Don't you dare, Jenn. We've got to entertain any and all ideas, even crazy ones. The way things are shaping up, my guess is that the truth is going to turn out to seem plenty crazy when we get this case solved."

Riley stopped herself from adding…

"If *we can solve it.*"

Failure wasn't an option, after all—especially now that there had been another victim. There was no reason to believe that this killer would to stop soon.

It was only a short drive west from New Haven to Wickenburg, a town right on the coast of the Long Island Sound. A quaint Colonial town like Wilburton, Wickenburg had a picturesque village green with a hexagonal gazebo that looked well-suited for dancing and musical ensembles.

The Fourth of July must get really lively here, Riley thought.

They followed Sturman through the little town to the beach, where several official vehicles had parked. She saw the medical examiner's van among them.

Jutting out from the shore, a curving row of enormous rocks protruded from the surf. Beyond the rocks a little lighthouse stood on a tiny isolated island.

They got out of their car and joined Agent Sturman, who was approaching a man in a police uniform and an official in a white jacket.

Introductions were exchanged. The two men were Terry Nilson, Wickenburg's chief of police, and Alex Kinkaid, the state medical examiner. The ME was an enormous man with a walrus-style mustache.

In a rough but almost cheerful voice, Kinkaid said, "Definitely looks like a serial killer, doesn't it? And I was thinking about retiring this year. I might have to think better of it if things stay this interesting."

By contrast, Chief Nilson looked badly shaken. He appeared to be much younger than the ME, and Riley guessed that he'd never dealt with anything this grim before.

Nilson and Kinkaid led Riley and her colleagues out onto the long, rocky reef. Kinkaid struck Riley as remarkably spry for a man his size, while Nilson negotiated the boulders with considerable caution.

So did Riley and her colleagues. The rocks were treacherous and slippery, and although the waves weren't nearly as high as they would be out on the ocean, they were pounding hard against the reef.

A handful of cops and the ME's team were gathered at the far end of the reef, surrounding a body that lay crumpled on a boulder. The dead man was facing to his left, his right hand extended toward a fishing rod that was wedged between a couple of rocks.

It looked to Riley like the rod must have flown out of his hands at the moment of the attack.

Chief Nilson said, "This is Ron Donovan, poor guy. He was a widower who owned a gift shop here in Wickenburg. He'd come out here to fish early mornings whenever he could. This morning he must have come out here shortly before dawn, when the tide was just starting go out."

Riley could see that the tide was definitely coming back in now, and the surf raised a mist in the air. She guessed that only a few minutes remained before the ME's team had to move Ron Donovan's body and his fishing gear before they were submerged or floated away.

Riley peered down at the body. The man didn't appear to be very old—maybe only fifty or so. His open eyes stared out over the water.

Bill asked, "Who found the body?"

Chief Nilson explained, "A couple of Ron's fishing buddies came out to join him and found him like this. Ron had a heart condition, so naturally they thought he'd died from a heart attack. They called nine-one-one, and an ambulance came with some paramedics."

Jenn asked, "Why did anyone guess it might be murder?"

Kinkaid said with a grunt of self-satisfaction, "I can take some credit for that. Of course, it's not public knowledge that Robin Scoville was killed with an ice pick—or that Vincent Cranston was murdered at all. We're trying to keep a lid on all that so the media doesn't go crazy about it. Still, I put out an APB to the appropriate medical personnel to keep a lookout for certain kinds of deaths—especially ones that involved bleeding from the ear."

The big man stooped down and pointed. Ron Donovan's left ear was pooled with thick, dark blood.

Kinkaid said, "Sure enough, this guy did not die of a heart attack. The paramedics called my office right away. My team and I got over here as soon as we could. Then I called Chief Sturman, and he brought you folks over here."

Riley looked all around, trying to assess her situation. Normally, a fresh crime scene like this would give her the perfect opportunity to try to get into a killer's mind. But the tide was already visibly higher than it had been when they got here. Riley knew she'd have to work fast.

Pointing to the dead fisherman's plastic bucket, she asked the police chief…

"How was his catch this morning?"

For a moment Chief Nilson looked surprised by the question. Riley knew it must seem odd that she'd be interested in such a seemingly irrelevant detail. But then he opened the lid and peered inside.

He said, "It looks like Ron caught five good-sized bluefish. He'd have been pretty happy with this."

Riley nodded, then retraced her steps some thirty feet back along the reef. Then she turned back around and looked out toward the end of the reef, trying to imagine the scene shortly before dawn when the tide was going out and the light sparkled from the east over the waves.

The killer would have seen Ron Donovan standing out there casting his line out into the water. She wondered…

Did the killer know him?

Had he chosen him as a victim before he'd even come here?

Riley had no way of knowing.

Even so, she tried to imagine herself in the killer's shoes as she made her way back out over the reef.

She asked herself another question...

Did he call out to Ron Donovan as he approached?

Had Donovan then turned and given him a welcoming wave?

She couldn't be sure, but she somehow doubted it. With the sounds of waves and crying gulls, it was easy to imagine the killer coming all the way out onto the reef without Ron Donovan even noticing him. And the killer might have wanted it that way.

Finally she arrived at the spot where Donovan had been fishing.

What happened here? she wondered.

She remembered the gut feeling she'd had back in Robin Scoville's house—that the woman had been struck with the ice pick before she'd even been aware of an intruder.

Had something like that happened here?

Riley looked down at the body again, trying to determine how the victim would have crumpled into this particular position as he fell dead.

She quickly realized...

Donovan was sitting down when he was attacked.

She didn't know much about surf fishing, but she did know that it was done from a standing position, just like the fly fishing she'd done with her father back in the Virginia mountains.

So he sat down when the killer arrived.

A hypothetical but remarkably vivid scenario began to play out in her mind.

Feeling prepared and ready for this new murder, the killer speaks to the angler when he gets directly behind him...

"Looks like it's going to be a nice day, doesn't it?"

The angler turns around with surprise as he winds his line back in from his previous cast.

The two men don't know each other. The killer figures the angler takes him for a tourist who is staying here in Wickenburg. The killer notices an irritated expression on the angler's face, and he guesses he's about to tell him to be on his way and leave him alone.

But the killer speaks before the fisherman gets a chance.

"How's the fishing this morning?"

The fisherman smiles, apparently pleased by the question.

"Have a look in the bucket yourself," he says.

The killer lifts the lid off the bucket and sees five large fish.

"Looks impressive," the killer says. "What kind of fish are these?"

"Bluefish," the angler says, sitting down on the rock. "Sit down with me, I'll show you the lures I've been using."

The killer sits down beside the man, pleased that things are going so well.

They chat pleasantly for a moment. The angler clearly enjoys showing off his equipment, talking about surf fishing to someone who doesn't know anything about it. Meanwhile, the killer fingers the handle of his concealed ice pick, waiting for the perfect moment to attack.

Then the killer points beyond the reef and says...

"That's a nice lighthouse. How long has it been there?"

The fisherman looks where he's pointing and nods. He opens his mouth to say something about the lighthouse's history.

But he doesn't get a chance to speak, because this is the moment the killer has been waiting for.

He lifts his ice pick and drives it into the fisherman's ear...

Riley shuddered as she snapped out of her reverie.

This time her sense of the killer was unusually vivid.

She had to steady herself a little and remind herself...

It's just conjecture.

As vivid as the scenario had seemed, she knew it was all nothing more than intuitive guesswork, especially details of the conversation. For all she really knew, Donovan and the killer hadn't spoken to each other at all. But that didn't strike her as likely. After all, Donovan had been sitting down at the moment of his death, which suggested that he had found the encounter to be relaxed and amiable—at least at first.

She felt pretty sure that she'd gotten some bits of the scene right. She heard Bill ask her...

"So what do you think?"

As Riley turned toward him, she saw that all the others except Bill and Jenn were staring at her with mystified surprise.

This again, she thought.

As so often happened, those who weren't accustomed to her strange, trancelike behavior didn't know what to make of it.

Riley stifled a sigh. She didn't want to explain it right now.

Riley replied to Bill's question with one guess she felt pretty sure of...

"I don't think Donovan knew the killer personally."

Jenn asked, "Anything else?"

As Riley tried to think of something else to say, she looked down again at the body. The tide would be lapping against it any minute now. And was that a bit of seaweed draped over the back of his right hand?

She stooped down and looked closely at the hand and saw that it wasn't seaweed. It was a blotch on the skin itself. She pulled up the sleeve a little and saw that the blotch spread up onto the victim's wrist.

She pointed to it and asked Kinkaid, "What do you think this is?"

The big medical examiner stooped down beside her and said, "I noticed it earlier. It's just a birthmark. Nothing to worry about. It doesn't have anything to do with anything. Anyway, we've got to get this guy out of here."

As Kinkaid gave orders for his team to remove the body, Riley saw Agent Sturman looking at his cell phone.

"I just got a message from my team in New Haven," he said to Riley and her colleagues. "They've been trying to track down people who've bought ice picks recently, and three names caught their attention. They don't look very promising to me, though. We can deal with them later."

Sturman pocketed his phone and added, "Niles Cranston's been waiting for us to come to his mansion and give him an update. I was hoping we could report something positive. He's sure as hell not going to be pleased to hear there's another murder."

Bill said to Sturman, "We'll follow your car to his place."

As Riley and her colleagues got into their borrowed vehicle, the image of that birthmark flashed through her mind, and she remembered the ME had just said…

"It doesn't have anything to do with anything."

Riley felt a tingle of anxiety as she thought…

Why do I get the feeling that's not true?

Chapter Thirteen

As Bill began to drive, following along behind Agent Sturman's car, Riley sat staring out the passenger window. Even as she watched the reef slip behind them, she couldn't get another image out of her head.

That birthmark.

The dark shape on the back of the victim's hand and wrist kept flashing in her mind like an afterimage from a bright burst of light. She didn't know why it nagged at her so.

She said to Bill and Jenn, "Were either of you bothered by Ron Donovan's birthmark?"

Her colleagues both glanced at her with surprise.

Jenn said, "No, why?"

Riley shook her head. "I don't know. It just concerns me somehow."

Bill scoffed slightly and said, "I can't imagine why. It's like the ME said, it doesn't have anything to do with anything."

Jenn added, "It's not like it was a wound inflicted at time of the murder. He'd had it all his life. Unless you think the ME was wrong, and it wasn't really a birthmark. But what else could it be? What could have caused it right then and there?"

Riley said, "I'm sure it is a birthmark, but…"

Her voice faded away for a moment.

Then she said, "Robin Scoville was an amputee."

"So?" Jenn said.

"So," Riley said, "both Robin and Ron were… imperfect."

"I don't understand what you're saying," Bill said.

Riley didn't reply. The truth was, she wasn't sure she did either. But she felt as though she'd gotten into the killer's head pretty vividly just now. And for some reason, she thought those two imperfections had mattered to him somehow.

Bill said, "They're nothing alike, Riley—a birthmark and an amputated leg, I mean. They just don't compare."

"And what about Vincent Cranston?" Jenn asked. "He was training to be a marathon runner. Judging from the crime scene photos, he looked pretty much perfect."

Riley stifled a sigh. She couldn't explain her feeling to Bill and Jenn. And it didn't really make sense, not even to herself. Anyway, she knew that Jenn was right. Riley had noticed nothing odd about the photos of Vincent Cranston except for that very slight but peculiar expression on his face. And of course, that had surely been the result of Vincent's surprise at suddenly being attacked. Otherwise, he'd looked like a healthy and remarkably handsome young man.

Just try to put it out of your mind, Riley told herself.

Not that she figured that was going to be easy to do. Once a glimmer of an idea got stuck in her head, Riley could rarely shake it off.

Still, she had other things to think about at the moment. For one thing, she wondered what Niles Cranston was going to be like.

The Cranston family had been famous since the nineteenth-century days of robber barons. They were part of American history. The first millionaires of that name had been well known for their philanthropy, a tradition their descendants upheld even today.

Nevertheless, the heirs to the family fortune were notoriously reclusive. Riley couldn't remember ever seeing photographs of any of them. She had no idea what to expect from Niles Cranston beyond what Agent Sturman had told her yesterday.

"He's really been leaning on us to solve the case."

Riley knew from experience that millionaires could be troublesome when it came to solving cases. Would Niles Cranston be any different?

Bill followed Agent Sturman's car back through New Haven, then farther east to the town of Levering. On the far edge of the picturesque and definitely upscale little town they arrived at the Cranston estate. They followed Agent Sturman to the front gate, where Sturman identified himself to a guard who admitted them into the grounds.

At first, Riley saw no sign of any houses or buildings as the vehicles wended their way along the curving road among several acres of tall, leafy trees. Finally, the Cranston family home came suddenly into view.

The sight of the place took Riley's breath away.

Her work had brought her to the estates of wealthy people before, but the Cranston mansion dwarfed any home she could remember. It seemed almost like the center of a feudal village—a huge, castle-like building surrounded by smaller structures and houses.

The two drivers parked the vehicles and they all walked up to the massive front entrance, where they were greeted by a stern, officious butler who was obviously expecting them. As the butler escorted them inside, their footsteps echoed eerily on the stone floor of a long hallway.

The four agents silently followed the butler along the cathedral-like hallway to a pair of wide-open doors at the end. Without a word, the butler waved his flock inside and then closed the doors, shutting himself outside the room.

They found themselves in a grand chamber with a high ceiling, dark paneled walls, and a long wooden banquet table. On the wall beyond the far end of the table hung a gigantic oil painting of a grim-faced, gray-bearded man dressed in old-fashioned clothes. Riley guessed it must be a portrait of Brenton Cranston, the Gilded Age steel magnate who had first built the family fortune.

At the end of the table nearest them, a man in his fifties stood staring up at the portrait, as if in conversation with the family patriarch. He was wearing an elegant silk housecoat and expensive slippers, and he was smoking a pipe.

He turned at the sound of approaching footsteps and said, "Hello, Agent Sturman. I see you've brought some visitors. I hope you've also brought some news."

"I'm afraid it's not good news," Sturman said. He introduced Riley and her colleagues, then said, "Mr. Cranston, I'm sorry to say there's been another murder."

Cranston squinted with surprise and dismay.

"Who was it this time?" he said.

"A man who was fishing this morning over at Wickenburg Reef."

"And he was killed in the same way as my nephew—and the young woman?" Cranston asked.

"With an ice pick, yes," Sturman said.

Cranston stared silently at Sturman for a moment, then sat down at the end of the long table, looking up at the portrait again as if he expected it to speak.

As Riley looked at him carefully, she noticed his resemblance to the man in the portrait—a hint of aristocratic breeding, a sense of privilege. Even so, Niles Cranston didn't have the same forceful gaze that his ancestor did. Somehow, he didn't strike Riley as an especially remarkable man. Nevertheless, he had inherited a much more than remarkable fortune.

Finally Cranston said to his visitors…

"Sit down. Tell me about it."

Riley and her companions sat down at the long table near him. Agent Sturman told him the news about Ron Donovan's murder without going into unnecessary details.

When Sturman finished, Cranston took a long puff on his pipe.

Then he said, "So you still have no idea who killed my nephew."

Riley could see Sturman wince a little.

"No," he said. "I'm sorry. We're doing everything we can."

Cranston glanced at Riley, Bill, and Jenn, and said to Sturman, "Even with the BAU's help, you're at a loss."

Riley said, "I wouldn't think of it that way, Mr. Cranston. My colleagues and I just got started on this case yesterday."

Cranston nodded. "Yes—after that poor woman's murder in Wilburton. Too little too late, it seems."

Cranston sounded bitter to Riley, but not really angry. She sensed that he felt deep disappointment and frustration at what he'd just heard—and that was hardly any wonder. She shared his discouragement.

Then Cranston said, "Agent Sturman, during your last visit I talked to you about my family's enemies. I gave you a list of people who might want to harm anyone in my family—including Vincent."

Agent Sturman nodded and said, "We checked your list thoroughly. We don't believe any of those people were connected, at least not with the first two murders."

Cranston's forehead crinkled skeptically.

He said to Sturman, "So you're absolutely positive Vincent wasn't targeted because... well, because he was a Cranston?"

Riley spoke up again. "Mr. Cranston, we aren't *positive* about anything. But we've got good reason to believe the three victims were murdered by the same killer. Do you know of any connection between your nephew and Robin Scoville in Wilburton, or that unfortunate fisherman at Wickenburg Reef?"

Cranston got up from his chair and started to pace.

"I don't see how that's possible," he said. "He'd just moved out here from San José in California—that's where his branch of the family lives. He barely knew anyone in Connecticut except for students he was starting to meet at Yale. I doubt he'd ever even been to Wilburton or Wickenburg. Those aren't places he would have been likely to visit."

Cranston looked hard at Riley again and said, "Agent Paige, I find it hard to believe that fate would single out my nephew... along with..."

His voice trailed.

Riley understood that he felt uncomfortable finishing his sentence.

She said in a reassuring voice, "Along with two perfectly ordinary people, you mean."

Cranston nodded.

Riley said, "You have every reason to feel that way. But please try to understand, Mr. Cranston... *fate* didn't single out *any* of the victims. A cruel and twisted human being did. For all we know, that person had no idea who your nephew really was when he chose him for his first victim."

"But you can't be sure of that, can you?" Cranston asked her.

Bill spoke up this time. "No, we can't be sure of anything at this point."

Jenn added, "Please try to be patient, Mr. Cranston."

Riley winced sharply inside. She knew that Jenn meant well, but it wasn't a tactful thing to say at the moment. A more experienced agent would know better. And she could see Cranston was ruffled by the remark.

"I believe I *have* been patient," Cranston said to Jenn. Then turning to Sturman he added, "I've abided by your wishes so far. I haven't told anyone that Vincent was murdered, not even in the family. God knows, it's been hard for anyone to believe that a perfect specimen like my nephew just dropped dead from some sort of natural cause, but that's exactly what I've been letting people believe. Am I supposed to keep on like that forever?"

Sturman shook his head and said, "No, just until we solve the case."

"And when will that be?" Cranston asked, his voice shaking a little. "The FBI hasn't inspired me with any confidence so far. I'm starting to think I should hire my own investigators—people who really know their work."

Riley could see that Agent Sturman was stung by his remark. Fortunately, she knew better than to take it personally.

She said to Cranston, "I understand how you feel. But we must ask you to please not bring anyone else into the investigation. I promise you, it will only lead to confusion and mistakes and make things much worse. Nothing good would come of it."

Riley saw Cranston's face soften a little. He asked Riley, "How long is this nightmare going to continue?"

Riley gulped. The last thing she wanted to do right now was make promises she wasn't sure she could keep.

Instead she said, "I don't know."

Cranston nodded silently. Riley sensed that he at least appreciated her honesty. Then he sat down again and stared off into space. Riley sensed he had something on his mind that he desperately wanted to say. But she knew better than to ask him outright.

Just let him come out with it.

Finally Cranston said…

"It was my fault—what happened to Vincent, I mean."

Riley felt a chill at the deep note of guilt in his voice.

What does he want to tell us? she wondered.

Chapter Fourteen

Riley waited eagerly for Cranston's next words. She glanced at her colleagues and saw that they, too, were anxious to hear what the man was about to say.

Cranston's face twisted with anguish for a moment.

Finally he spoke. "Forget I said anything. It doesn't matter."

Of course that wasn't what Riley had expected to hear, but she forced herself to wait. She could see that Jenn was about to insist, and stopped the young agent with a subtle gesture. From her own experience conducting thousands of interviews, Riley knew that the least bit of prodding could shut certain types of people down.

Silence was the best way of drawing Cranston out.

Finally he said in a slow, agonized voice, "It was my idea. Vincent coming to Yale, I mean. He wanted to stay near his parents—my brother and sister-in-law—in California. He wanted to go to Stanford. The truth was... I barely knew the boy. I hadn't seen him since he was a baby, hadn't shown any real interest in him. It wasn't any of my business. Still, I insisted. I told his parents that he had to go to Yale."

"Why?" Riley asked.

Cranston's lips twisted into a bitter, painful, ironic trace of a smile.

"Tradition," he said.

Then he pointed at the portrait. "My great-great grandfather Brenton Cranston got only a third-grade education. He was truly a self-made billionaire—a titan of a man. He sent his own sons to Yale and declared that he wanted all of his male descendants bearing his name to go there too. He made it a condition of inheritance in his will. And so it began. And for some damn fool reason, I…"

He heaved a long, grim sigh.

He said, "If it weren't for me, Vincent would have gone to Stanford instead. And he'd be alive today. This feels like fate's way of telling me how wrong I was, how indifferent I am to the happiness of others. It never occurred to me… that a tradition could kill."

Riley felt a deep pang of sympathy. She'd often seen this sort of guilt among relatives and loved ones of murder victims. Murder had a terrible way of reminding people of their personal failures, causing them to blame themselves.

And now he's troubled about fate again, as though he'd given fate the opportunity to strike the young man down.

She said in a slow, gentle voice…

"Mr. Cranston, it's like I told you before. Fate had nothing to do with your nephew's murder. But I understand how you feel. This is a terrible thing to have to deal with alone. Do you have anyone you can share these feelings with, someone who can understand and help?"

Cranston drew himself up and relit his pipe.

He said, "I can manage. I'll be all right."

Stifling a sigh, Riley thought…

I take that as a no.

"We'll go now," she said to him. "I promise we'll be in touch as soon as we have any news at all."

"I hope so," Cranston said.

As Riley and her colleagues got up to leave, something Cranston had just said rattled in her brain. It was the way he'd described his nephew.

"… *a perfect specimen.*"

Jenn, too, had said something similar about the crime scene photos…

"… *he looked pretty nearly perfect.*"

Riley hesitated, then said…

"Mr. Cranston... did your nephew have any...?"

She paused and asked herself...

Any what?

What was it exactly she wanted to ask?

And how could she put it tactfully?

She cautiously continued, "Did he have any—distinguishing characteristics? Some sort of visible—imperfection?"

Cranston looked puzzled by the question.

"Imperfection?" he asked.

"A birthmark, for example," Riley said.

"No, nothing like that at all," Cranston said. "He was... well, very good-looking. Everyone who knew him said so. And of course, he was also an aspiring athlete."

Riley thanked him again, and she joined Bill and Jenn on their way to the double doors where they'd come in. Bill turned the doorknob and pushed the door open. The butler who had led them here was standing in the hallway, apparently waiting for them to come out, looking as forbidding as he had before.

Riley paused in the hall to look back at Cranston. He was still seated at the end of the table, looking up again at that stern portrait on the wall as if expecting it to speak.

It troubled her to think about the man's isolation in this vast, drafty, unwelcoming home. There was the butler, of course, and there must also be a fairly large household staff lurking about unseen. But did any of them really care about their employer?

Niles Cranston seemed to have no companionship at all except that grim, ghostly image of his ancestor on the wall.

Such a lonely man, she thought.

His inherited fortune had brought him no happiness that she could detect. Instead, it seemed more like a burden that he could never, ever shake off.

And now his nephew is dead.

As Riley and her colleagues stood in the hall, the butler pulled the double doors shut again and said coldly...

"Kindly allow me to show you out."

Riley and her colleagues followed the butler back the way they'd come, through the vast hallway and out the impressive front door.

As they left the house and walked toward their cars, Agent Sturman asked...

"What do we do next?"

Riley exchanged glances with Bill and Jenn. She could tell that they, too, felt stymied.

She said to Sturman, "What about those names you mentioned a little while ago? The list of people who had bought ice picks?"

Agent Sturman took out his cell phone again and looked at the message he'd received earlier.

He shrugged and said...

"Well, like I said, the three names don't look that promising. My team found ice pick purchases made by people with criminal records, but none of them for violent crimes. One guy got busted five days ago on a parole violation."

Jenn said, "Well, he certainly didn't kill Robin Scoville or Ron Donovan."

"What about the others?" Bill asked.

Agent Sturman shook his head and said, "Another guy bought his ice pick just last week—too recently to have killed Vincent Cranston. But the third guy... I don't know..."

"Tell us about him," Riley said.

Sturman said, "Well, his name is Bruno Young, and he bought an ice pick a week and a half ago, long enough to have killed all three victims. He's on parole after serving time for heroin delivery."

"Heroin delivery," Bill grumbled. "You're right, that doesn't sound promising."

Riley said, "We'd better check it out anyway."

"That shouldn't be much trouble," Agent Sturman said. "I've got his address right here. He lives in New Haven."

"Let's pay him a visit," Riley said.

Riley and her colleagues got back into their borrowed car and followed Agent Sturman's vehicle back into New Haven. Sturman led them into a seedy, rundown neighborhood. Riley guessed that it had once been a quaint and charming area, with small shops and pleasant apartment buildings. But now the businesses were mostly boarded up, and many of the buildings were in terrible shape.

Riley saw women lurking in the doorways—prostitutes, she guessed, although they weren't openly parading their bodies. Police cars were prowling the streets on patrol, so the women probably stayed in the shadows as much as they could, luring their johns instead of boldly approaching them.

Bill parked their car behind Agent Sturman's as he parked in front of a decrepit apartment building, one of a row that had probably once been individual houses. Sturman led Riley and her colleagues into the building and up to the second floor. When they found the apartment they were looking for, they saw that the door bore multiple locks. They could hear the sounds of a TV and noisy children's voices inside the apartment.

Sturman knocked on the door, and a woman's voice called out from inside…

"Who is it?"

"The FBI," Sturman called back. "Is this where Bruno Young lives?"

After a pause, the woman said…

"I guess."

Sturman exchanged glances with Riley and her colleagues.

Riley called out, "May we come in?"

After another silence, they heard the woman say…

"Let them in, Andy."

After the rattle of several locks, the door was opened by a teen-aged boy with a blank expression on his face. The apartment was tiny and a terrible mess, with dirty clothes scattered everywhere and a mountain of dirty dishes in the kitchen area. Four younger, raucous children were running around making lots of noise.

An exhausted-looking woman sat in a battered armchair staring at an old television screen, smoking a cigarette and watching what looked like a soap opera. She didn't look away from the screen as Riley and her colleagues came inside.

She grumbled, "FBI, you say?"

Sturman, Riley, and her colleagues all produced their badges and introduced themselves.

Still staring at the TV, the woman said…

"And you're looking for Bruno?"

"That's right," Bill said.

With a hoarse, asthmatic-sounding sigh, the woman said…

"Then you're here to arrest him, I guess."

Chapter Fifteen

Riley exchanged startled looks with her colleagues.

What does this woman know that we don't? she wondered.

The woman in the battered armchair had immediately assumed she and her colleagues were here to arrest Bruno Young. They'd actually come just to talk to him, to try to determine whether he was a possible suspect.

Now Riley didn't know what to think.

The woman glanced up from the TV screen at the four agents and added...

"Well, isn't that why you're here? Bruno did kill somebody, didn't he?"

Riley's perplexity deepened.

Bill asked the woman, "Is Bruno Young on the premises?"

Looking back at the TV, the woman said, "No, but you don't have to take my word for it. Have yourselves a look around. Be my guest. Maybe pick up some of the mess while you're at it."

Neither Riley nor her colleagues bothered to move from where they were standing. The apartment was tiny and crowded, not a likely place for anyone to hide. Riley was sure the woman wasn't bluffing. Apparently the other agents felt that as well, because none of them was poking around checking into closets.

The woman seemed to be apathetic from sheer exhaustion—and Riley thought she looked much too young to have so many children.

She asked the woman, "Are you his wife?"

"Sure am," the woman said. "My name is Doris."

Then with a wave of her hand at the raucous children she added, "And these are Bruno's kids. Not that he cares much about them— or about me. Hell, he probably couldn't tell you all their names."

Doris looked quickly around and said sharply to the teenaged boy...

"Andy, stop your little sister from swallowing that thing."

The boy snatched a small plastic toy out of the little girl's mouth. She immediately started crying. The woman muted the TV but kept on watching it.

Speaking over the growing noise of the children, Riley said to the woman...

"Why do you think your husband killed somebody?"

Doris shrugged and said, "He keeps talking about it, that's why. He's been an angry man since he got out of the Danbury Prison a couple of months ago. You'd barely recognize him from how he was before. He was easier to live with when he was hooked on smack."

She pointed toward the kitchen area and said...

"Have a look at the tabletop over there."

Riley and her colleagues walked over to have a look at the kitchen table. The checkered tablecloth was gouged and torn, and the Formica top under it was badly scarred by something sharp and hard.

Doris said, "He keeps coming and going all hours, sometimes disappears a day or two. Whenever he's home, he just keeps sitting over there, saying he's going to get his own back, somebody's going to pay for what happened to him. All the while he keeps stabbing at the table with that damned ice pick of his. Scares me and the kids half to death."

Riley felt a deep chill of anticipation.

An ice pick.

Had the search for ice pick purchases conducted by Agent Sturman's team found the killer after all?

Riley had barely dared to hope so, but now it was starting to seem likely.

Bill said, "Do you have any idea where Bruno is right now?"

Doris said, "He's mentioned hanging around the corner of Redmond and Wilson, about a half a block east of here. I couldn't tell you why."

Riley and her colleagues hastily thanked Doris Young, then rushed out of the sad little apartment, down the stairs, and out of the building. As they continued on foot along the street, Agent Sturman remarked…

"We'd better find out what he looks like."

Sturman used his cell phone to log into a database of mug shots. Soon he found one of Bruno Young, a bearded young man with hollow eyes.

When they got to the street corner Doris Young had mentioned, they saw nobody in sight. There were vacant lots on three of the corners where buildings had recently been torn down. On the other corner stood a narrow, four-story building with sagging porches on each of its floors. A yellow sign in front read…

THIS PROPERTY IS CONDEMNED

Sure enough, the windows were all boarded up.

Riley remembered something Doris had said…

"He was easier to live with when he was hooked on smack."

Riley had a gut-churning feeling that she knew what she'd find inside.

Am I ready to deal with this? she wondered.

The only alternative was to wait outside while her three companions went on in. And she couldn't accept that as an option.

Pointing to the building, she said to her colleagues…

"We'd better search that place."

Riley drew her weapon as they crossed to the dilapidated structure and climbed up onto the sagging porch. She saw that the other agents had done the same.

The front door was hanging loose on broken hinges, so they all stepped inside. The hallway was littered with trash and crumbling plaster. There were three apartment doors on the ground floor.

Jenn rapped sharply at one of the doors and shouted…

"FBI. Open up."

When no reply came, Riley, Bill, and Agent Sturman clustered on each side of the door, their weapons ready.

Jenn opened the door and gasped at what she saw.

"Jesus," she said. "You all had better get a look at this."

Riley felt a deep tingle of anxiety. She already thought she had a pretty good idea what to expect.

Sure enough, when they all walked through the door, they found that the room was lit only by candles. The floor was strewn with five human bodies. Some of them looked as though they might actually be dead, but Riley felt pretty sure that they weren't. They were surrounded by debris that included bags of white powder and hypodermic needles.

"What's the matter with them?" Jenn murmured.

"They're high on heroin," Riley said, thinking…

"High" doesn't seem like the right word.

The inhabitants of the room were practically unconscious, except for a man and a woman who crouched in a corner. The man was giving the woman an injection, right there and then. He looked up at Riley and her colleagues as he pulled out the needle.

"Did you say you were FBI?" he said in a weirdly detached voice. "What do you want?"

Riley felt sure that the man was too deep in a drug-induced euphoria to care about the arrival of law enforcement agents.

Bill said, "We're looking for a man named Bruno Young."

Jenn added, "Is he on the premises?"

The man sat heavily beside the young woman and closed his eyes.

"Bruno Young, you say?" he said. "Maybe, I'm not sure. Names don't count for much in a place like this."

Riley felt a chill at those words…

"… a place like this."

Just as she'd suspected, he meant that the whole building was a so-called "shooting gallery"—a place where heroin addicts gathered to keep getting their fixes. Riley figured the people in this room practically lived here...

And they're probably going to die here.

Her weapon was shaking in her hand now, and she really wasn't sure if she could deal with what she was seeing.

The last time she'd been in such a place was November of last year. She'd been searching for her daughter April, who'd been abducted by a vicious young punk. He had injected her and then tried to sell her body. When Riley found them, she'd had to fight her inclination to kill the young monster.

Bill took Riley by an arm and steered her out of the room and back into the hallway, His voice was flat as he said, "We'd better check the rest of the building."

Riley nodded and added, "We should split up, each take a floor."

As Jenn knocked on another door just across the hall, Riley, Bill, and Agent Sturman climbed the stairs. Each step felt as though it might collapse under them.

Bill began checking rooms on the second floor, and Sturman on the third floor, while Riley continued on her way to the top floor.

She was panting and felt sweat breaking out on her forehead, but she knew it wasn't just from the climb.

The ugly smells of the house were triggering a grim memory— of how she'd walked into a bedroom of another shooting gallery and found April lying drugged on a bare mattress, whimpering "no, no, no," while a young man tried to undress her for another man's sick pleasure.

She also remembered the violent rage the sight had triggered in her—how she'd brutally and deliberately crushed the abductor's hand, first with a baseball bat and then under her foot.

Shuddering deeply, she reminded herself...

Keep your head in the game.

She had a job to do, and she couldn't let herself be overwhelmed by the past.

She called out near the top of the stairs, "This is the FBI. We're looking for Bruno Young. Show yourself, with your hands in sight."

When she reached the top of the stairs, she saw three open doors. She looked into one of them and saw just one man sitting hunched over against a wall with a needle and a spoon on the floor beside him.

Is that him? she wondered. *Is that Bruno Young?*

Riley stepped into the room.

Someone grabbed her from behind, spun her around, and slammed her hard against the wall.

Her gun flew from her hand.

A strong shadowy man held her fast, and she felt something sharp against her throat.

An ice pick, she realized with alarm.

"What do you want with me?" the man hissed at her.

Chapter Sixteen

Riley stared into the angry face that loomed just inches from her own. She immediately recognized those hollow eyes and that shaggy beard.

Bruno Young.

She had seen his mug shot just a few minutes ago, and now he had her pinned against the wall.

He pressed the point of an ice pick against her throat.

For a few moments, all movement seemed to freeze.

Riley wanted to shout to her companions in the floors below, but she barely dared to breathe. She knew that with a single hard punch, Young could drive the ice pick's sharp, long shaft all the way through her windpipe and into the vertebrae of her neck.

She'd probably be dead before she hit the floor.

The man snarled, "Answer my question, FBI lady! What do you want from me?"

"I just want to ask you some questions," Riley said hoarsely.

"Questions, huh?" he growled. "What did you need a gun for if you just wanted to ask me questions?"

Panic seized Riley's body as she tried to decide what to do. Any move she tried to make could well be her last.

Just then Riley heard another voice in the room.

"Bruno, you son of a bitch."

Riley realized it was the man she'd seen when she'd first entered the room—the man who'd been huddled against the wall in a drug-induced stupor.

Bruno yelled back to him, "Shut up, Jim. Mind your own business."

The distraction was brief, but it was exactly what Riley needed.

She jerked her whole body sharply to her left, then heard the dull thud of the ice pick as its shaft plunged into the wall.

A quick glance around the room didn't reveal her gun. It must have disappeared somewhere in the room's deep debris.

The man on the floor cried weakly...

"Look out, lady."

Riley whirled back around just in time to dodge a lunge from Bruno Young.

He had pulled the ice pick out of the wall and swung it at her, but his body weight carried him harmlessly past her.

Then the heavy man turned toward her again, holding the ice pick in his fist with the point upward. This time he seemed to be considering what to do next.

Riley recognized the stance of an experienced street fighter. She also knew that she was still dazed from his initial attack. She stood facing him, waiting for his next move.

When it came, she seized her chance. She deftly grabbed his arm and twisted it.

The ice pick fell from his hand.

In another second, she had the man on his knees on the floor, holding his arm behind his back.

In a violent surge of adrenaline, Riley's whole body was dangerously charged with energy.

She flashed back again to how she'd crushed the hand of April's abductor, and she remembered how close she'd come to killing him.

The same uncontrollable rage came over her now.

She knew that one sharp twist would be enough to dislocate her attacker's elbow, and then with another she could break his wrist...

And after that...

Image after sadistic image filled her imagination.

She didn't know if she could control the urge to strike this man, injure him badly, or perhaps kill him.

Agent Sturman's voice interrupted.

"Agent Paige, are you all right?"

Riley snapped around and saw him standing in the doorway.

She wondered just how long he'd been there. She hoped it had been long enough to see that Bruno had tried to kill her.

Riley nearly blurted...

"Yeah, but you probably saved this bastard's life."

Instead, she gasped for breath and said, "I'm OK, but I could use a hand with this guy. Get a pair of cuffs on him. He's under arrest."

As Jenn and Bill came into the room, Riley crouched down and searched for her missing weapon. She found it and put it back in its holster. Then her eyes fell on the other man still sitting next to the wall—the man Bruno had called "Jim."

He'd been watching the scene with the weird, detached tranquility of someone immersed in a heroin high.

Riley said, "Sturman, call the local cops to come and clean out this hellhole. They'll have a lot of arrests to deal with. Then you and Agent Roston take Bruno Young here to the local FBI headquarters. Bill and I will catch up with you shortly."

Jenn dragged Bruno out of the room, and Sturman followed her, calling the police on his cell phone. Riley could hear the man loudly protesting as they hauled him down the stairs.

Riley saw that Bill was watching her closely. She knew her partner was aware that something dramatic had happened here. She turned away from him and whispered...

"We've got to talk to this guy. I'm hoping he can give us some answers."

Bill looked a bit surprised at the suggestion, but then he turned his attention to the man on the floor.

The two agents crouched down in front the drugged man.

Riley said to him, "You're name is Jim, I take it."

The man nodded, and his eyes rolled back in his head.

"Yeah," he said. "Jim Gibney. Who are you?"

Riley's hopes wavered. She knew she'd called out that she was FBI when she'd gotten to the top of the stairs. Jim was still awfully deep in his drug state.

Does he even remember what just happened? she wondered.

Riley said, "I'm Special Agent Riley Paige, FBI. This is my partner, Agent Jeffreys."

The man seemed to be making an effort to hold his head up. When he spoke again, he sounded as if he were talking in his sleep.

"Don't arrest me, OK? I mean, if that's what you're here for. I'm not worth the trouble. This place is full of other junkies. You don't need me. Anyway, I saved your life just now, didn't I?"

Riley didn't reply. But the truth was…

He might be right.

As stoned as he was, he'd managed to alert her just in time to keep Bruno Young from stabbing her with that ice pick. Still, she wasn't going to grant his request. Soon the police would be here, and Jim would be hauled away along with everybody else in the building.

Riley said to him, "What can you tell me about Bruno Young?"

Jim squinted and said, "Bruno was here? Again?"

Riley suppressed a sigh. Jim's memory of what had just happened seemed to be very dim. Was she going to be able to get any useful information out of him?

She said, "Jim, he just attacked me with an ice pick, remember?"

"You too, huh?" Jim said.

Riley said, "Are you saying he attacked *you* with his ice pick?"

Jim breathed deeply, in and out.

"Not exactly," he said. "But he's been threatening to kill me with it. It's been going on for days and days, maybe a couple of weeks. He comes up here and sits beside me and holds that ice pick to my throat, talks about how easy it would be to finish me off, and how he'll do it sooner or later. Sometimes he really scares me, but…"

He inhaled and exhaled again and said…

"Other times I tell him to go ahead, it's not like I give a damn."

Bill said, "Why does he keep threatening to kill you?"

"You'd have to ask him that," Jim said. "If you can find him. Did you say he was here just now? If not, I sure don't know where he is. Maybe you can catch him at home."

"We arrested him just now," Bill said. "Right here in front of you."

Jim smiled ever so slightly.

"Did you?" he said. "Hey, good for you. He's a mean son of a bitch. Has been since he got out of the joint. It really changed him. It's like I don't know him anymore. We used to be pals..."

Jim seemed to be fading off into a semi-conscious stupor. Riley shook him by the shoulder.

"We need for you to tell us more," Riley said.

Jim shook his head and said, "I'm not a narc."

"Why did he want to kill you?" Riley said.

Jim repeated, "I'm not a narc."

Then he closed his eyes and seemed to slip completely away from them.

Riley was about to shake him again when she heard the sound of footsteps and voices down on the ground floor.

Bill said, "The cops are here. Maybe we should haul this guy in separately. Maybe we can question him when he can make more sense."

Riley said, "You know that's not going to happen any time soon. As soon as he comes down from this fix, he's going to want more. When he can't get it, he'll go into withdrawal, and he still won't make any sense. Anyway, we'll know where he is if we think we need him."

Bill nodded.

"Wishful thinking," he admitted.

They both got back on their feet.

Riley said, "Besides, I think he already told us something."

Bill scoffed a little and said...

"Yeah? Like what?"

Riley still wasn't quite sure. But she realized that something was nagging at her mind.

She said, "Let's head on over to FBI headquarters."

As she and Bill walked down the stairs, multiple arrests were already in progress. Riley felt troubled by what was going on around her. She remembered all too well how hard it had been for April to recover from her fleeting experience with heroin. It had taken some rigorous rehab, but April had gotten through it, and now she'd put the whole ugly experience behind her.

And now Riley couldn't help but wonder…

What if April had gone to jail instead, just like the people here?

Would she ever have gotten better?

Were these people likely to get better in jail or prison?

Riley tried to put such thoughts out of her mind as she and Bill headed out of the house and walked toward their borrowed car.

Now she kept hearing Jim's protest in her mind…

"I'm not a narc…"

On one hand, he'd pretty obviously meant that he wouldn't inform on Bruno to an FBI agent.

But Riley suspected that he'd meant something else as well.

Chapter Seventeen

As they walked toward the FBI headquarters in New Haven, Riley reviewed the shooting gallery episode in her mind. Her thoughts were interrupted by Bill's deep sigh of despair.

"It's started," he grumbled.

Riley looked up and immediately saw what he was talking about.

A small group of reporters, some with TV cameras, were gathered around the building's front entrance. Their hopes of keeping the media away from this case were about to get wrecked.

As Riley and Bill pushed past them, the reporters called out questions.

"Are you FBI agents?"

"Are you investigating the murder this morning at Wickenburg Reef?"

"Is it true that the fisherman's death was connected to an earlier murder in Wilburton?"

"Have you got a suspect for both murders?"

Riley and Bill kept saying "No comment" and managed to get inside the building without answering any questions. Then they asked a receptionist for directions to the interrogation room. As they continued on their way through the building, Bill said...

"It doesn't sound like they know about the ice pick angle."

"Not yet," Riley said. "But they've found out that those last two murders have something in common. The weapon used is liable to leak pretty soon. Let's hope we can keep the cause of Vincent Cranston's death quiet for a while longer."

Bill chuckled a little and added, "At least none of them seemed to recognize you."

Riley understood what he meant. She'd gotten quite a bit of unwanted publicity for her brilliant work on some cases. Some crime reporters knew a lot about her. She hoped all of that wasn't going to turn out to be a liability while they were working on this case.

When Bill and Riley arrived outside the interrogation room, they found Jenn and Agent Sturman looking through a two-way mirror at Bruno Young. Riley's recent assailant was manacled and sitting at a table.

Bill asked Jenn and Agent Sturman...

"Has he lawyered up yet?"

Agent Sturman scoffed. "Not yet. He's an arrogant bastard. Says he doesn't need a lawyer because he didn't do anything wrong."

Riley said, "Well, he did assault a law enforcement officer."

Sturman nodded and said, "Yeah, I got there just in time to see him lunge at you with that ice pick. You subdued him before I could come to your aid. You've got some moves there, Agent Paige."

Riley wondered—had Sturman also seen the rage in her eyes when he'd called out to her? Did he know how close Riley had come to doing Bruno some serious bodily harm—perhaps even killing him?

If he does know, he's not making an issue of it, she realized.

She felt a renewed rush of relief that Sturman had saved her from her own violent impulses.

Bill asked Sturman and Jenn, "What have you been able to find out about Bruno Young since you brought him here?"

Sturman said, "It's like his wife said—he'd been paroled from Danbury Prison a couple of months ago. The charge was heroin delivery. He served just eighteen months on a much longer sentence. He got out for good behavior, but the terms of his parole are as strict as hell. Just hanging around a place like that shooting gallery is enough to send him back to prison."

Jenn nodded and said, "And of course he wouldn't be allowed to own a firearm. But an ice pick is another matter."

Bill said, "Now we need to know what he's been doing with it."

"Maybe we can get him to tell us," Sturman said. "Should all four of us go in and interrogate him? Maybe we can intimidate him with numbers."

Riley thought about it for a moment. She knew it would take some pretty sharp interrogation skills to get the truth out of Bruno, if it were even possible to do so. And he could still demand a lawyer at any moment. Too many interrogators would likely make a mess of things. She didn't want everybody piling on with this one.

She said, "Agent Jeffreys and I will go in and talk to him. Agent Roston, Agent Sturman, you two stay out here and watch and listen. Keep track of whatever gets said."

When Riley and Bill walked into the room, Bruno looked up at Riley and snarled...

"You again! You're the one who should be in cuffs right now, not me."

"Why do you say that?" Bill asked.

Bruno said to Bill, "Because she attacked me, that's why. It was police brutality."

Riley knew, of course, that he couldn't make that case. She hadn't injured him in any way, and besides, Agent Sturman had seen enough of the incident to testify otherwise.

Bill and Riley produced their badges and formally introduced themselves.

Bruno shrugged and yawned, trying to act bored.

"So what do you want to know?" he asked.

Riley said, "First of all, what were you doing hanging around that shooting gallery?"

Bruno drummed his fingers on the table.

"It was therapy," he said.

"Therapy?" Bill scoffed.

"Yeah, therapy. You probably know I'm a recovering heroin addict. Lately I've been dealing with really bad cravings. I figured it would help if I went back to my old stomping grounds, reminded myself what my life was like in the old days. Believe me, it worked. It's enough to keep me sober, let me tell you."

Riley felt a tingle of excitement. He was lying, and she knew it. The trick now was to keep the lies coming until he tripped himself up.

That shouldn't be hard, she thought.

She said to Bruno, "You know that you broke parole by going back to that place."

Bill added, "We could send you back to Danbury for that alone."

Bruno scoffed. "So—I'm getting questioned by the FBI because of a measly parole violation? I don't think so. You've got bigger fish to fry. What do you really want from me? Just come out with it."

Riley knew better than to get too direct, at least not yet. And she knew that Bill did too.

She asked, "What were you doing with that ice pick?"

Bruno shrugged again and said, "Nothing. I just found it lying around on the floor."

"And then you attacked me with it," Riley said.

"That was self-defense," Bruno said.

Bill leaned across the table toward him and said, "Now we know you're lying, Bruno. That ice pick was why we were looking for you in the first place. We know that you bought it a couple of weeks ago."

For the first time during the interview, Bruno began to look uneasy.

"I don't know what you're talking about," he said.

Riley said, "Tell me about the other guy who was in that room."

"Just some junkie," Bruno said. "I never saw him before in my life."

"I heard you call him by name," Riley said. "'Shut up, Jim,' you said."

"OK, so he'd just introduced himself," Bruno said. "Big deal. Why do you care if I know him? And while we're at it, why do you care whether I had an ice pick or not? It's not against the law."

Riley said, "According to Jim, you'd been threatening him with that ice pick for a couple of weeks."

Bruno let out a forced-sounding sarcastic chuckle.

"And you believe him?" he said. "He's a lying junkie."

Riley's curiosity was growing with every lie.

And the lies are coming on hard and fast.

She knew the man's type. Like many addicts she'd encountered, recovering or otherwise, Bruno Young was a thoroughgoing bullshit artist. Lying was his default reaction to even the most mundane queries...

But what's he trying to hide?

Riley's mind clicked away as Bill kept asking him questions and getting one lie after another in response. She found herself remembering something Jim had said to her back in that room, about how mean Bruno had gotten since he'd gotten out of prison...

"It's like I don't know him anymore. We used to be pals."

She asked him, "Why have you been threatening Jim?"

"I haven't been threatening him," Bruno said, his voice starting to crack under the strain. "I told you, he was lying."

Riley flashed back again to something else Jim had said...

"I'm not a narc."

She'd been harboring a vague gut feeling ever since she'd heard Jim say that.

Now that gut feeling was starting to really make sense.

She said to Bruno, "Tell me, Bruno—what's the absolute worst thing you could ever say about another person? The worst thing you could call him?"

"Huh?" Bruno said.

"I think you know what I mean," Riley said. "What's the absolute lowest kind of human being, as far as you're concerned?"

Bruno's face twisted into an expression of violent disgust.

He said, "A goddamn narc."

Riley struck her fist against the table and said...

"And that's what Jim is, isn't he?"

Bruno snapped back at her, "You're damned right, he's a narc. He narced me out to the cops, got me sent to prison."

Bill chimed in...

"And how did that happen, Bruno?"

Bruno suddenly seemed eager to tell the story.

"He called me in the middle of the night, said he'd run out of smack, wondered if I had any to spare. How was I to know he'd made a deal with the police? He'd gotten busted himself, was looking at a lot of prison time. But the cops offered him a 'get-out-of-jail-free' card if he'd turn narc, rat out his friends. And I walked right into the trap. The cops were waiting for me right there at his door."

He was trembling with rage now.

He said, "Heroin delivery, they called it! Until that night, I'd done nothing but use the stuff. I minded my own business, kept my own stash. I wasn't a pusher, never sold a gram of it to a living soul. But Jim sounded so desperate that night, and I felt bad for him, so I was willing to share some, that was all. I was just trying to be a good friend. And look where it got me."

Bruno sneered and added, "And yeah, the ice pick was mine. I bought it. All I wanted to do was scare him with it, make him regret what he'd done to me."

Bill said, "But that wasn't all you did with that ice pick, was it?"

"I don't know what you're talking about," Bruno growled.

"Oh, I think you do," Bill said. "And you may as well tell us the truth. Even if you scrubbed that thing real good, we can still get DNA samples off it."

Bruno's eyes widened with alarm.

"What the hell are you getting at?" he said.

Bill leaned in close to him and said, "Where were you around dawn this morning?"

"I don't need to tell you that," Bruno said.

"What about a week ago?" Bill said. "Where were you when Robin Scoville was killed?"

"Robin who?" Bruno said

"You know exactly who I'm talking about."

Bruno looked panic-stricken now.

"I want to see a lawyer," he said.

"Why?" Bill demanded. "I thought you hadn't done anything wrong."

"I won't say another word without a lawyer," Bruno said

Bill was about to keep pushing him, but Riley gave him a nudge. When Bill looked at her, she shook her head, silently telling him...

We've got to quit now.

Bill let out a growl of disgust. Then he and Riley went back out of the room to rejoin Jenn and Agent Sturman.

Bill grumbled to Sturman, "Looks like you'd better call in a public defender."

Sturman said, "He's our man, isn't he?"

"We'll have to get forensics to check out that ice pick to be certain," Bill said.

Nevertheless, Riley sensed from Bill's tone that he felt pretty sure of Bruno's guilt.

But now that the interview had been cut short...

I'm not so sure, Riley thought.

Chapter Eighteen

While Riley was hard at work in Connecticut, her ex-husband, Ryan Paige, was getting into the car after his flight. He found himself wondering...

Am I sure I want to do this?

Is this really a good idea?

Even as he asked himself those questions, he realized how odd it was for him to be so hesitant. Not too long ago, he'd never have doubted his own decisions. But now a lot had changed in his life.

For several long minutes, Ryan sat in the Mercedes he'd just rented at the Tweed– New Haven Airport and tried to think things through.

His life as he'd known it—his high-paying career as a lawyer, his prestige and reputation, the countless beautiful young women he'd been involved with—all that was over now.

His stupid little affair with an associate named Kyanne had provoked a sexual harassment suit and gotten him kicked out of his own law partnership.

His last attempt to reconcile with Riley had been worse than humiliating.

He sat up straighter in the driver's seat and shook of his indecision.

What else could he do? He started the car, grateful that some of his credit cards were still functional.

Now it was time to start picking up the pieces of his life.

But how could he do that without Riley?

What other choice did he have except try to put things back together with her?

Ryan set his turn-by-turn navigation to the FBI headquarters in New Haven. As he drove through the city following the spoken instructions, he remembered waking up this morning in that vast, empty house he'd once shared with Riley and April.

He'd burst into tears at the thought of being so alone. Then he'd pulled himself together, downed a cup of coffee, and summoned up his courage to give Riley a call. The phone had been answered by Jilly, that girl from Arizona Riley had adopted earlier this year.

When Jilly had said that her mother wasn't home, Ryan had pushed the girl to tell her where Riley was. Jilly had reluctantly told him that Riley was in Connecticut, but she hadn't explained what she was doing there.

Not that Ryan had needed an explanation.

She's surely working on a case.

If he was right about that, someone at the FBI headquarters in New Haven could tell him how and where to find her. Then he could he could go meet with her and…

And what?

Did he really expect her to meet him with open arms? Did he really think she'd be glad to see him? No, of course not. He'd been crying and drunk the last time she'd seen him—hardly the young man she'd fallen in love with many years ago. He knew he'd been strong and attractive back then. Well, he didn't think he'd lost all his charm. Not completely. And maybe she'd be impressed by his romantic gesture.

Even so, Ryan knew that it was ridiculous for him to imagine that this would be easy. Nor did he deserve for it to be that easy, after all the heartbreak and disappointment he'd caused Riley for so many years.

It was only fair that it would take some work to win her back.

And that was what he was going to do.

Ryan parked in front of the FBI building and got out of his car. As he walked toward the front entrance, he noticed a bunch of people clustered there, some of them wielding TV cameras.

Reporters, he realized.

He figured something important must be going on.

Did it have anything to do with Riley?

He wouldn't be surprised.

He knew that Riley often worked on high-profile cases that attracted the media. If so, was this a good time to be stepping back into her life?

Maybe not, but on the other hand...

Maybe she could use my support.

Then again, for all he knew, maybe that boyfriend of hers—that restaurant owner, Blaine—was here already.

But how likely was that, really? Ryan couldn't remember ever having traveled with Riley to be with her when she was working on a case. Would things be different with Blaine? Would Riley encourage him to come along?

Ryan doubted it—which gave him new cause to hope. Now might be his perfect chance to prove that he was more interested in her work than he'd ever been.

More so than that boyfriend of hers, even.

Besides, he'd gone to a lot of trouble to make sure that he looked his very best. His hair, still remarkably full for a man his age, was perfectly combed, and he was wearing his finest three-piece suit. He did still have a decent wardrobe, after all.

As he neared the building, Ryan was surprised and somewhat alarmed when the reporters suddenly clustered around him and started to badger him with questions.

"Are you an FBI agent?"

"Are you investigating the murder this morning at Wickenburg Reef?"

"Was the fisherman's death connected to an earlier murder?"

Ryan stammered...

"I—I'm sorry, I... don't know anything about..."

But the questions just kept coming, and Ryan couldn't push the rest of the way through the reporters to the front door.

Finally, not knowing what else to say, he called out...

"I'm sure the situation is in good hands."

"How do you know?" one reporter yelled.

Ryan blurted, "Because my information indicates that Special Agent Riley Paige is here working on the case."

Now the reporters really went crazy. They started yelling Riley's name at him and at each other.

One reporter shoved a microphone in his face and demanded...

"Who are you?"

Ryan felt completely overwhelmed now.

"I—I'm Agent Paige's husband," he said. "Ryan Paige."

The reporters closed in tightly around him, and Ryan thought...

Oh my God.

Did I just make a really stupid mistake?

Should he stop and explain that he was actually Riley's ex-husband?

No, he reminded himself. *I'm here to win her back.*

And maybe this was playing out exactly as he needed it to.

The reporter with the microphone in Ryan's face harangued him louder than the rest.

"Mr. Paige, I've got an anonymous source in the Connecticut Medical Examiner's office. He says that the recent death of Vincent Cranston was actually a murder, and the authorities are covering it up. Also, that Cranston was killed in the same way as the victim in Wilburton—with an ice pick. Can you confirm that?"

The sense of surprise in the other reporters was palpable. The reporter nearest to Ryan apparently knew something that rest of them hadn't.

"Is that true?" another reporter asked Ryan.

"Are all three of these deaths connected?" yet another asked.

"Is there a serial killer at large?"

An odd feeling started to come over Ryan. He was starting to enjoy being the center of attention. It felt a lot like arguing a case in front of a courtroom.

Just keep your cool, he told himself.

Just do your stuff.

With a surge of self-confidence, he yelled back…

"I'm sorry, but I'm not at liberty to discuss any of that."

He flashed his most winning smile at a renewed onslaught of questions, and managed to quiet the reporters at least a little with an authoritative gesture he'd often used in the courtroom.

Then he said…

"But I'd be glad to answer other questions about Agent Riley Paige."

Riley was sitting in a conference room with Bill, Jenn, and Special Agent Sturman, discussing the interrogation that had just taken place. Bruno Young's public attorney had now arrived and was conferring with him privately back in the interrogation room.

Agent Sturman struck Riley as perhaps overly enthusiastic.

"I think we've got him," Sturman said. "I think we've got our man."

"Maybe," Riley said

"What do you mean, maybe?" Sturman asked. "He threatened a junkie with an ice pick, and he tried to kill Agent Paige with it. Is it just a coincidence that he had an ice pick at all?"

Riley stifled a sigh. Was she going to have to explain to this seasoned agent that coincidences were a fact of life in investigative work?

She was relieved when Jenn spoke up.

"Not necessarily. Ice picks are coming back into style as weapons. Gang members are using them a lot these days. They like them because they're scary. They make them feel like gangsters of the old days. Maybe Young was telling the truth—that he was just trying to scare that junkie."

Then Bill said, "But Young certainly acted guilty. He seemed downright scared when we brought up Robin Scoville's murder. Too bad he lawyered up before we could start leaning on him about Vincent Cranston and the fisherman at Wickenburg Reef this morning."

Riley shook her head and said, "Maybe he was just scared because he really hadn't known anything about any of the murders until that very moment, and he thought he might get convicted for a crime he didn't commit. That would be a scary possibility, especially to a convict out on parole."

Jenn drummed her fingers on the table and said, "You might be right. Still, do you remember what his wife told us? She said he comes and goes at all hours, sometimes disappears for a day or two. And just now, he didn't even try to think of an alibi for where he'd been around dawn this morning."

Agent Sturman let out a grunt of discouragement.

He said, "If it weren't for that damned lawyer, maybe we could lean on him harder about his whereabouts. It's going to take some serious work to try to track his past movements. If it's even possible."

"At least we've got his ice pick," Bill said. "If he killed anybody with it, forensics might still be able to find traces of blood on it. And if they can find blood, they'll also find the victims' DNA. Then we'd have him dead to rights."

Riley and her colleagues sat in silence for a few moments.

Then Riley said, "Look, I felt like I got at least some sense of the killer at all three of the crime scenes. And Bruno Young doesn't fit my impressions."

"Why not?" Agent Sturman asked.

Riley was about to try to explain her doubts and feelings when there came a knock on the door.

"Come in," Sturman said.

A young FBI employee stepped inside.

He said nervously, "I'm looking for Special Agent Riley Paige."

Riley felt a tingle of alarm.

Is something wrong at home? she wondered.

"I'm Riley Paige," she said.

The employee said, "We've got a situation out at the front entrance. A man who says he's your husband is talking to the press."

Riley squinted with confusion.

"I'm not married," she said.

The employee shrugged and said, "Well, that's what he keeps saying. Please come with me. Things are really getting out of hand."

As Riley got up and followed the employee out of the room, she wondered who might be calling himself her husband.

Blaine, maybe?

Surely Blaine wouldn't do anything that ridiculous.

Then she felt a jolt as it occurred to her...

Oh my God! It's Ryan!

Chapter Nineteen

As Riley followed the young FBI employee down the hall toward the front entrance, her mind was racing with questions.

"How bad is it?" she asked breathlessly.

"Really bad," he replied. "Your husband—"

Riley interrupted, "He's not my husband."

"Well, whoever he is, he seems to have told the reporters that Vincent Cranston was murdered, and that there's a serial killer at large."

Riley could hardly believe her ears.

She said, "But Ryan doesn't even know anything about the case!"

The employee said, "I don't know what to tell you. It's what he said. And now it's what a lot of reporters believe."

Riley and the young man stepped out through the front entrance.

For a moment, Riley stopped and stared.

She saw that considerably more reporters were now gathered out here. Even worse, some of them had TV cameras. Worse still, they were clustered tightly around her ex-husband.

Even worse, Ryan appeared to be thoroughly enjoying himself...

Like he's holding court.

Riley charged forward and grabbed him by the arm.

"Come with me," she ordered.

As she tried to pull Ryan away from the reporters, they started clamoring...

"Are you Riley Paige?"

"What can you tell us about Vincent Cranston's murder?"

"Is it true that his killer has also murdered two other people?"

Ignoring the questions and hoping not to be caught by the TV cameras, Riley shoved Ryan through the door and into the building.

Fortunately, a couple of security guards were stationed just inside, and they kept the reporters from entering.

Ryan seemed shocked and surprised as she dragged him into the building.

"You don't act very glad to see me," he said.

Riley didn't bother to reply. As they continued down the hallway, she looked around for a place where they could talk in private. They passed the open door of the conference room, where Bill, Jenn, and Agent Sturman sat staring at them.

Sturman got to his feet and called out to her, "Agent Paige, where are you going?"

Riley jerked Ryan to a halt.

Good question, she thought.

She asked Sturman, "Is the interrogation room free?"

"As far as I know," Sturman said.

Dragging Ryan by the arm again, Riley called back to Sturman...

"That's where you can find us."

She roughly escorted Ryan to the little room and shoved him inside, then shut the door behind them.

"Sit," she said sharply to Ryan.

His mouth hanging open, Ryan sat down in the same chair where Bruno Young had been sitting just a little while ago. Riley paced back and forth in front of the table, trying to bring her anger under control.

"First things first," she said. "How did you know I was in Connecticut?"

Ryan knitted his brow with worry.

"Oh, Riley, I don't know if I should tell you that."

"You'd damn well better," Riley snarled.

Ryan sighed deeply and said, "OK, if you must know, Jilly told me."

Riley was aghast now.

"Jilly?" she said.

"Don't be mad at her," Ryan said. "She meant well. I think she wants us to get back together."

Riley doubted that very much. Ryan had bitterly disappointed Jilly in the past. Jilly had never forgiven him for treating her like a true daughter for a time, then bailing on her like he always did with his family.

She asked, "Why did you even call the kids?"

Ryan smiled that familiar rakish smile of his.

"Come on, Riley," he said. "You know how much I love the kids. I always try to stay in touch."

Riley felt a flash of anxiety. Ryan seemed to be genuinely out of touch with reality. He seemed to have convinced himself that he'd been acting out of the best intentions. She wondered—how much harm had his delusions caused just now?

Riley asked, "How did you know Vincent Cranston was murdered?"

"I didn't know," Ryan said.

"You must have known," Riley said. "It's what you told them, isn't it?"

Ryan looked confused by the question.

"No, I didn't tell them anything like that," he said. "I've never even heard of Vincent Cranston."

"You must have said something about him," Riley said. "What was it?"

"Well, a reporter got in my face and said something like…"

Ryan seemed to think for a moment.

Then he said, "Oh, yeah. He said he had a source with the medical examiner's office who said Cranston was murdered, and it was being covered up. He wanted to know if I could confirm that."

"So what did you tell him?" Riley asked, dreading the answer she was likely to get.

Ryan shrugged and said, "I told him I wasn't at liberty to discuss it."

Riley let out a groan of despair.

She knew that, as far as all the reporters were concerned, Ryan had as much as confirmed that Cranston had been murdered.

"What's the matter?" Ryan asked with a nervous look. "It was the right thing to say, wasn't it?"

"No, it wasn't!" Riley said. "You should have said, 'I don't know.' Better yet, you shouldn't have said anything at all."

Ryan thought for a moment and then shrugged.

"Well, anyway, don't worry," he said. "I changed the subject right away."

"What did you tell them?" Riley asked, her dread rising by the second.

Ryan smiled again.

"Just what it's like to be married to the great Riley Paige," he said. "I had them eating out of my hand, Riley. I was just starting to tell them about how you had to rescue April and me from that crazy killer last November. Remember that?"

Of course I remember, Riley thought.

Riley had been hounded by a psychopath seeking revenge because she had killed his girlfriend in an arrest many years before. The man had threatened Riley's family, so she had hidden April in a safe motel room guarded by FBI agents. Then Ryan had gotten the smart idea that April would be happier in a nice rented house in Chincoteague and had taken her there—where, of course, the killer had found it easy to find them both. She'd never told Ryan that the criminal mastermind Shane Hatcher had actually been the one who stopped the killer and tied him up so Riley could free her family.

If Hatcher hadn't arrived when he had...

She couldn't bear to think about what would have happened before she could have gotten there herself.

She said to Ryan, "Did you tell them you damn near got both you and April killed?"

Ryan said, "I didn't get a chance to tell them much of anything before you came out and broke things up. Riley, I had no idea how well-known you are. You really should exploit that to your advantage. I could help with that. You know what they say—there's no such thing as bad publicity."

Riley grumbled, "In your line of work, maybe. In my line of work, there's no such thing as *good* publicity. It's essential for me to be able to operate under the radar. And it's essential to keep some information out of the media. People's lives are at stake. Do you have any idea how much damage you did just now?"

"No, I don't know," Ryan said. "Maybe if you'd talked to me more, I'd know more about your work. Whose fault is that?"

Riley felt stung. It was true that Riley had tried to keep the grim facts of her FBI work to herself, to protect her family from them. Had she maybe carried her reticence too far?

But then she caught on to what was happening.

Stop it, she scolded herself. *Don't let him manipulate you—again.*

Ryan looked around uneasily.

"I don't like this room," he said. "I feel like one of your suspects. Am I being interrogated or something? I didn't do anything illegal, did I?"

Riley growled, "You're the lawyer, Ryan. You tell me. How about stalking? Because this sure feels like it."

Ryan's eyes fell on the two-way mirror.

"Is someone watching?" he said. "Is someone listening?"

Riley found herself wondering the same thing. She'd just told her colleagues she was coming here. Had they followed and gathered around that mirror to watch and listen? Or were they still back in the conference room discussing the case? She didn't know, and she realized that she really didn't care very much. She was glad to have something that might impress Ryan with the seriousness of the situation. Maybe he needed to feel a little paranoid.

Riley crossed her arms and demanded…

"Tell me right now. What the hell are you doing here?"

"Riley, I just want to put things right between us. I didn't like how we left things the last time we were together."

Riley bit her tongue to keep from saying…

"Do you mean with you drunk and crying?"

Ryan leaned on the table with his chin in his hands, gazing at Riley as casually as if he were sitting at a kitchen table.

He said wistfully, "Do you know what our problem was, Riley?"

Riley's mind boggled...

Where do I even begin?

Ryan continued, "We never made plans for all the changes we'd have to face. Because, you know, life is all about changes. We let ourselves get into a rut. We never faced the future."

Riley's mouth hung open with disbelief.

She said, "No, our problem was that I couldn't count on you—for anything at all."

Ryan said, "Riley, how many times do I have to tell you, I can change?"

Riley stifled a gasp.

"And how many times are you going to disappointment me and the girls? We've had enough, Ryan—all three of us. All four of us, if you count Gabriela."

Ryan leaned back in his chair and said, "You don't get it, do you? Our problem is the future. I mean here I am, between careers..."

Riley interrupted, "Between careers? You got thrown out of your own firm! And for good reason!"

Ryan continued as if he hadn't heard her.

"And what about you? You can't spend the rest of your life playing the hero. It was fine when you were younger. But you can't keep risking your life forever. You'll have to stop sometime for the sake of the people who love you. Your luck will run out, and then where will we all be?"

Riley felt stung again. Ryan had hit another nerve—the hardships her career had caused her family.

Don't let him get to you, she told herself again.

Ryan said, "Let's start from scratch, make things like the old days. We were a great team, remember?"

Then he snapped his fingers and said...

"Hey, I've got a great idea. With your fame and all your past adventures, you ought to write a book. Of course, you'd need my help. I've done a lot of writing, you know, doing my kind of work. I'm good at it. Between the two of us, we could write a surefire bestseller. I'd never have to work in a law office again. And you'd never have to go out into the field."

Riley could hear a change in Ryan's voice as he kept babbling. It grew fainter, sounded farther and farther away, as if Ryan knew how farfetched his fantasies of reconciliation were getting, knew how pathetic he really was really sounding.

I hope he doesn't cry again, she thought. *I can't deal with that right now.*

Then she realized her own throat was tight and her eyes were stinging.

She was on the verge of crying herself.

It's time to put a stop to this, she thought.

"Ryan, I don't have time for this," she said. "And neither do you. I've got a family to raise—a new family, with a new man. And you—well, you've got to pick up the pieces of your own life. I can't do that for you. No one can. You've got to find the strength to do it yourself."

Try as she might to feel otherwise, her heart went out to him. She wanted so much to reach across the table and take him by the hand or touch him on the shoulder…

Don't do it.

Then with a shaky voice she added, "And I know you can do it, Ryan. The man I married all those years ago is still in there. You've got the strength to start again."

Ryan said nothing, just stared at her with soft, sad eyes.

Riley said, "You've got to go home now, Ryan. You do know that, don't you?"

He nodded slowly.

Now a new problem occurred to her. How was she going to get Ryan out of the building without attracting the media's attention?

"Stay right here," she told him.

As she left the interrogation room, she saw that no one had been watching through the two-way mirror after all. It was just as well. The scene had been painful enough for her without having to face an audience afterward.

She walked down the hall to the conference room, where she found Jenn and Bill in earnest discussion.

Bill gave her a concerned look. "Is everything all right?"

Riley wanted to say yes, but somehow she couldn't get the word out.

Instead she asked, "Where is Agent Sturman?"

Jenn said, "He's out in front of the building, trying to fix things with the media."

Riley felt a fleeting but welcome trace of relief. She was glad somebody was trying to clean up the terrible mess Ryan had just made.

She stepped back into the hallway and saw that one of the young agents stationed there was approaching.

Riley said to him, "Excuse me, but do you know a way out through the back of this building?"

The agent nodded. Riley led him to the interrogation room, then called for Ryan to come on out. She instructed the agent to escort Ryan outside as quietly as possible. And she sternly advised Ryan to slip around the building and back to his car without attracting any attention.

"No more interviews," she said firmly.

"No more nothing," Ryan replied morosely.

Obediently, he turned and followed the agent down the hallway.

As she watched him walking away, Riley was struck by how bowed and broken her ex-husband looked from behind.

She fought back tears again as she remembered the words she'd said to him in the interrogation room...

"The man I married all those years ago is still in there. You've got the strength to start again."

But now she realized she'd been lying to Ryan—and possibly to herself. The man she'd thought she'd married had never existed. He'd been an illusion—a hollow, empty shell from the start.

And now that shell was hopelessly broken.

Riley shook off her grief and told herself...

Get your head back in the game.

You've got a job to do.

Chapter Twenty

When Riley walked back through the FBI building, she saw that Jenn and Bill were standing with Agent Sturman outside the conference room, apparently waiting for her.

Riley felt a surge of expectation.

While she'd been talking with Ryan, Sturman had been dealing with the reporters.

She hoped he'd managed to salvage the situation.

"How did it go?" she asked him.

Sturman replied, "As well as could be expected, I guess. Agent Jeffreys tells me that guy who made such a mess of things was your ex-husband. Just what the hell did he think he was doing out there?"

Riley sighed guiltily and resisted the urge to say...

"Crying for help."

Instead she said, "I'm sorry it happened, Agent Sturman. Ryan's—well, he's going through a rough time right now. He's not thinking straight, I'm afraid. Not that that's an excuse."

Sturman asked, "What was he doing confirming or denying anything about this case? I was about to have him arrested, but Agent Jeffreys assured me he was harmless."

Riley tried again to explain, "He was mostly just trying to make me look good."

When Sturman didn't comment, she added, "He's a lawyer."

Sturman frowned and asked, "Did he think he was working on this case?"

"Actually he didn't know anything about the case. He was just bouncing his replies off of the reporters' hints and questions."

Sturman nodded. "They kept feeding me lines too. One of them said an anonymous source in the ME's office told him an ice pick killer was at large."

Riley remembered Ryan mentioning the same thing. She said, "Well, Ryan didn't give them any actual information because he didn't know any."

Sturman shrugged and said, "Well, what's done is done. No offense, Agent Paige, but I hope we've seen the last of your ex for a while."

No more than I do, Riley thought miserably.

Sturman continued, "Naturally, the reporters kept asking whether Vincent Cranston had been murdered—and if so, whether he was killed by the same person who killed Robin Scoville a week ago and Ron Donovan just this morning. I kept saying 'no comment,' of course. What else could I say?"

Bill said, "Sounds like a mix of anonymous leaks and pure speculation."

"Right," Sturman said. "I'll make sure that ME Kinkaid knows about what happened. If I know Kinkaid, he'll find the leaker soon and kick him the hell off his team. Anyway, I didn't confirm the ice pick thing one way or the others, but I'm sure the reporters believe it already and are going to go with it. In fact, it's probably all over the Internet already."

Looking thoroughly dismayed, Jenn said, "That's bad. Ice picks are sure to scare the public. That's why the mob liked them back in the old days, and why gangs still like them now. I'm afraid we'll have a widespread panic on our hands."

Sturman chuckled a little and said, "I don't think so. At least I was able to tell them we've got a likely suspect in custody and the killings are probably over. That ought to keep the public reasonably calm."

Riley started at those words…

"… *a likely suspect…*"

"… *the killings are probably over…*"

Had Sturman made up his mind that Bruno Young was definitely their killer?

For that matter, what did Bill and Jenn think?

Before their meeting had been interrupted by Ryan's arrival, Riley had sensed that Bill was pretty confident about Young's guilt. She hadn't been able to tell exactly what Jenn had thought.

Sturman shuffled his feet and exchanged glances with Riley and her two colleagues.

"Look, the three of you have been a great help. I'm pretty sure your work is done as far as this case is concerned. It's up to my team and the forensics guys from here on in, to check out Bruno Young's alibis and scour the ice pick for DNA samples. I'll be surprised if they don't come up with pretty solid proof that Young's the killer. You guys go ahead, go back to Quantico, get a well-deserved rest."

Riley was about to voice her disagreement when Bill gave her a nudge and said quietly…

"Come on, Riley. Let's all three of us get out of here."

Riley stifled a sigh. She knew that Bill was right, of course. It was never a good idea to argue with local authorities when they said it was time to leave. She said goodbye to Agent Sturman and followed Bill and Jenn through the back entrance where Ryan had left. They made their way around the building to their borrowed car without being noticed by reporters.

Riley and her colleagues said little during the short drive back to Wilburton. She sensed that all of them felt vaguely unsure of how they would be leaving things in Connecticut.

It was dinnertime by the time they got back to the Ramsey Inn, so they went straight to the restaurant and ordered another delicious seafood meal. As they waited for their food, Bill looked at Riley and Jenn and said one single word…

"Thoughts?"

Riley felt relieved that they were finally going to clear the air.

Jenn said, "I guess it really looks like Bruno Young is our killer. I mean, all the evidence points that way, but…"

She hesitated, then shrugged and added...

"But I don't feel like I've got much business offering an opinion. After all, I was pretty much convinced that Wesley Mannis was our killer. Then that fisherman was murdered, and we knew that Wesley wasn't anywhere near where it happened, let alone in any kind of mental condition to commit a murder. I was flat-out wrong."

Riley leaned toward Jenn and said, "Remember what I told you, Jenn. We've got to keep coming up with ideas, even when they're wrong. Tell us what you're thinking right now."

Jenn inhaled slowly, then said, "I don't know. But Bruno feels like the wrong guy to me somehow. I can't put my finger on just why. It's just a gut feeling, I guess."

Riley breathed a little easier to learn that Jenn was nearly on her own wavelength.

"What about you, Bill?" Riley asked.

Bill took a sip of his beer and thought for a moment.

Then he said, "I could go either way. But he sure acted guilty during our interrogation. And he really began to panic when we started talking about the murder victims. That's usually a sign of guilt."

A word Bill had just said caught Riley's attention.

Panic.

She felt a sharp tingle as her own feelings started to come into focus.

She spoke slowly and cautiously...

"You're right, Bill. Bruno started to panic. And I don't think our killer is the kind of guy who panics—about anything."

Bill looked at her with interest. He asked, "Does this have to do with the impressions you got at the crime scenes?"

Riley nodded and said, "Think about it, Bill—the icy coolness it must take to approach someone with an ice pick and drive it cleanly into the softest part of the human skull—a small target if ever there was one, but he never missed. And all three victims were perfectly conscious and alert. You'd need a steady hand, and a steadier temperament. Does Bruno Young strike you as that kind of a man?"

Bill tilted his head and said, "When you put it that way, I've got to say no. He's a typical recovering junkie—defensive, deceptive, and as nervous as hell."

Bill took another sip of his beer, then added...

"Anyway, Riley, I learned ages ago to trust your instincts. They're very rarely wrong. If you think Bruno's not our killer, my guess is you're probably right."

Jenn asked, "So where does that leave us?"

Bill let out a low growl of discouragement and said, "Exactly where we started. We've got nothing tangible to prove Bruno isn't the killer—nothing to persuade Agent Sturman or anybody else we should stay in Connecticut. Now if we're right, forensics is likely to bear us out. His ice pick won't have a trace of blood on it, and it will be obvious it was never used as a murder weapon. But until then..."

Bill's voice trailed off, but Riley knew what he was leaving unsaid.

We've got to go back to Quantico.

We've got no choice.

Bill messaged Special Agent in Charge Brent Meredith that they'd be on their way back tomorrow, and they'd give him a full report. He asked Meredith to have a plane ready for them in the morning at the Tweed–New Haven Regional Airport for their flight back.

Over dessert, the three of them decided that they'd return their borrowed vehicle to the Wilburton police station early in the morning, then ask Chief Brennan to have somebody drive them to the airport.

Finally, they finished eating and returned to their rooms.

Riley sat on the edge of her bed, trying to piece things together in her mind. It was of some comfort to know that she, Bill, and Jenn had much the same opinion about the status of the case. Even so, there was nothing they could do except go back to Quantico and wait for forensics to prove, as they probably would, that Bruno Young had nothing to do with the murders.

Then they'd surely fly back to Connecticut in a hurry.

Riley shuddered deeply as she wondered...

Is the killer going to strike again in the meantime?

It was a race against time—a race that she, Bill, and Jenn weren't even allowed to run in, at least not until the forensics team finished its work.

Meanwhile, Riley's nerves were on edge, her breathing was quick, her muscles were tight all over, and her senses were uncomfortably keen.

I'm having a fight-or-flight response.

She'd been in this situation many times over the years—braced and ready for action, but with no course of action to take. She hated this feeling.

As she tried to put such thoughts out of her mind, she realized it was time to call home and check in on how things were going there.

As she picked up her cell phone, she suddenly remembered what Ryan had told her about how he'd found out she was in Connecticut.

"OK, if you must know, Jilly told me."

Riley groaned with discouragement.

Jilly!

She hadn't given it any thought until now, but...

Why would Jilly do such a thing?

Riley felt a flash of anger. She was afraid if she called home right now, she'd start yelling at Jilly. With a scowl she thought...

Jilly deserves it.

She knows better than to do something like that.

But *why* had she done it?

Riley also remembered Ryan saying...

"She meant well. I think she wants us to get back together."

Riley gasped as she wondered—could that be true? She remembered the last two times Ryan had been at home, and both girls had been cold to him to the point of being rude. It would never have occurred to Riley that Jilly still wished Ryan could be her father.

But had Riley been wrong? Jilly had become very attached to Ryan when he'd lived with them for a short time.

Riley now wondered whether she should make the call at all. What kind of a confrontation might she have with Jilly? Could Riley deal with such drama, with everything else that was on her mind? Might it be better to just wait and deal with things when she got home tomorrow?

No, Riley decided. *I've got to do it now. This is my family.*

The phone shook in her hands as she made the call. Then she heard April's voice.

"Mom! I'm glad you called! Something's really wrong!"

Chapter Twenty One

Riley was terrified by the sound of desperation in her daughter's voice.

"What is it, April?" she asked.

"It's Jilly. She's locked up in her room. She won't talk to anybody."

Riley could scarcely breathe now. Less than a month ago, she'd found that her younger daughter had been cutting herself out of feelings of unworthiness. With the help of a therapist and good mother-daughter conversation, they seemed to have gotten past that.

She managed to gasp, "What happened?"

"I don't know," April said. "Neither does Gabriela. It started just a little while ago when we were all watching the news on TV in the family room. A reporter started talking about some murder case in Connecticut—something to do with a serial ice pick killer. And then—oh, Mom, I thought I'd gone crazy or was dreaming or something, but…"

April hesitated, but Riley was pretty sure she knew what was coming next.

"They ran a tape of Dad, and he was standing right in front of the FBI building in New Haven, talking to reporters about the case! Then we got just a glimpse of you pulling Dad away from the reporters and into the building. Mom, what was Dad doing there, anyway?"

Riley didn't want to explain all that right now.

Instead she said, "What about Jilly?"

"Well, Jilly freaked out when she saw Dad on TV. She ran out of the family room and all the way upstairs. We heard the door to her room slam up there. Gabriela and I have both been trying to get her to open the door and let us in and tell us what's wrong. But she just keeps telling us to go away. We keep hearing her sobbing in there."

Riley's heart felt like it would fall right through the floor.

This is worse than I'd imagined, she thought.

She said to April, "We can't let her shut herself up alone. Could you tell her I'm on the phone and want to talk to her?"

"I'll try, Mom."

Riley could hear April's footsteps as she carried the phone through the upstairs hall to Jilly's room. She heard April knock gently on the door and say...

"Jilly, Mom's on the phone. She wants to talk to you."

Riley heard Jilly's muffled reply from inside her room.

"I can't talk to her."

"What do you mean, you can't talk to her?" April asked.

"I just can't. Not right now."

Riley heard April heave a deep sigh, then say...

"Jilly, you've got to talk to *somebody*. If you won't talk to me or Gabriela, then somebody. I really think you should talk to Mom. She's really worried about you."

A silence fell. Then came the sound of Jilly's door opening.

Riley heard Jilly say, "April, I've got to talk to her alone."

April said, "OK," and Riley heard Jilly's room door closing again.

Jilly let out a couple of sobs and said, "Oh, Mom, I really screwed up. I did something terrible. It's all my fault."

"What's all your fault?" Riley said.

"We saw him on TV," Jilly said. "Da... Ryan."

Riley realized that Jilly was now unable to call him "Dad." She'd started calling him that when they were all living together, but Ryan had let Jilly down too many times now.

"April and Gabriela and me, we all saw him. I'm sure you didn't want him to be there, and I could see how he made a mess of things. And it was my fault he went there. You see, I..."

Jilly swallowed hard and added, "I told him you were in Connecticut."

Riley said, "I know you did, sweetie. He actually told me that. How did it happen?"

"He called the house, and I answered the phone, and he sounded... well, he sounded bad, that's all, like something was really wrong. He said something had come up, and he needed to find you and talk to you, and it was really, really urgent. I had no idea he was going to up to Connecticut and act like..."

Riley couldn't help but smile as she finished Jilly's thought...

"Like a raving idiot?"

Jilly gasped a little, then let out a nervous giggle.

"Yeah, pretty much," she said.

Riley was starting to breathe easier.

She said, "It's OK, Jilly. I understand."

"But I told him..."

"I know, and you shouldn't have done that," Riley said. "You shouldn't tell people anything about what I'm doing when I'm working on a case. But this time you couldn't help it. You were worried about Ryan, and you meant really well, and..."

Riley paused, then said...

"And you had good reason to worry. He's not doing very well, Jilly. He's going through a bad time. And he's doing some rash and stupid things because of it. I wish there were something we could do about it, but there's not."

Another silence fell as Riley waited for a reply.

Then Jilly said, "He's got to work things out for himself, doesn't he?"

Riley felt her throat catch at Jilly's words.

What a mature thing to say!

Her younger daughter really was growing up.

She said to Jilly, "Yes, he does. He really does. But he's having trouble understanding that. He keeps turning to other people to fix his life for him. Nobody can do that but him, and if any of us give in and try to fix things for him, we'll only make things worse for all of us, including him. But you've got a good heart, Jilly. And I'm really proud of you for that."

Jilly let out another last sob and said, "Thanks, Mom. I'm proud of you too." Then she added, "Hey, an FBI guy was on the news after you and Ryan went into the building. He said you got the killer. Congratulations."

Riley's spirits sank a little.

Given all the doubts she shared with Bill and Jenn, she didn't feel like being congratulated right now.

But she knew she'd better not go into all that with Jilly.

"Thanks, Jilly," she said.

"Does this mean you'll be coming back home soon?" Jilly asked.

Riley stammered, "Uh, yeah, we—we'll be flying back tomorrow."

Jilly sounded really happy now.

"It'll be so good to see you! I know you've only been gone a couple of days. But it always seems like a long time when you're gone. I really miss you."

Riley swallowed down a lump of emotion.

"I miss you too, Jilly," she said. "And I love you."

"I love you too. We'll see you tomorrow."

They ended the call, and Riley sat on the edge of the bed feeling sad and discouraged.

Jilly's words echoed through her head...

"It always seems like a long time when you're gone."

It made Riley sad that she couldn't feel the same way. Certainly she missed her daughters, and missed them badly. But the work she was doing always absorbed her full attention, and time often seemed to fly while she was doing it. It was hard to think much about home when she was away.

And now...

What kind of mom will I be when I get home tomorrow?

Doubtless she'd be edgy and anxious after leaving matters so unsettled here in Connecticut. She'd have a hard time giving all her attention to the girls. And of course, they'd feel like she was being distant with them.

If only Bill and Jenn and I could stay a day or two longer, she thought.

If only we could solve this case once and for all.

Then she could go home with a clear mind and spend some great time with her kids—time that they all could enjoy.

Riley got up from the bed and went to the bathroom to take a shower, then went straight to bed. She was tired after a long, hard day, and she went to sleep quickly.

Riley found herself standing on the edge of a precipice, staring down into a seemingly bottomless darkness. Strange sounds emerged from those depths—screams, cries of torment, evil laughter, clanking chains, gunshots…

"What is this place?" Riley asked herself aloud. "What's down there?

To her surprise, she heard a voice answer in reply…

"It's the abyss."

She turned to see who had spoken. Also standing on the precipice just a few feet away was Wesley Mannis, staring fixedly in those depths.

She was astonished to realize he was right. This was an abyss—her own personal abyss, filled with all the evils, pain, injustice, and horrors she'd faced and struggled against her whole life. It was also full of her own faults and failures, weaknesses and lapses that had cost so much to herself and other people—sometimes even their lives.

It terrified her deeply to think…

All of it.

Everything that frightens me.

All of it is down there.

But then she wondered—what was Wesley doing here, standing next to her?

And most of all…

She asked him aloud, "How do you know? About the abyss?"

Wesley kept staring silently. Riley remembered how hard it was to reach Wesley, to get him to say as much as a single word. Surely he wouldn't speak to her now.

But then, still staring downward, Wesley said…

"I know because I've been there."

Riley felt jolted with astonishment. How was it even possible? This was her abyss, crawling with her own personal demons and horrors. How could Wesley know anything about it?

And yet she knew…

He wouldn't lie.

She looked down and listened again. This time, amid the tangle of noises and voices, she could just barely make out a terrified cry for help. Someone needed her. Someone's life was in danger, and Riley had to save that life.

But how?

The abyss was so deep, she could think of no other way to enter it but to jump.

But even if she did, what could she do?

She'd be lost and confused and of no help at all.

Then she realized something. She turned to Wesley and said…

"We've got to go down there—both of us. I can't do it on my own. We've got to jump in, both at the same time."

Wesley didn't reply, just kept staring.

"Did you hear me, Wesley?" she said. "I need your help."

Wesley stood silent for another few moments, then said…

"I'm not a peeper."

Riley was startled to hear those words he'd said over and over again yesterday.

She pleaded with him, "This isn't about peeping, Wesley. This is about doing the right thing. This is about saving someone's life."

"I'm not a peeper," Wesley repeated.

Then, to Riley's alarm, he turned and started to walk away.

She called after him…

"Wesley, please don't go! I need your help! Someone down there needs our help! We have a life to save! Maybe more than one life!"

But Wesley kept on walking away, muttering over and over again…

"I'm not a peeper… I'm not a peeper…"

Riley tried to run after him, but her own feet were frozen where she stood.

She turned and looked again into the abyss and thought…

I've got to go down there.

But I can't do it alone.

I need Wesley to help me.
But how could she possibly get him to do that?

Riley's eyes snapped open, and she lay gasping from the nightmare she'd just had. She saw morning light coming in through the curtains.

As she remembered the dream, she thought...

Wesley has been through a trauma.

He saw something he thinks he shouldn't have.

He's probably endured other traumas too.

Riley had suffered through her share of traumas and had experienced terrible bouts of PTSD. Could she reach him through their common experience? Could she get him to tell her what he'd seen that night?

I've got to try, Riley thought, jumping out of bed and pulling on her clothes.

Chapter Twenty Two

When Bill awoke at the sound of a knock at the door of his room, he knew right away…

It's Riley.

He called out to her in a hoarse, sleepy voice.

"Give me a minute, Riley. I'll meet you downstairs for breakfast, OK?"

"OK," Riley called in reply. "I'll go wake up Jenn."

Bill grinned as he got out of bed. This was no surprise. When he'd gone to sleep last night, he'd been aware that Riley was still ruminating on the case. His longtime partner often got powerful intuitive hits by way of nightmares or late-night insights. And those hits often went contrary to the expectations of her co-workers.

Right now, Bill was glad of it.

He knew that Riley's ex-husband turning up out of the blue yesterday had shaken her up a bit. Despite all his years working with Riley, Bill had never gotten to know Ryan Paige very well. But Bill had never really liked him, and Riley had made no secret that Ryan didn't like him either.

What did Ryan think he was doing here, anyway? Bill wondered.

Whatever he'd had in mind, the man had certainly caused his share of trouble. And Riley had seemed discouraged for the rest of the day.

This early wakeup call suggested to Bill that maybe she was back to her old self. If she'd gotten a new idea, the team badly needed one right now.

Yesterday Riley had pretty well convinced him that Bruno Young wasn't their killer, which surely meant that the real murderer was out there somewhere, ready to strike at any time...

If he hasn't already.

Bill hated the idea of leaving Connecticut without solving the case. He was sure they'd just have to come flying back after someone else got killed. If Riley had thought of something new, that could give them a fresh start.

He brushed his teeth and got dressed and headed down to the restaurant, where Riley and Jenn were already getting settled at a table. The three of them quickly ordered coffee, then Bill and Jenn both looked at Riley expectantly.

Riley took a deep, long breath and said...

"We've got to go talk to Wesley Mannis."

Bill's spirits sank a little. A repetition of a fruitless meeting wasn't what he had expected.

Jenn asked bluntly, "What good will that do, Riley?"

Sounding a bit anxious, Riley explained, "He saw something the night Robin Scoville was killed. He may have seen it happen."

Bill said, "We already know that, Riley. But nobody seems to be able to get through to him right now, not even his mother."

Jenn added, "Even that strange therapist, Dr. Bayle, didn't seem to be making much progress the last time we were there."

Riley hesitated, then said...

"I can get through to him."

Jenn looked at Riley with an expression of disbelief.

"Oh, Riley, I don't know," Jenn said.

Bill added, "I'm not sure you understand what you're saying."

Riley sounded impatient now.

"I *do* know what I'm saying," she said. "We've got—well, we've got something in common, Wesley and me. Something that I can use to make a connection."

"What's that?" Jenn asked.

"I don't know," Riley said. "That's what I've got to find out."

Bill exchanged a doubtful glance with Jenn.

Riley said, "Look, just let me try, OK?"

Bill shrugged and said, "Well, it depends on whether you can even get permission to see him. That's going to be up to staff over at Wilburton House—Dr. Rhind and Dr. Bayle, especially. I'm not sure they're going to want you to do that."

The three of them fell silent for a moment. Riley's taut expression was familiar to Bill. She often wore it when she was building up her resolve to take some kind of action, no matter what anybody else thought.

Bill knew from experience that could mean trouble.

The server arrived with their coffee and took their orders. Then Riley abruptly took out her cell phone and started to make a call.

"Who are you calling?" Bill asked.

Riley didn't say anything, just waited for someone to answer.

Then she said, "Hello, this is Special Agent Riley Paige with the FBI. Could I speak with Dr. Rhind, please?"

She's calling Wilburton House, Bill realized.

He whispered to her, "Riley, are you sure this is such a good idea?"

Riley didn't answer his question. She waited for a moment, then said...

"Good morning, Dr. Rhind. My colleagues and I would like to pay Wesley Mannis another visit."

After another pause, Riley said...

"I understand your concerns, Doctor. We won't do anything you disapprove of. We'll stop by Wilburton House in just a few minutes and speak to you first about this."

Bill was also familiar with that determination in her voice. He knew that it was very hard for anyone to say no to Riley when she came on that strong.

"Thank you, Doctor," Riley said. "We'll drive right over."

Riley ended her call and said, "We're skipping breakfast. Let's go."

Bill stifled a sigh. "OK, but at least let me call Quantico and notify Chief Meredith. I also need to let Chief Brennan know we aren't bringing his car back right away."

As Riley settled the bill for the coffee, Bill stepped aside and took out his cell phone. He called the police station and left a message for Brennan, then called Quantico. When he got Meredith on the line, the first thing the chief said to him was…

"Are the three of you on your way back yet?"

"Um, not exactly," Bill said nervously.

Meredith growled, "I'm not sure I like the sound of that, Jeffreys. A plane is already on its way to Tweed–New Haven to pick you up. You need to get to the airport."

Bill said, "I'm afraid we—won't be there to meet it right away."

"Why not?"

Bill said, "Agent Paige thinks she might be able to…find out something about the case."

"What for? Don't you already have a suspect in custody?"

Bill hesitated, then said…

"Yeah, we do. But the truth is, Roston and Paige and I don't think he's the right guy."

A tense silence fell.

Then Meredith said, "Remember what I said before you went up there. No more shenanigans. I expect you to do everything by the book."

"Yes, sir," Bill said. "You can count on us, sir."

The call ended, and Bill and his two colleagues headed on out to the car.

Bill's own words rattled again through his head.

"You can count on us, sir."

He stifled a sigh as he started the car engine.

I sure hope we can keep that promise.

During the short drive to Wilburton House, Riley couldn't help but remind herself…

Sometimes a dream is just a dream.

Maybe the nightmare she'd had didn't mean anything at all, and this visit to Wesley Mannis was going to be a waste of time—or perhaps worse, troubling and difficult for Wesley.

Still, she couldn't shake that image out of her head, of standing beside Wesley on a precipice, and him saying to her...

"It's the abyss."

It had felt as though she and Wesley shared an understanding of the dark side of human nature. Somehow, the dream seemed to fit with her impressions of Wesley when she'd first met him. If she could find common ground with him, maybe she could coax him into telling her whatever he'd seen on the night of Robin Scoville's murder.

When Riley, Bill, and Jenn arrived at Wilburton House, they found Dr. Rhind waiting for her, not looking as cheerful as she had on their previous meeting.

The doctor said to them, "I'm afraid this visit comes as a bit of a surprise. I saw on the news yesterday that you had a suspect in custody. Isn't the murder case closed?"

Riley didn't want to say outright that she and her colleagues thought they had the wrong man.

Instead she said, "We've still got some work to do. We're hoping that Wesley might be ready to help us."

"I'm not sure I like this," Dr. Rhind said, squeezing her hands together anxiously. "Wesley is doing so much better. He's interacting with other people again, functioning really well. We've been hoping he could start spending time outside the facility again, maybe even go back to his old job, or else get a new one. The last thing I want is for him to have a setback."

"I understand," Riley said. "I promise we'll be careful. But tell me, did Dr. Bayle ever get him to say anything about what he saw on the night of the murder?"

Dr. Rhind shook her head. "Not as far as I know. I think he would have told me. Dr. Bayle decided to stay here for another day or two to help, so we gave him a room of his own."

Bill asked, "Where is Dr. Bayle right now?"

Dr. Rhind sighed and said...

"I wish I knew. He's an odd sort of man. Absolutely brilliant, but with some peculiar habits. He comes and goes a lot, seemingly at random. He'll be talking with me or working with Wesley, then suddenly he'll get up and leave, walk right of the building without saying anything at all. Sometimes he'll be gone for several hours, then he'll come back and get right back to work without any explanation."

Riley felt a tingle of worry at what she was hearing, although she wasn't sure just why. She remembered being unsettled by the therapist's demeanor, and especially in his unexplained interest in Riley herself.

"I know quite a bit about you," he'd said when they'd first talked on the phone.

And Dr. Rhind had said he hadn't been interested in Wesley's condition right away, but...

"As soon as I mentioned your name, Agent Paige, he was suddenly eager to come."

His curiosity made Riley uncomfortable, almost as if he were some kind of a stalker.

And why was he coming and going in such a mysterious manner?

Should she and her colleagues try to find out?

Perhaps he's not what he seems to be, she thought.

As Riley made a mental note to try to learn more about Bayle, Dr. Rhind led her, Bill, and Jenn to the pleasant sitting room Riley had noticed during their previous visits. Among the relaxed-looking residents lounging, playing games, and eating snacks, she saw Wesley sitting at a table playing chess with another young man. Wesley's mother was standing nearby, still looking tired but watching her son intently.

Wesley's chess partner looked lively and friendly and seemed to be carrying on a one-sided conversation with Wesley as they played. By contrast, Wesley kept his eyes focused on the chessboard, apparently unperturbed by his partner's distracting chatter.

Riley remembered the last time she'd seen Wesley, recovering from a meltdown in that strange contraption called a "squeeze machine."

Yes, he's definitely doing better, Riley thought.

The last thing she wanted to do was cause him a setback. Or, she wondered, was the last thing she wanted to do actually to leave town without finding the killer?

Somebody else is going to die if we don't get ahead of this, she thought.

When Gemma Mannis looked up and saw the agents approaching with Dr. Rhind, she appeared uneasy.

"I wasn't expecting you back again," she said. "I thought the murders had been solved."

This time Bill spoke up tactfully, "We do have a suspect in custody, but we've still got a few things to sort out."

Riley knew she'd better ease into the issue of whether she could be allowed to talk to Wesley. For one thing, she still wasn't sure just what she hoped it could accomplish.

She said to Gemma, "I can't imagine how hard life has been, for you and Wesley both. I just need to ask you whether you can think of specific traumatic incidents that might have had a longstanding effect on him?"

Gemma sighed deeply and said, "Traumatic incidents! Oh, Agent Paige, I'm afraid life has been one long traumatic incident for poor Wesley."

Dr. Rhind nodded and added, "Researchers have only just recently started to discover the extent of post-traumatic stress syndrome among autistic people. It's a much more widespread problem than anybody realized."

Gemma continued, "Things are only just now beginning to get better for Wesley. But growing up with his disability was terribly hard. He was always bullied and shunned by other kids, never had any real friends, and…"

Gemma hesitated for a moment, then said…

"I remember once when he was a little boy, he got invited to a party at the local swimming pool. My husband and I—we were still married back then—had such hopes that he'd have a good time, maybe get drawn out of his lonely little world. But while he was there, we…"

Gemma gulped hard and said, "We got a call from the lifeguard, saying Wesley had almost drowned and we needed to come and get him."

Gemma seemed on the verge of tears now.

"We were never able to find out exactly what happened. The kids he was with just said it was an accident. Wesley didn't know how to tell us anything, even if he understood what happened himself. But I've always feared that he fell victim to some prank that went wrong. Children can be awfully cruel, especially to a child who is different. But I've also feared… that something even worse might have happened at some point. Something I still don't know about."

Gemma turned away for a moment, trying to bring her emotions under control. Then she turned back to the group and said…

"Back in those days, he'd tell me from time to time, 'Mom, I don't want to live anymore. I just want to die.' The way he said it wasn't self-pitying at all, more like a statement of fact. And I've often wondered if maybe at that party he'd decided he'd had enough, and…"

Gemma's voice faded away, but Riley knew what she was leaving unsaid. Maybe the sensory overload of the party, all those other kids laughing and shouting and sharing in joys that he couldn't even understand, had gotten be too much for him. And of course, the kids there had probably shunned or teased him.

Maybe he'd had enough, Riley thought.

Maybe he'd decided to kill himself.

It shocked her deeply that no one who cared about him could know for sure. The secret was locked away inside Wesley's lonely mind, probably never to be revealed.

Riley gulped hard. She felt truly out of her depth now.

Maybe this is a bad idea, she thought.

Maybe I shouldn't even try.

Then Gemma said to her, "I take it you want to talk to Wesley."

Riley nodded and said, "Only if you give me permission."

Gemma sighed again. "Well, I'm not the one whose permission counts, am I? It's up to Wesley as far as I'm concerned."

At that moment, Wesley's chess partner toppled over his king, conceding the game with a good-natured grin. Wesley sat staring at the board as if he were still analyzing the game.

Gemma walked over to Wesley and whispered something in his ear. Riley saw his lips move as he whispered something in reply. Then he got up from his chair and walked with his mother toward Riley and the others.

Looking a bit surprised, Gemma said...

"He says he wants to talk to you."

Wesley nodded and said in a flat, toneless voice...

"Someplace more quiet, though. We should go back to my room."

Without another word, he turned and walked out into the hallway.

Riley and the others followed him.

Riley felt breathless with anticipation. She had no idea what to expect.

When they got to the room, Wesley went on in ahead of the others. Riley glanced at Bill and Jenn. They both nodded and stepped aside to wait outside the door. After a moment's hesitation, Dr. Rhind and Gemma also stood aside.

Riley stepped inside the room. Wesley was sitting at his table, so she sat down across from him.

Staring at the tabletop, Wesley said to her...

"Mom says you're an FBI agent."

"That's right," Riley said.

"I think that's really interesting," Wesley said. "I'd like to know more about it. Not that I could ever be an FBI agent myself. Obviously, I'll never be able to do anything like that. I just don't have the... abilities. Still, I'd like to know a few things."

Riley was startled at the flow of words. Although his voice was still expressionless, Wesley was obviously capable of more communication than she'd realized.

Then he fell silent, still staring at the tabletop.

Riley wondered if he was waiting for her to say something.

How should she start?

Without looking up, Wesley spoke again. "You must see and experience a lot of awful things, doing the work that you do. Evil things. Terrible things"

Riley nodded slowly and said, "That's right."

Wesley raised his eyes little without looking at her directly.

"Well, what I'd like to know is... how do you cope? How do you deal with all that? Emotionally, I mean."

Riley felt a tingle of fascination as she wondered...

Is this his way of starting to open up about what he knows?

Or was he really just curious about what it was like to be an FBI agent?

Anyway, he'd just asked her a very good question—and amazingly, it was a question that few people ever bothered to ask her.

She realized that she had no reason not to answer it honestly.

"It's hard, Wesley," she said. "There's all kinds of evil out there in the world, and it's my job to try to stop it. But nobody can stop it, not really. Certainly not all of it."

Wesley nodded slightly and said...

"You can't change human nature."

Riley felt a jolt of amazement at this remark.

So perceptive—so right.

At the moment, it was almost hard to remember that Wesley suffered from a mental disability.

"That's true," Riley said, feeling strangely free to speak honestly about things she usually kept to herself. "And sometimes it makes my job seem—well, futile, as if I'm not doing any good at all."

Looking off to one side, Wesley said...

"But you *are* doing good. You're stopping killers. You're putting them in prison. You're making the world just a little bit safer. What more can you ask of yourself?"

Riley's eyes widened, and she felt her breath catch.

His strangely mechanical monotone made his insightful comments all the more disarming.

"I don't know," she said. "But it comes with the job, I guess—expecting the impossible from yourself. Anyway, in answer to your question about how I cope... I try to compartmentalize a lot, keep different aspects of my life as separate as I can. For example, I've got a family, but I try not to bring all that evil home with me."

She couldn't keep a note of despair out of her voice as she added...

"I don't always succeed."

Wesley's brow crinkled with thought.

Then he said, "You say you compartmentalize. I understand that. So do I. I guess that's part of my problem. I do it too much. I do it pretty much all the time."

Riley could hardly breathe now as she realized...

He really, really wants to tell me something.

This strange discussion they were having seemed to be his roundabout way of trying to say it.

She said slowly and cautiously...

"Wesley, I know you saw something the last time you went out on your garbage route. It was something awful, something very hard for you to talk about. But I need for you to tell me... if you possibly can."

Wesley looked down at the tabletop again.

In a barely audible whisper, he said...

"Windows."

Riley leaned toward him a little.

She said, "You saw something through a window, didn't you?"

"I'm not a peeper," he said.

"I know you're not a peeper," Riley said.

Wesley seemed to be slipping further away from her.

She wondered, *Am I going to lose him?*

Then he repeated that word again...

"Windows."

After a pause, he added, "The first time I was looking out. The last time I was looking in."

He took a long, slow breath.

Then he said...

"I think I can...Agent Paige. I think I can tell you something...I've never told anybody else."

Chapter Twenty Three

The man felt a twinge in his foot and ankle as he strolled along the sidewalk. He groaned a little at the realization...

It's starting again.

Why did the pain always have to strike when he was out and around, trying to be inconspicuous, looking for his next target? For that matter, why did he have to suffer this pain at all?

This cruel reminder of his childhood suffering had come and gone several times during his life, but in the most recent decade or so it had faded completely. For years he'd thought he had put it behind him for good.

But the pain was back again. For several months now, it had been recurring at rare but unexpected moments.

It was getting worse.

What did I do to deserve this? he asked himself.

He shook his head at the pointless rhetorical question. He knew perfectly well...

Nothing. I did nothing to deserve this.

Life had done him a grave injustice, pure and simple.

He also knew perfectly well what would make the pain stop.

Fortunately, the man could see a charming sidewalk café just at the end of the block. Small tables and chairs were clustered behind a low wall, and flowering plants hung overhead. It was nice, he thought, that the weather was mild enough for the outdoor part of this restaurant to be open. He could sit there and enjoy the sun and fresh air for a little while. If he was lucky, the pain would ebb a bit before he had to be on his way, searching for new prey

Taking care not to limp or otherwise show his discomfort, he walked to the entry and waited until the hostess approached him with a menu and offered him a small table off to one side. Once he was seated, he let out a quiet sigh of relief. Just getting off his feet eased the pain a little. But what would happen when he tried to get up again? He'd take a pain pill when the server brought him some water, but lately the pills hadn't been doing him any good at all.

He knew what was required. He knew that when he fulfilled his duty, the pain would disappear like magic and he would have at least some days of comfort.

Meanwhile, he was glad he'd gotten here when he did. A line was starting to form at the café entrance. He'd been spared the ordeal of standing there waiting for a table.

Second in line was a young woman who immediately captured his attention. She was remarkably beautiful, with exquisitely sculpted facial features and an equally well-shaped body.

A model? he wondered.

No, her clothes didn't suggest it. She was wearing was a nice outfit, but he could tell that it had been chosen off the rack—possibly even at some thrift store, a shrewd and sensible purchase that spoke well of the woman's intelligence. Stirred by her beauty, he wished he could walk over to her and introduce himself to her. But then he reminded himself...

Those days are over for me.

With the recent recurrence of his pain, he'd discovered a burning purpose in life, and it precluded fleeting, pleasurable entanglements like the fantasy that was now forming in his mind.

When the server arrived, the man ordered a tuna melt sandwich. He gulped down a pain pill with a glass of water. Then he saw that the hostess was escorting the young woman to her table. As he glimpsed her from behind, he noticed something he couldn't have seen before.

There were small, reddish scars in the bends of her knees.

Right then he knew...

Liposuction.

This woman's good looks had been manufactured very recently. Just a few weeks ago, or maybe even a few days ago, she'd been markedly less sleek and attractive than she was now.

As he watched her sit down, he wondered—how much surgical work had she gotten done?

A lot, he guessed.

Which meant that those two little scars he's spotted weren't the only ones. She was bound to have similar scars all over her body—tiny pinpricks in her thighs, her back, her buttocks, and low on her belly. If he could only see her closer up, he'd surely spot similar little marks on her arms.

Artificial, he thought, suppressing a shudder.

Now that he studied her face more carefully, he noticed a mannequin-like stiffness about her features.

Plastic surgery.

He wondered—how had she looked before all that surgery? And why had she gotten it done? A couple of scenarios ran through his head. Maybe she'd been in some terrible accident and had been disfigured. Or maybe she simply hadn't been very good-looking from the start, with unsightly features and a dumpy body.

Either way, she'd been just the sort of prey he was hunting…

Imperfect.

The surgery hadn't corrected anything, not really, not below the surface. Those old flaws would still be there, visible to anyone who knew how to look. Even worse, in trying to make herself perfect, she'd just created new flaws. Her various scars might heal and become nearly invisible, but they would still be there.

He felt a flash of anger toward her at the thought of those flaws.

She herself was a scar on a world that should only consist of the perfect.

But he quickly reminded himself…

Don't be angry.

You must remain composed.

After all, he was carrying out a kind of surgery all his own, extracting imperfections from human society. A surgeon never let himself be controlled by emotions. And his own mode of killing required an extraordinary degree of precision and skill.

So far, he'd managed carry out his mission with the necessary purity of focus.

But when and how was he going to remove her?

A bold possibility occurred to him...

Why not right here and now?

It would be a challenge, of course, but hardly impossible. He was carrying his ice pick in his briefcase, and he could conceal it in his cloth napkin and walk right over to her. He could act like he just wanted to introduce himself, then move so deftly that nobody would notice his swift stabbing movement to her ear. She might not even slump over right away. Maybe he could slip out of the restaurant before she mysteriously collapsed, apparently from some natural cause.

Then he silently scolded himself...

Don't be ridiculous.

Customers and staff here had gotten a good look at him. They'd be able to identify him sooner or later. No, he had to lure her away to some other location and kill her there.

He felt a sudden twinge of alarm as her eyes met his.

She sees me staring at her.

But then she smiled and got up from her table and walked toward his.

She said in a flirtatious voice...

"I see we're both here alone. Would you like some company?"

He smiled back at her and said, "Thanks, that would be nice."

He sometimes forgot that he was considered to be a reasonably handsome man who was attractive to some women. As things were turning out, his good looks were likely to prove quite opportune for his purposes.

The woman sat down and introduced herself as Dawn. He lied and said that his name was Scott. As they began to exchange pleasantries, he found himself thinking of a different woman who had been on his mind lately...

Agent Riley Paige.

She was far more intriguing than this fake beauty who was chattering away about nothing of interest to him.

Riley Paige was a healthy, vigorous, good-looking woman. He knew that some people would consider her beautiful. Although he was sure that Riley Paige had never used surgery to improve her looks, he had to wonder if she harbored imperfections that weren't immediately visible. Yes, surely a life of crime-fighting would leave its share of scars, both emotional and physical.

He would like to find out.

He wondered if maybe he should target her next, after this victim.

Or maybe he should leave this one alone, go after Riley Paige much more promptly.

The notion of luring one of them to some more private place was beginning to appeal to him. It would be entertaining to toy with his prey for a while. That would certainly be a change of pace, a way to keep things fresh and interesting.

But he reminded himself that he wasn't doing this for his own gratification.

He was performing a service to humanity.

Of course he couldn't begin to rid the world of all its flawed people. But it was his duty to do so whenever and wherever he could.

It seemed sad that no one would ever know the good he was doing for the world. But it had to be sufficient that he knew, and that he could take satisfaction in his work.

It's lonely work, he thought. *But it has to be done.*

And anyway, he did get one private reward.

As soon as he killed, the pain would ebb. He'd feel fine, at least for a time.

That's something to look forward to, he thought with a smile.

Chapter Twenty Four

Riley sat across the table from Wesley Mannis, breathlessly waiting for him to speak again. He'd just said he thought could tell her…

"… *something… I've never told anybody else.*"

But then he'd stopped.

He was just staring at the tabletop, saying nothing.

His lingering silence worried her. She wondered whether she should call Dr. Rhind and his mother back into the room to see if they could help.

No, Wesley had made one thing clear. He felt some rare sort of personal connection with Riley. He thought that he could communicate with her in a way he couldn't communicate with others.

Riley knew she had to wait until he was ready to say whatever was on his mind.

Did he want to tell her exactly what he'd seen on the night when Robin Scoville had been killed? If so, could he really do it? Was he capable of communicating anything so profoundly traumatic? She'd interviewed people with far fewer cognitive problems who had trouble recalling, much less describing, such disturbing experiences.

If that's what Wesley was trying to do, she had to help him through it without any outside assistance.

She couldn't remember ever feeling so daunted by an interview, so desperately out of her depth.

To make matters worse, Wesley seemed to her to be slipping away into his own world again. She wished she could simply pressure him into make eye contact, like she would with any normal interview subject.

But of course she remembered what Dr. Rhind had said about eye contact.

"Just trying to make that kind of personal connection overloads him, sends him into a meltdown."

She remembered his last meltdown with dread. Anything like that would put an end to his attempt to communicate.

Don't push things, she thought.

She saw that the "squeeze box" was still in the room, ready and available in case he did have a meltdown. But she also remembered how skillfully Dr. Bayle had coaxed him into the contraption. Bayle wasn't here now to do that. Was Dr. Rhind up to the task?

And where the hell is Bayle, anyway?

Dr. Rhind had said about Bayle, *"He comes and goes a lot, seemingly at random."*

The more Riley thought about Dr. Bayle, the more uneasy she felt about him—and vaguely suspicious as well. But now was no time to let herself worry about the peculiar therapist…

Keep focused.

The best tactic seemed to be to stay alert, attentive, and silent, and let Wesley speak whenever he felt ready.

Finally Wesley muttered…

"There was a cage."

Those four words rattled through Riley's head…

A cage?

What did a cage have to do with Robin Scoville's death?

Then Wesley said…

"There was a cage. There was a window."

Riley's mind clicked away, trying to make sense of this…

A cage? A window?

Then she reminded herself of how she'd hoped to get through to Wesley. If she could find common ground, some shared experience, he might trust her enough to share what he had witnessed.

She gulped hard when she realized...

A cage.

Yes, she knew something about cages.

But should she tell him about that terrible episode in her own life? Would it help get him to open up to her?

I've got to try, she thought.

In a slow, cautious voice, she said, "Wesley—I've been locked in a cage."

Wesley lifted his head—and for what seemed like a fraction of a second, his eyes actually met Riley's.

Looking down at the table again, he said, "Tell me about it."

Riley's mind boggled. Where could she even begin? Sam Peterson had been a sadistic madman who had captured and tormented women until he finally killed them.

One of the women he had captured had been Riley herself.

His last intended victim had been April.

Then Riley and April had killed him together.

Both of them had suffered from terrible PTSD during the weeks afterward. Even now those memories were raw and terrifying when they surfaced. What could Riley say about that hideous experience without becoming very shaky right here and now?

Forcing herself to speak calmly, she said, "A terrible man locked me in a cage. He kept me in total darkness for days at a time. He...threatened me with a blowtorch, which was the only light I ever saw while I was his prisoner. I didn't think I'd ever get out. I thought I was going to die horribly."

But I did get out, Riley thought.

Then later, after she'd saved April from Peterson's clutches, she'd savagely and vengefully beaten him to death. April had helped her get the better of him and watched while she stuck him down.

Was she going to have to tell Wesley about all that?

What possible good could it do?

She was relieved when Wesley spoke quietly.

"That must have been terrible."

Riley nodded and said, "It was terrible. I don't think I've ever been through anything worse. And I don't talk about it to most people."

Wesley ran his finger back and forth across the table, watching it closely.

He's stimming again, Riley realized.

Then he said, "It was different for me. You were inside a cage. I was not inside. I was outside. And I…"

His voice trailed away.

"Tell me," Riley said.

He squinted and knitted his brow, as if deep in thought.

"I was nine years old," he said. "I was looking out the living room window. It was a sunny day. In the yard next to ours, Mrs. Roberts's roses were blooming. She had watered them earlier that morning. There were two cars parked on the street, a blue Chevrolet and a black Volkswagen. The Volkswagen needed washing. I could see three boys across the street—they were bullies who always treated me badly. They had a small cage with a puppy locked inside. They were…tormenting the puppy, teasing it, poking it with a stick through the cage. And I…"

Even though Wesley described all the details in the same flat tone, Riley sensed that he was struggling hard with the memory.

"I didn't do anything," he said. "I stayed inside looking out the window. I didn't go out and try to stop them. I didn't go out because Mom told me to stay inside the house. I wasn't supposed to go out because the boys were bad to me. But I…"

He paused again, then spoke in a tight voice…

"I should have gone outside anyway. I should have stopped them from doing what they were doing. They bullied me all the time, but that wasn't as bad as what they were doing to the puppy. The puppy didn't deserve it."

Riley was shocked by his comment.

"You didn't deserve it either, Wesley," she said.

"Maybe not," Wesley said. "But I could at least figure out why they hated me. They hated me because I was different, and they didn't understand why I was different. I didn't understand them either. But the puppy didn't understand *anything*. The puppy had no idea why it was being mistreated. What the boys were doing was wrong. I should have done something."

His body slouched a little, as if he were letting go of some inner burden.

Riley felt heartbroken with pity for the poor young man. He'd been carrying this guilt around inside himself for many years. He'd lived with some form of PTSD far longer than she had, and of course it had been made worse by his inability to tell anyone about it. Both Riley and April had sought out a therapist in order to regain balance in their lives. Wesley had seen plenty of therapists, but had never made full use of their skills.

Whatever he'd seen in Robin Scoville's window had renewed his trauma with even greater force.

And the reason he was able to tell Riley was because…

He knows something about me.

He knows that I also understand how cruel people can be.

People have been cruel to him all his life.

Like him, I've looked into an abyss.

Riley could sense a deep pain in the convoluted mind of this young man, different from the darkness that she sometimes encountered in herself. For a moment, she felt herself recoil as she watched him try to find his way through a strange jungle of emotions and confused thoughts.

But in spite of her own qualms, she had to keep him moving toward a specific event…

She remembered something he'd said at the beginning of their conversation about windows.

"The first time I was looking out. The last time I was looking in."

Something was beginning to make sense to her.

He'd been trying to say that he'd had two traumatic experiences looking through windows. The first time he'd been looking out—that was when he'd been a child watching those bullies torment the puppy.

The second time he'd been looking in…

At Robin Scoville's murder.

As he continued running his finger back and forth across the table, Riley wanted to reach out and squeeze him gently by the hand.

But she remembered something Dr. Rhind had said about autistic people like Wesley.

"They desperately need physical security, an embrace or a hug—and yet they can't tolerate human contact."

Don't touch him, Riley told herself.

He'd surely have a meltdown if she did.

She said to him, "Wesley, can you tell me about the second time you looked through a window—when you were looking in? Can you tell me what you saw?"

His face tightened, as if he were trying to summon his courage and resolve.

But then he went slack again.

"It's no use, Agent Paige," he said. "I can't tell you that. I want to tell you, but… it's like I'm in a cage. In the dark. I think you know… what it's like."

Riley suppressed her own sense of horror…

Yes, I know.

I know what it's like all too well.

She also knew that he'd told her all that he possibly could, at least right now. It was discouraging, but she also recognized the slight touch of her own relief. She had to overcome that, she knew, in order to help Wesley get at his own ugly memories.

What would that take?

Just then came a knock on the door.

I guess now is as good a time to be interrupted, Riley thought.

"Come in," she said.

Dr. Rhind came into the room carrying her cell phone.

"I hope I'm not interrupting, Agent Paige," she said. "It's just that I've got Dr. Bayle on the line. And he wants to talk to you."

"To me?" Riley said with surprise.

Dr. Rhind nodded and handed Riley the phone.

She heard Dr. Bayle say in his strange, flat voice...

"I was just calling to check in with Dr. Rhind. She says you're there right now. Have you been talking with Wesley?"

Riley felt a flash of worry.

Is he going to disapprove? she wondered.

She said, "Yes, I was talking to him just before you called."

"Are you through talking to him?" Bayle asked.

"I think so."

A long silence fell. Riley wondered if maybe the call had been disconnected.

Then Bayle said in a tone that struck her as vaguely sinister...

"I want to meet with you, Agent Paige. Right away. You'll find me at the Szymko Aquarium."

"All right," Riley said. "Agents Jeffreys and Roston and I will come right over to see you."

"No," Bayle said, his voice sharpening a little. "I must insist on talking with you alone. Privately."

Riley felt puzzled now.

Alone?

"What about?" Riley said.

"I just want to talk," Bayle said. "I'll see you shortly."

Without another word, Bayle ended the call.

Riley looked at Dr. Rhind and said, "How far away is the Szymko Aquarium?"

Dr. Rhind shrugged. "Not far, just outside of town. Maybe a fifteen-minute drive. I can give you directions."

Dr. Rhind explained how to get to the aquarium and Riley brought it up on her cell phone. Then she stepped out into the hall, where Bill and Jenn stood waiting.

She said to them, "I've got to take the car for a little while. I need to drive over to the Szymko Aquarium."

"What for?" Jenn asked.

When Riley told them about the odd phone call just now, Bill and Jenn exchanged wary glances.

Bill said, "This sounds pretty weird, Riley."

Riley didn't reply, but she certainly couldn't disagree.

Jenn took a long, deep breath and said, "Look, I hadn't meant to say anything, since we don't have any evidence pointing to him... but I've been kind of suspicious of Dr. Bayle ever since we met him."

Bill looked at Jenn with surprise and said, "You too?"

Riley was startled to hear of her partners' mutual suspicions. The truth was, it hadn't occurred to Riley until just now to imagine that Dr. Bayle was anything but eccentric.

Jenn said to Dr. Rhind, "You mentioned that he comes and goes at odd times and in an odd manner. Do you know where he was yesterday morning, right around dawn?"

Dr. Rhind's mouth was hanging open with shock.

"Do you mean when that man was killed?" she said. "Surely you don't think...?"

She paused, then shook her head and added, "No, you mustn't suspect Dr. Bayle. He's got a sterling reputation. I'm sure he'd never do anything like... what you imagine."

"Even so, could you check for us?" Riley asked.

Using her cell phone, Dr. Rhind was able to bring up a record of sign-ins and sign-outs to and from the building.

She said, "I don't see anything here to suggest that Dr. Bayle wasn't right here, probably in his room."

Riley's worry was mounting now.

That doesn't necessarily mean anything, she thought.

While the building's security seemed to be fairly adequate, it was easy to imagine someone who knew the building well slipping out and coming back in without being noticed, especially that early in the morning.

Riley said to her companions, "Anyway, he's expecting me. I'd better head on over there."

Jenn squinted and said, "I'm not sure I like this, Riley."

"I'm not sure I do either," Bill said.

Riley forced a slight chuckle and said...

"Look, you're both worried over nothing. I'm meeting him at an aquarium—a safe public place. He won't try anything there. And anyway, there will be security guards around to help if he does. Not that I can't take care of myself. I think you both know that."

Bill shuffled his feet and said, "At least let's drive over there together. Jenn and I can sit outside the aquarium in the car. We'll be right there in case you need to text us for help."

Riley saw no reason not to agree with that plan.

She and her colleagues left the facility and got into the car. During the short drive to the aquarium, Riley kept replaying in her mind what Bayle had said to her over the phone.

"I must insist on talking with you alone. Privately."

She wished she had some idea why he'd said that.

But I guess I'm about to find out.

Chapter Twenty Five

Her partners were obviously unhappy with her decision, and Riley understood their concern. She herself felt apprehensive, at the very least.

When Bill parked the car in front of Szymko Aquarium, Jenn made one more try at changing Riley's mind.

"Are you sure you don't want Bill and me to come inside? Just into the building, anyway? We can stay outside the room where you meet with him."

"No, I think I'd better do exactly as Bayle says," Riley said. "I don't want to do anything that might spook him into running off."

"I'm not worried about you spooking him," Jenn grumbled. "I still don't like this."

"Neither do I," Bill said to Jenn. "But it's Riley's call and I think she's up to handling the doctor if he turns out to be the one we're looking for. Besides, we'll be right out here if she needs help."

Riley got out of the car and went on inside the building and bought a ticket. As she continued on into the maze of displays, she was dazzled by the huge glass windows that revealed colorful sea creatures moving gracefully and languidly through the water. She realized it had been a long time since she'd actually visited an aquarium.

I'm not here to sightsee, she reminded herself.

She found the location of the shark tank on the display map and walked directly there.

Sure enough, she saw Dr. Bayle sitting on a bench staring into the tank. Swimming restlessly inside the tank were a number of sharks, all of them six or seven feet long. Riley shivered a little. She'd forgotten how disturbed she was by sharks, with their ridged gills and dead eyes and hungry mouths.

Nobody else was in the room at the moment. Riley reminded herself...

If he's the killer, he's fast and precise.

She had to be on the alert.

She stood next to Dr. Bayle, who said without even looking at her...

"Tell me, Agent Paige—how did your interview with Wesley go?"

It seemed like an abrupt way to begin a meeting that Riley already found to be puzzling.

And anyway, what am I supposed to tell him?

Since Dr. Bayle was Wesley's therapist, should she give him all the details—including Wesley's story about the bullies tormenting the caged puppy? That didn't seem right somehow. She remembered Wesley saying...

"I think I can tell you something I've never told anybody else."

And then he'd told her what he apparently thought to be one of his deepest, darkest secrets.

He trusts me, she thought.

She didn't want to violate that trust.

On the other hand, there was no reason to lie.

She said, "He didn't tell me what I needed to know."

"Which is who killed Robin Scoville," Bayle said, without taking his eyes off the sharks. "Or at least give you a description of her killer."

"That's right," Riley said.

"Yes, I've been trying to coax that out of him as well. I'm pleased with the progress he and I have been making in terms of his condition. But when it comes to telling anyone what he saw that night..."

Bayle paused, then added, "Well, I'm afraid that might never happen. Right now, he doesn't dare even think about what he saw. I don't think he'll ever be able to talk about it."

Then he locked eyes with Riley and added, "But then, I guess it's possible that you consider *me* a suspect."

Riley stopped herself from saying...

"Yes, it was starting to cross my mind."

Turning back to the sharks again, Bayle continued, "It only makes sense, really. I understand perfectly if you feel that you and your colleagues think you have to investigate me. If you do, please consider my life an open book—especially everything I've been doing for the last week or so, my comings and goings and so forth. I'll be glad to tell you everything, and I'll make certain that you can confirm everything I say. The sooner you eliminate me as a suspect, the better, I'm sure."

Riley studied his handsome but expressionless features closely, looking for some clue to what he was really thinking.

But he might as well have been a blank sheet of paper...

I can't read him at all.

"Please sit down, Agent Paige," he said. "I think we'd both be more comfortable."

Riley stood for a moment, weighing the risk.

Although she still couldn't determine whether he was the killer or not, she had a gut feeling...

He's not interested in killing me right now.

She wasn't sure why she felt that way so strongly, but she sensed that this man actually did want to talk about other topics.

Riley sat on the bench beside him, but turned slightly toward him so she would be aware of any sudden move on his part.

She said, "Dr. Bayle, could you please tell me why you asked me to come here?"

With just a trace of surprise in his voice, Bayle said...

"Why, to talk with you, of course. I told you yesterday—I know a lot about you, and I've always wanted to talk with you. Of course, with all that's been going on, we haven't had much of a chance to get to know each other. This seemed like an excellent opportunity."

"But—alone?" Riley asked.

"Naturally. Why wouldn't I prefer to talk to you one-on-one?"

Riley was surprised to realize...

That's a perfectly sensible answer.

Or at least it seemed *almost* sensible. She still didn't understand his mysterious behavior, especially why he'd chosen this place for their meeting. But little by little, something about Dr. Bayle's personality was starting dawn on her. He was in some way different from most other people. She couldn't yet put her finger on whatever it was.

Still staring at the sharks, Bayle said...

"I'm fascinated by these creatures—how wonderfully flawless they are. Natural selection has fashioned them into such perfect eaters. Did you know they have amazing digestive systems? Their expanding stomachs break down everything they eat with acid that's strong enough to dissolve metal. They can eat just about anything."

Pointing at a shark that was passing near the glass, he continued...

"And look at what great swimmers they are. They've got cartilage rather than bones, making them supple and resilient. And they've got that sleek shape and that tail and all those perfectly shaped fins, almost aerodynamic in design. There's nothing clumsy about them, nothing that's not graceful and efficient."

Riley shrugged slightly and said, "I hear they have to keep moving in order to breathe."

"That's true of most sharks, including these," Bayle said.

"That doesn't sound so efficient to me," Riley said.

"But it's not like they *miss* standing still," Bayle said. "It's not like they wish they could do it. It doesn't occur to them that there's such a thing as being still. It's completely outside their experience. Movement is all they know."

Then he added without a smile, "So I would guess that they're fine with it."

Bayle fell silent, then took up a different topic.

"I guess Dr. Rhind has told you that I have a way of wandering off from time to time. I know it puzzles people. But I really need those breaks. Wherever I happen to be working at any time, I make sure there's a place nearby where I can get away and lose myself, preferably in animal life. For instance, Bridgeport has a wonderful zoo with a reptile room. I could stare at lizards and snakes for hours at a time."

Riley squinted as something began to dawn on her.

"You can only deal with people for just so long at a time. Is that right? People drain your energy. If you're around people too long, you get…"

She paused as the word came to her…

"Overloaded."

Bayle nodded silently.

Riley stifled a gasp, then added…

"You're autistic."

Bayle tilted his head slightly.

"Well, I'm on the spectrum, anyway. There are many kinds and degrees of autism, so it's useful to think of it as a spectrum. When I was a kid, everybody thought I was retarded. But I was eventually diagnosed with Asperger's syndrome, if you want to put a label on it. I don't much care for labels myself. Anyway, I eventually proved to be…very functional, I'm sure you agree."

Functional—and brilliant, Riley thought.

Bayle continued, "I suppose the idea of someone like me becoming a therapist must strike you as strange. It's true that I'm extremely short on empathy. But I more than make up for that with my strengths for analysis. And autistic patients often appreciate having a therapist who can relate to their experience. That can work out especially well for certain patients, including Wesley Mannis."

"Please explain," Riley said.

"Well, Wesley's problem isn't a lack of empathy at all. His empathy is so powerful and overwhelming that he can't control it. It floods through him all the time. He feels whatever everybody around him is feeling. It gets terribly painful for him, which is why he withdraws into his shell and sometimes tries to stay there. But when he's around someone like me, he doesn't feel overloaded. So he doesn't mind opening up. It often works that way."

Riley's mind rushed along as she tried to grasp what she was hearing. Wesley's condition suddenly made much more sense to her now. He'd felt such empathy for a tormented puppy that it had haunted him for many years—until he'd finally told Riley all about it.

She said cautiously, "Wesley... opened up to me too."

"And why do you think that was?"

Riley thought back to the conversation she'd had with Wesley and wondered...

How can I put our connection into words?

Instead she said to Bayle, "Maybe you can tell me."

Bayle turned his head and looked Riley straight in the eye. "Riley—is it OK for me to call you Riley? I'd like very much for you to call me Kevin."

"That's fine," Riley said.

"As I said before, I've been extremely interested in you for a long time. I'm a student of human nature, after all, and you're... well, a very unique human. I've read everything I could get my hands on about the cases you've solved. And I'm fascinated by your ability to get into a killer's mind. That rare ability you have, that uncanny intuition—my guess is that Wesley relates to it. He thinks of you as a kindred spirit. As do I."

Riley's eyes widened with astonishment.

"Are you saying that I'm... autistic?"

Kevin Bayle shrugged and said, "I wouldn't put it that way. Like I said, I don't like labels. But I think we can both agree that you're not what anyone would describe as normal—or to use a term that I prefer, *neurotypical*. Your experience of the world is different from almost anybody else's. It's so different that you take it for granted—like the way sharks don't know anything else but swimming, so it doesn't occur to them that there's such a thing as standing still. You never stand still, Riley Paige. You don't even think about standing still. That's why I'm fascinated by you."

Riley felt absolutely speechless.

Kevin leaned toward her a little and said, "Riley, I've always wanted to ask you—what's it like? Getting into the mind of a killer,

I mean? Sensing his presence so strongly that you can share his point of view?"

Riley shuddered and said, "It's terrifying. A lot of the time I wish I couldn't do it. But I can, so... I guess you could say it's kind of my duty to make the best use of it I can. But there's always a danger—of becoming a monster myself."

She gulped hard and added, "Sometimes I worry that I *am* some sort of monster. It's hard, keeping those dark parts of my mind hidden from people, protecting people I love from... myself."

Riley suddenly found herself talking freely with Kevin, going into details about cases he'd read about, telling him about specific moments when her terrifying ability came into play. She also talked about things she barely spoke of with anyone else. She described moments when her inner darkness had consumed her, for example when she'd crushed the hand of the young man who had injected April with heroin, or when she and April had pulverized the man who had imprisoned them.

When she finished talking, she felt limp and tired—but also strangely relieved.

It had felt good to talk to someone who really wanted to understand all those terrible things about her...

Someone who would never judge me.

Finally Kevin smiled at her—the first time she'd ever seen him smile, she thought.

He said, "Thank you for sharing all this, Riley. I'm truly grateful—and honored to make your acquaintance at long last."

Without another word, Dr. Kevin Bayle got up from the bench and headed out of the room.

Riley realized that she was no longer surprised by such brusque behavior. It was just his way. Besides, she was pretty sure she knew that he was on his way back to Wilburton House to take care of his patient. She hoped he could continue to help Wesley Mannis.

When Riley walked out of the building, she saw Bill and Jenn sitting in the borrowed car, staring at Kevin as he walked on toward his own vehicle.

Bill looked like he was about to climb out of car and accost Bayle. Then he saw Riley and settled back into the driver's seat.

When Riley got into the car, Bill asked her...

"What happened in there?"

Riley's mind boggled at the question.

How can I begin to explain?

Instead she said simply...

"Kevin Bayle isn't the killer."

"Then who the hell is?" Bill said. "Didn't you get any information out of him at all?"

"He doesn't know anything about it," Riley said, trying not to sound defensive.

As Bill started driving them back into Wilburton, Riley remembered something Kevin had said about Wesley.

"Right now, he doesn't dare even think about what he saw. I don't think he'll ever be able to talk about it."

She felt sure that he was right, which meant that Wesley Mannis was another dead end in their investigation.

Riley let out a sigh of despair.

We're back at square one, she thought.

And they were surely running out of time before the killer claimed another victim.

Chapter Twenty Six

As Bill drove back to the Ramsey Inn, Riley's head was still spinning from her encounter with the brilliant therapist. She was trying to get her mind around what Kevin Bayle had revealed to her when Bill grumbled...

"Are you telling us Dr. Bayle didn't give you any information at all?"

Jenn added, "You sure did spend some time with him. He must have had something to tell you."

He had a lot to say, all right, Riley thought.

And I told him some things as well.

Bayle, who, as it turned out, was himself on the autism spectrum, had revealed something Riley hadn't really understood—that her own mind wasn't exactly normal...

Not "neurotypical."

It was a lot to process. But Riley knew this was not the time to try to deal with it. She needed some time to think it over. She'd known for a long time that she had abilities that most people lacked, but she'd never thought about it as possibly an actual difference in her brain.

She replied to Bill and Jenn, "He didn't tell me anything useful about the case."

Jenn said, "And you're sure he's not the killer himself?"

Riley felt slightly startled by the question. The very idea now seemed utterly impossible to her.

"I'm absolutely sure," she said.

"Could you tell us why you're sure?" Bill said.

Riley stifled a sigh. "You'll just have to take my word for it."

She heard Bill let out a growl.

She knew he didn't like it when she went all cryptic. The truth was, she didn't like it either. He was her best friend, and she liked to think she could talk to him about anything. Maybe she could tell him about the conversation some other time. Or...

Maybe not.

Maybe it was something she should just keep to herself.

Bill said, "Well, Meredith sent the plane for us early this morning. We've left it waiting at Tweed–New Haven for hours now. He was pretty grouchy about our delay when I talked to him back before we paid Wesley Mannis a visit. He's probably furious by now."

Jenn added, "We've got to get packed and get out of here fast. He'll probably be OK when he knows we're on our way back."

Riley's heart sank at that idea.

She said, "But we've got the wrong guy in custody. We all agree on that, don't we? Bruno Young isn't the killer, and we all know it. The real murderer is still out there."

Bill said, "It doesn't matter what we think. The only suspect is locked up. We've got no other leads to follow. There's nobody else to interview. We've got nothing else to do here."

Riley knew there was no point in arguing. After all, Bill was right. She also knew that that they would almost certainly have to fly back here again—probably after yet another murder.

Some unknown person's life was at risk. If she could only figure out some other track to investigate, maybe she should prevent that next murder.

When they got back to the inn, Riley went straight to her room and sat down on the edge of her bed. She knew Bill and Jenn would be ready to go within minutes. But somehow she couldn't make herself pack up her go-bag.

In fact...

I really want a drink.

She opened the room's little refrigerator and looked inside. It was stocked up with soft drinks, nothing alcoholic. She had half a mind to head downstairs to the bar...

Stop it!

She reminded herself that it was still before noon, and the bar probably wouldn't be open. Besides, she ought to know better than to suppose a drink would really make her feel better. Things tended to get out of control when she tried to drink her troubles away.

Don't even think about it, she told herself.

She gazed around at the comfortably decorated room with its flowered bedcover and matching stuffed chair. A watercolor on the wall featured the billowing sails of boats in a regatta. She realized that she had taken no previous notice of these surroundings and that she wouldn't miss them when she left. Maybe it was time to get back to a more practical world where she could actually do some good, perhaps solve somebody else's problems.

With a sigh, Riley picked up her go-bag and went into the bathroom to pack her toiletries.

Then she heard a knock at the door.

It's Bill already, she thought. *Or Jenn.*

Her colleagues must have packed faster than she'd even expected.

She called back impatiently, "Give me just a few minutes."

But then came another knock. This time Riley noticed that the knocking was soft and hesitant...

Not like Bill or Jenn.

Who was it, then?

She walked to the door and called out...

"Who is it?"

She heard a muffled voice on the other side of the door.

"Who is it?" she asked again.

Again came that muffled voice, but she couldn't tell what the person was saying.

Suddenly wary, Riley wondered whether she should have her weapon ready. But when she looked through the peephole, her heart quickened.

Wesley Mannis was standing outside her door.

Riley swung the door open.

"Wesley!" she said. "Come on in."

Wesley shifted his weight from one foot to other shyly for a moment, as if unsure of what to do.

"Come in," she repeated, standing aside.

Then he said, "Thanks," and came on into the room.

He looked around and said, "It looks like you're getting ready to leave. I hope this isn't a bad time."

"No, not at all," Riley said.

She figured that Bill and Jenn and the plane were going to have to wait just a little longer. If Meredith wound up angry, she'd take the blame for her two partners. Meanwhile, she was surprised by Wesley's perfectly normal tone of voice.

"Would you like to sit down?" she asked, offering him the stuffed chair.

Wesley looked at the chair for a moment, as if trying to make up his mind.

Then he tilted his head and said, "No, I don't think so."

Riley couldn't help but smile at his slightly odd response. Then she remembered Kevin Bayle's abrupt departure from the Szymko Aquarium. She'd assumed he was on his way back to Wilburton House.

She asked Wesley, "Does Dr. Bayle know you came here?"

Wesley stood a bit straighter. Riley sensed that he was rather proud of himself.

"Yes he does," he said. He still wasn't making eye contact with Riley, but otherwise he seemed quite self-assured. "So does Dr. Rhind. So does the whole staff at Wilburton House. They're all pleased that I'm doing so much better. They say I can start coming and going on my own again. Dr. Bayle was especially pleased that I wanted to talk to you."

Riley asked, "Did Dr. Bayle drive you here?"

With just a flicker of a smile, Wesley said…

"No, he offered me a ride, but I told him I'd rather call a cab. It feels good to be independent again. I was really going through a hard time for a while."

Then he nodded and said...

"But now I'm better."

Riley was starting to dare to hope. She figured Wesley must have had some good reason to come and see her.

Unless he's just here to be friendly.

The thought suddenly worried her. As happy as she was that Wesley was doing so much better, she really didn't have time to spend just visiting with him. Besides, she wasn't sure she even had the skills to carry on a conversation with him. But what would happen if she asked him to leave? Would that set him back? Might he even have another meltdown? If so, she knew better than to think she could cope with it.

In the meantime, Wesley just stood there, looking around as if he'd forgotten that Riley was in the room. She was just wondering whether to say something when he spoke up.

"I keep thinking about this morning, when you told me about being locked in a cage. I think it was very brave of you to tell me that."

Riley almost said, *"It was nothing."*

But of course, it hadn't been nothing, and telling Wesley anything less than the truth right now was surely a bad idea. She wouldn't have been surprised to learn that Wesley had never told a lie in his life, and he certainly didn't deserve to be lied to, even out of politeness. It had been very hard for Riley to share that trauma with somebody she barely knew, let alone someone whose mind she really didn't understand.

Instead she said, "It was kind of you to listen."

"I was glad to listen," Wesley said.

Wesley fell quiet for a long moment, then added...

"Before you left, I told you... I felt like I was in a cage in the dark, and I couldn't tell you what you wanted to know."

He took a long, slow breath and then continued speaking in his flat, emotionless voice.

"But I feel better now. I don't feel like I'm in a cage anymore. I think I can tell you what I saw."

Chapter Twenty Seven

Riley waited breathlessly for Wesley to speak again. He was still standing, and for a few moments he stared off into space, again shifting his weight back and forth from one foot to the other.

Is this really happening? she asked herself.

Is he going to tell me...?

As she forced herself to be patient, there came another knock at the door—a much sharper knock this time.

Riley fought down a groan of despair.

That's got to be Bill this time.

She really didn't want any interruption right now. She didn't want anything to spoil Wesley's attempt to communicate.

Riley said to Wesley nervously...

"Please sit down. I'd feel better if you do. I'll be back with you in just a moment."

Wesley nodded and obediently sat in the big flowered chair.

She opened the door just a little and saw that both Bill and Jenn were standing in the hallway. She whispered through the door opening...

"You've got to give me more time!"

Bill looked at his watch, then looked at Riley incredulously.

He said, "Riley, we're really, really late."

"What's going on in there?" Jenn asked.

Riley let out a moan of frustration, slipped out into the hallway, and pushed the door nearly shut behind her. Standing with her back to the door, she kept her voice low as she told her partners...

"Wesley Mannis is in there. He says he's ready to tell me what he saw."

Bill and Jenn both stood there with their mouths hanging open.

"Give me just a few minutes, please," Riley said.

Neither of her partners made any objection.

Without another word, Riley ducked back into the room and closed the door. She pulled one of the room's smaller chairs over near Wesley and sat down facing him.

To her surprise, he looked utterly unperturbed, as if he hadn't noticed that any interruption had taken place.

"Now please tell me what you were going to say," she said.

Wesley nodded, and, looking off somewhere over his shoulder, he began.

"It happened on Victoria Street. There was a broken gate at one-forty. I saw a swing on the porch at two-thirty, and another at two-forty-five..."

Riley was seized by an odd feeling of familiarity.

Is this déjà vu?

She could swear that she'd heard Wesley describe exactly those same places before.

She listened as he continued...

"The garage door was open at three-fifty-two like it always was..."

As he kept on talking, she realized—he was repeating almost word for word what he'd said to Dr. Bayle yesterday. She was starting to panic now.

Is that all he's going to tell me? she wondered.

Just exactly the same stuff he said before?

But she knew better than to interrupt his flow of words. He was either going to tell her the whole story or he wasn't. Any effort to force him might lead to disaster. She knew she had to let him do this his own way.

So Riley sat quietly as Wesley continued...

"No cars are allowed to park on Victoria, but there was a new car in the driveway at four-sixty. I didn't see any pedestrians, but I saw the same fluffy black cat that I often see walking around in that neighborhood…"

As she listened, Riley couldn't help but be impressed by the photographic detail of his descriptions. It seemed like everything he saw was permanently imprinted on his memory. She figured he could be a great detective if it weren't for his disability.

He said, "I had to stop to pick up a milk carton that had fallen out of its bin, then I had to run to catch up with the truck, and…"

His flow of words slowed to a stop, and he seemed to turn inward. Riley wondered if maybe he was going to get stuck again while trying to relive his trauma.

But he nodded and said…

"Then the truck and I got to four-sixty-five on Victoria Street."

Riley's breath caught with excitement.

Robin Scoville's address!

Finally looking into Riley's eyes, Wesley said…

"I want you to know, I'm not a peeper."

"I know you're not, Wesley," Riley said.

"It's just that…well, the woman who lived at four-sixty-five sometimes had her lights on at that time of morning. Whenever that happened, she'd be standing right there in her living room at her big window. She wore some kind of cuffs on her arms—they were crutches, I think. I guessed there was something wrong with her legs, although I could never see her legs. She'd look right out at me. And she'd take one arm out of the cuff, and she'd wave at me."

He leaned toward Riley and added…

"So you can see, I'm not a peeper. I just couldn't help noticing her. I always worried that maybe she'd think I was rude, pretending not to see her, not waving back to her. She was just being friendly. But I didn't wave because I'm not supposed to be looking at people in their homes. I'm not supposed to be looking through anybody's window."

"I understand," Riley said.

And indeed, she felt as though she was understanding Wesley better with every word he said. He not only noticed physical details, he was extremely sensitive to people's moods.

He knew she was being friendly.
He was afraid she'd think he was rude.

She remembered something Dr. Bayle had told her about him.

"His empathy is so powerful and overwhelming that he can't control it. It floods through him all the time."

Riley realized now that it must be painful for him to live with that kind of rampant empathy. Small wonder that he tried to shut himself off from the world, tried to stay emotionally disconnected from everyone around him.

He lowered his eyes and said…

"But this time, when she was standing there looking out the window, I saw someone else. It was a man who came in from another room. He was behind her. She was looking at me, not at him. I'd never seen him before. But I figured she at least must have known he was in the house with her. I thought maybe he was…"

Wesley paused, seeming to search for polite words.

"Spending the night with her," he said. "I had no idea…"

He looked off into space, as if slipping into his own world again.

Riley said in a firm but gentle voice…

"Then what did you see?"

He seemed to be struggling with his thoughts now.

"The time before, when I was nine years old, that time I told you about… I was looking outside through a window, when I saw what the boys were doing to the puppy…"

Trying to coax him back on track, Riley said, "But this time you were looking *in*. Please tell me what you saw. What did the man look like?"

Knitting his brow with concentration, Wesley said, "He was taller than she was. He had brown hair, slicked back, parted on the right. And when he walked toward her from behind, he was…"

Wesley fell quiet again, then said…

"He was limping."

Riley felt a tingle of excitement.

"Limping?" she asked. "Are you sure?"

"Yes, I'm sure. He limped toward her through the room. He was moving slowly and he definitely dipped down with every other step."

He limped! Riley thought.

She sensed immediately that this was an important detail, but she didn't have time to consider why.

Wesley continued, "I realized that he must be moving very quietly and I thought maybe he was going to surprise her with a hug. But then he held up something in his left hand. It glittered a little under the light from the ceiling fixture. I thought maybe it was a knife, but it wasn't, it was too thin for that."

An ice pick, Riley realized.

She suspected that no one had ever mentioned to Wesley that Robin Scoville had been killed with an ice pick. In fact, probably no one had talked to him in detail about the murder at all. This gave Riley further assurance that his account was accurate and reliable—not that she'd had any doubts so far.

Wesley said, "Just when she raised her hand to wave at me, I realized he was going to do something bad to her. I raised my own hand and pointed... trying to tell her that someone was behind her. But..."

He gasped for breath and said...

"He stabbed her... in the ear," he said. "The narrow shiny thing went in and out of her ear. And when it came out, she dropped straight to the floor."

He was trembling and gasping now.

"I should have done something," he said in a thick, agitated voice. "I should have..."

He fell silent again, shivering almost convulsively.

"There was nothing you could do," Riley said. "You pointed. You tried to let her know."

He nodded and echoed Riley's words...

"I pointed. I tried to let her know. But it was like with the puppy. There was a window between us. I couldn't... go through the window."

Afraid he was on the verge of another meltdown, Riley said, "Listen to me, Wesley. Take a couple of deep, long breaths. Very slowly. In and out. You're right here with me. Everything's all right."

Wesley inhaled and exhaled slowly.

Then, seeming to recover from his agitation, he said in a calmer voice, "After she fell, the man looked out the window, but I don't think he saw me. I think I had stepped back out of the streetlight."

Riley asked, "Do you think he saw the garbage truck?"

"No, he couldn't have. The truck had driven on while it was happening. The man stood and smiled down at her for a moment. Then he just... turned around and walked back the way he'd come, walked out of the room, and..."

Wesley squinted curiously, as if something had just dawned on him.

"He wasn't limping anymore," he said.

Riley felt that tingle of excitement again.

"Are you sure?" she said.

"I'm sure. He walked out of the room just fine."

He shook his head and said, "After that, I don't remember much. Everything went blank, and the next thing I knew I was back in my room. They told me I'd walked off my job, but that I wouldn't tell them why. I guess I... really didn't want to remember."

Then he slumped in his chair.

"That's all I can remember," he said. "That's all I can tell you. I wish I could have done something to help her."

Riley wanted with all her heart to take his hand and offer him some comfort.

But no, he can't deal with that.

"You didn't do anything wrong," she said.

"Maybe when I got home I should have called the police," he said. "I think that's what you're supposed to do..."

"You were in shock," Riley said. "You were traumatized. You couldn't talk to anybody about it... then. But you talked to *me*, right *now*, and that was very brave..."

And it might save someone else's life, she thought.

He looked thoroughly drained now, but hardly on the verge of a meltdown.

"I'm tired," he said. "I think I should go back to Wilburton House."

Riley briefly wondered whether it might be possible for him to tell her anything else. But she quickly decided that he'd already said everything he possibly could, down to the very smallest detail.

She suggested, "My partners and I can drive you back."

Wesley shook his head. "No, I'll call for a cab. It's important for me to do things like this on my own."

He got up from the chair and walked over to the room phone and started to punch in a number. Meanwhile, Riley opened the door to the hallway, where Bill and Jenn were still standing with anxious expressions on their faces.

Bill said, "Riley, what the hell's been going on in there?"

Where do I begin? she asked herself.

Her own head was buzzing with questions.

She could think of only one thing she could say to her partners for certain.

"We're not flying back to Quantico. Not yet."

Chapter Twenty Eight

Jenn Roston glanced up at Bill. He looked even more flabbergasted than she felt.

As they'd been standing there in the hallway wondering what was going on, Riley had popped out of her room and announced…

"We're not flying back to Quantico. Not yet."

Then Wesley Mannis had come out of Riley's room, spoken to them shyly, and wandered down the hallway to the stairs.

It all boggled Jenn's mind, and she didn't know what to say.

Bill didn't seem to have that problem.

"What are you talking about?" Bill barked at Riley. "What the hell happened just now? Did you and Wesley just solve the case between the two of you?"

"Not exactly," Riley replied calmly.

"Then what's going on?" he asked.

Riley said in a determined voice, "We've got some work to do, that's what's going on. And we've got to do it right here and now."

"But the plane…" Bill began.

"The plane will have to wait," Riley said. "Come on into my room, both of you, and let's get started."

Bill growled, "I'll call Meredith. He's going to have a fit about this."

"That's too bad," Riley said. "I'll call room service. We didn't have breakfast, so we'd better get some food in our stomachs. We'll think better."

Reluctantly, they both followed Riley into her room. As Bill started his phone call, Jenn crossed to the window and looked outside. She could see Wesley Mannis standing down by the curb with his hands in his pockets.

"What's Wesley doing down there?" she asked Riley.

"Waiting for a cab," Riley said. "That's how he got here. He's headed straight back to Wilburton House."

Jenn was thoroughly baffled now.

He's catching a cab?

How could Riley be sure where he was really going?

The truth was, Wesley gave Jenn the creeps. She'd felt that way since the very first time she'd met him. He'd reminded her too much of Gerard, the autistic kid she'd known when she'd been living in Aunt Cora's so-called "foster home."

Now, gazing down at Wesley standing out there, she flashed back to Gerard holding a screwdriver to her throat. He'd cornered her alone in the house and was threatening to rape her. Fortunately, one of the other kids happened to show up, and Gerard had pretended nothing had happened.

The thing that had really scared Jenn was that Gerard hadn't been having a meltdown.

He hadn't seemed frantic or agonized or even angry.

He'd seemed cool and in perfect control of himself.

It had made Jenn wonder just how "disabled" Gerard had really been.

Had he been faking at least some of his autistic symptoms?

That was why she couldn't help but wonder now—was the meltdown Wesley had the day before yesterday even real, or just feigned? And why did Riley seem to trust him so much?

Jenn turned away from the window.

Riley was on the room phone ordering sandwiches while Bill talked to Meredith on his cell phone.

Bill was sputtering over his phone, "I—I know, sir... I'm sorry, sir... Agent Paige seems to really think she's got something—a break in the case, maybe... I'll tell her that, sir."

Bill ended the call, put the cell phone in his pocket, and said...

"Meredith is calling the plane back to Quantico without us. He said other BAU agents need to get to their assignments. And Riley, he, uh... made some rather colorful threats. He said we'd better get some results before the day's over. All our asses are seriously on the line—especially yours."

Riley said, "If we don't get results before the day's over, someone else is liable to wind up dead. I'm more worried about that than I am by Meredith's threats. Sit down with me, both of you."

Jenn knew this wasn't the first time Riley's job had been threatened. In fact, she'd been fired or suspended more than once. Jenn wondered if she herself would ever be so intent on her goals and so sure of her decisions that such threats wouldn't stop her.

Jenn and Bill sat down at a table with Riley.

Bill said, "Riley, you've really left us in the dark. First there was that meeting you had with Dr. Bayle. When are you going to tell us what was up with that?"

"It doesn't matter," Riley said.

"Well, what *does* matter?" Bill demanded.

Riley took a long deep breath and said, "What Wesley told me is what matters. He was finally able to talk about what he saw through the window that morning, when Robin Scoville was killed."

Bill gasped with surprise.

"Was he able to describe the killer?" he asked.

Riley replied, "Somewhat. He said the man was taller than the victim. He had slicked-back brown hair parted on the right."

Bill squinted skeptically and said, "Is that it? That's hardly any kind of description at all. Thousands of guys could fit it."

"I know," Riley said. "But I'm sure it's all he could make out, at least as far as a simple description goes. He was watching through the window from the street, quite a ways off."

Jenn suddenly got a mental picture of Bruno Young, with his beard and his scraggly hair.

She said, "If his description is right, Bruno Young definitely isn't the killer."

Riley nodded and said, "Which is what I've been saying all along. But Wesley said something a whole lot more important."

Riley leaned toward Bill and Jenn and added...

"He also said that the killer walked with a limp."

"A limp?" Jenn asked.

"Yes, but only when he was creeping up on the victim from behind. After he killed her and walked away, the limp was gone."

Jenn wondered...

Does that even make sense?

Bill apparently had the same reaction.

He said, "I don't get it. Why would a killer, or anybody, limp and then not limp?"

"That's what we've got to figure out," Riley said. "But all along, I've been thinking..."

Riley paused, apparently searching for the right words.

"I think the killer is obsessed with imperfection. He picks out his victims because they have... flaws."

Bill drummed his fingers on the table and said...

"Yeah, you said something like that when we were at looking at Ron Donovan's body at Wickenburg Reef. Donovan had a birthmark on his hand and wrist. Robin Scoville was an amputee. And it's like I told you before, the two things just don't compare. They don't add up to anything. Besides, Vincent Cranston doesn't seem to have had any imperfections at all."

Riley's face was tightening with determination.

"It *does* add up," she said. "I can feel it in my gut. And now we know that the killer himself is somehow... imperfect. He limps, at least some of the time."

Jenn felt like she could no longer keep her doubts to herself.

She said, "You're grasping at straws, Riley. For one thing, we don't have any idea if what Wesley said is even true. He might be lying, or he might simply have imagined what he claims he saw. He's mentally disabled. That makes him just about the most unreliable witness we've ever had to deal with."

Riley stared straight at Jenn and said...

"He's not unreliable. And he's not lying."

"How do you know?" Jenn asked.

"For one thing, he's got a photographic memory," Riley said. "For another thing... I just don't think he's capable of telling a lie. He just hasn't got it in him. I'd be surprised if he's ever told a lie in his entire life."

Jenn rolled her eyes and said, "Oh, Riley, come on..."

"That's enough, Jenn," Bill said, interrupting her.

Jenn stared at him, startled by his sharp tone of voice.

Bill said to her, "When Riley says she's sure of something, I've learned to trust her instincts. She knows what she's talking about. And she's right—we've got work to do, right here and now. So let's get to it."

Then there was a knock at the door.

Jenn took the opportunity to hide her confusion. She got up from the table, went to the door, and opened it. An inn employee had arrived with their sandwiches.

As she and her colleagues set the table for both work and lunch, Jenn thought about what Bill had just said...

"I've learned to trust her instincts. She knows what she's talking about."

She found herself amazed and touched that Bill trusted Riley so much. And she knew that Riley felt the same way about him. And...

I feel that way about both of them.

They were, after all, the best friends she had ever had. If it weren't for Riley especially, Jenn surely would have fallen back into Aunt Cora's clutches well before now. But she hadn't. These two great people had been her salvation...

And now I'm free of Aunt Cora for good.

At the realization, a lump formed in Jenn's throat

She told herself sternly...

Don't cry, damn it.

She opened up her laptop computer on the table next to her sandwich and said to Bill and Riley...

"OK, what do you want me to do?"

Chapter Twenty Nine

Dawn Bowen sat curled up on a velvety blue sofa gazing out a huge glass window at the carefully tended grounds outside. She was half-wondering...

Is this a dream?

No, she was sure it wasn't. She'd been asking herself that question over and over again since this whole thing started, and she was perfectly sure it couldn't be a dream. But there was definitely another word for it...

An adventure.

Yes, that's exactly what this must be.

Dawn wasn't used to adventures. She didn't really know how this sort of thing was supposed to go.

She had to admit that this one was off to a thrilling start. It was also just a bit scary, which only made things more delicious as far as she was concerned.

She could still hardly believe she'd invited herself to sit down with a strange man in that outdoor café back in Holloway. She'd never have dared do such a thing just a few short months ago, before she'd had all the work done on her body and face. But now she felt like a new woman.

So I might as well act like one.

She heard him call out to her from the kitchen, "What would you like to drink?"

"A whiskey sour," she said.

"My favorite as well," he said. "I'll make them for both of us. I'll fix us a snack too."

"Thanks, Scott," she said.

She'd sensed from the moment she'd met him that Scott wasn't his real name. That, too, helped make things exciting. She almost wished she hadn't told him her own real name...

Dawn!

God, what a boring name!

Why hadn't she adopted some exotic, foreign name—something Eastern European, maybe...

Irina, Katya, Magda, Masha...

She grinned as she imagined faking a foreign accent, inventing some wild story about her life before coming to America.

It was a silly fantasy, of course. She could never have carried it off.

But this man who called himself Scott—she found him to be the very stuff of fantasies.

As she listened to him working in the kitchen, she remembered how they'd talked for over an hour at the café—almost entirely about her, a subject she couldn't imagine why he'd find so interesting. What could possibly be interesting about the life of a small-town real estate agent, a single woman with few friends who scarcely thought about anything but work?

Nevertheless, he'd coaxed her along her with considerate questions, and she'd wound up telling him everything...

Or almost everything.

She certainly didn't tell him about the surgery, or what life had been like when she'd been plain and overweight. He might have been put off to know all that, and she was glad that he didn't seem to have guessed it, at least not so far.

After lunch, things had gotten really strange and exciting. He'd told her that he wanted to take her home with him—straight from the café, right at that moment.

It had been a scary proposal—almost too scary.

She remembered how they'd left the café and walked a block or so to where his expensive SUV was parked. Before they'd gotten into the vehicle, he'd offered her a large, black silk handkerchief.

"*What's this for?*" she'd asked him.

With a debonair grin he'd replied...

"*A blindfold. Let me help you put it on.*"

"*Why?*"

"*I don't want you to see where we're going.*"

She'd definitely been taken aback by that. But when she'd hesitated, he'd gently, teasingly taken back the handkerchief and started putting it back in his pocket.

"*Too bad,*" he'd said, still smiling. "*I had such a lovely afternoon in mind.*"

Dawn had changed her mind right then and there.

She'd turned around so he could tie the handkerchief around her head. Then he'd helped her gallantly into a back seat of the SUV. She'd already noticed that the vehicle had tinted windows, so probably nobody would see that she was riding around blindfolded with this handsome stranger. She'd figured that was just as well. If she'd been seen by anyone she knew, sooner or later she'd wind up having to make awkward and embarrassing explanations.

Anyway, it had seemed silly to be scared of him. He was well dressed and handsome and had perfect manners. She was sure he couldn't possibly mean her any harm. But he certainly knew how to create a feeling of romantic intrigue.

And she liked that about him.

She liked it a lot.

The drive had been surprisingly long, and she'd had no idea where he might be taking her. Finally the SUV had stopped, and he'd helped her out and taken off the blindfold. She'd gasped with delight when she found herself facing a perfectly charming little house, like something out of a fairytale.

And here she was right now, looking out the window at the surrounding grounds. Even at this time of year, gold and orange mums were still blooming in the little garden just outside the windows. Rows of tall hedges and a grove of trees concealed much of what lay beyond, and she thought the grounds seemed unusually spacious for such a small house.

As she continued to wait for him to return from the kitchen, she wondered what these grounds would look in a few weeks, when the leaves changed colors. And what would they look like in the winter? How would it feel to sit here looking out this window at the snow while a fire roared in the fireplace?

She was starting to entertain a new fantasy—that he'd soon tell her his real name and all about himself, and their relationship would blossom into something more than a brief adventure, and...

Maybe I'll never have to leave this place.

Her fantasy was interrupted by the sound of Scott's footsteps coming from the kitchen. She turned and saw him carrying a silver tray with two drinks and a plate of sliced cheese, olives, crackers, and other treats.

As he walked into the room, she was startled to notice that he was limping.

She asked with concern, "Did you hurt yourself?"

"No, why?" he asked.

"Well, it's just that..."

She shrugged and nodded toward his leg.

His smile widened, and he said, "Oh, that. Just an old... problem that bothers me now and then."

He set the tray on the coffee table in front of her chair and added...

"It will go away very soon."

Chapter Thirty

Riley breathed a sigh of relief. Both of her partners were willing to take the risk of backing her up in spite of the case supposedly being closed. Of course, now the pressure was on Riley herself.

She had to prove that she was right.

If she couldn't do that, she wouldn't be the only one to face Meredith's wrath. She didn't want Bill and Jenn to wind up regretting their loyalty to her.

Meanwhile, both Jenn and Bill were staring at her expectantly. Jenn had just now asked Riley...

"OK, what do you want me to do?"

Jenn's laptop was open on the table in front of her, but Riley had no idea what to tell her to do with it.

She thought for a moment, then said...

"Look, we all know about one big flaw in my theory. Robin Scoville was an amputee, Ronald Donovan had a birthmark. But as far as we know, Vincent Cranston had no physical flaws at all."

Jenn drummed her fingers on the table and muttered...

"As far as we know. How closely has anybody checked?"

Bill shrugged and said, "Well, the medical examiner and his team must have gone over his body pretty carefully."

Jenn asked, "Yeah, but are we talking about something they'd bother to notice? Remember, none of us were exactly impressed when Riley pointed out the birthmark on Donovan's hand and wrist—including the chief medical examiner. But if she's on the right track, we'd better start thinking differently."

Riley couldn't help but smile.

That's what I want to hear.

She thought back to the photos that had been taken of Vincent Cranston when his body had still been at the crime scene. She remembered noticing a certain detail that had fleetingly caught her attention. What had it been?

Riley got a tingling feeling when she realized...

Oh, yeah. His mouth.

His eyes had been open, and his lips had been shaped into an expression that resembled a slightly smirk. It had struck Riley as slightly odd at the time, because facial muscles usually relaxed after someone died. But she'd barely given the matter a moment's thought since then.

She pulled out her cell phone and said to her partners...

"I want to call the chief ME. Maybe he can tell me something. Jenn, find the phone number of the ME's office in Farmington."

Jenn went to work on her laptop and found the number within seconds. Riley made the call and put it on speakerphone so her colleagues could listen in. They all soon heard Alex Kinkaid's familiar gruff but jovial voice.

"Well, if it isn't Special Agent Riley Paige. Calling from Quantico, are you?"

"No," Riley said, "my partners are still right here in Wilburton. Agents Roston and Jeffreys are also on the line."

"Well, isn't that interesting. I thought I'd heard the last of you folks. Didn't you wrap up that ice pick killer case? Don't you have a surefire suspect in custody?"

"We don't think we've got the right man for this one," Riley told him. "We need your help."

Kinkaid chuckled and said, "Just when I was thinking again about retirement. Well, I do like to stay busy. What kind of help do you have in mind?"

Riley thought for a moment, then asked, "Did you happen to notice any physical imperfections on Vincent Cranston's body?"

"Do you mean a birthmark, like the one the fisherman had? I still don't know why you got all excited about that."

"Not exactly," Riley said. "I mean...something about his face, especially his lips."

"Huh! Now that you mention it..."

She could hear Kinkaid thumbing through a file.

Then he said, "I wonder if I could send you folks an autopsy photo attached to an email."

Jenn spoke loudly so Kinkaid could hear her.

"That would be great. I'll give you my email address."

Jenn told him the address, and the three of them ate their sandwiches while they waited. The email with the image came in just a couple of minutes. Jenn turned her computer so they all could look at it.

It was an autopsy close-up of the victim's face. Riley noticed that odd expression again. But as she looked closer she said...

"Chief Kinkaid, are you still on your phone?"

"Right here," came the reply.

"Isn't that a slight scar I see over his upper lip?"

"Yep," Kinkaid said. "He was born with a cleft lip."

Bill asked, "Do you mean a harelip?"

Kinkaid said, "Well, that's an old colloquial term that we prefer to avoid these days, but yes, that's what it is. A cleft lip develops during early pregnancy, when the upper lip fails to fuse properly. In Cranston's case, the cleft was unilateral, a single rift under one nostril. He was lucky. A bilateral cleft is harder to fix."

Jenn asked, "Fix? How?"

"Through surgery. It looks like his cleft was accompanied by a slight deformity of his nose, and also some dental malalignment. Those problems are pretty typical. Cranston probably got the cleft and his nose worked on when he was about three months old, then had some dental work done as he got older. It looks like good work overall. But there was no way the surgeons could avoid leaving a slight telltale scar. He carried that with him all his life."

Riley heard the ME scoff a little. "I still don't see what this could have had to do with his murder—nor why Donovan's birthmark had anything to do with his murder. Who would want to kill somebody over little things like that?"

Riley didn't answer his question. But she could tell by her colleagues' expressions that they now shared her suspicions.

All three victims had some kind of imperfections.

With no other connections of any kind, that one had to mean something.

Riley thanked the ME, who told her to get back to him if she needed any other information. Then they ended the call.

Riley, Bill, and Jenn sat looking at each other for a moment.

Then Jenn said, "OK, now we've got a real theory. We've got a killer who hates physical imperfections, and it doesn't matter whether they're big or small. To him, an amputated leg and a repaired cleft lip are equally intolerable."

"That's right," Riley said. "And my guess is, he considers it sort of a twisted mission to rid the world of such imperfections."

Bill added with a growl, "Meaning he kills anyone who has them. We're lucky he hasn't killed a lot more people already. But the question still remains—how exactly does he pick them out?"

Jenn said, "Maybe he just wanders around from town to town looking until someone stands out. He must stalk them for a while. Then he plans his killings carefully. He learned Vincent Cranston's jogging route, probably stopped him for a friendly chat, then drove the ice pick in his ear. Then he planned his break-in at Robin Scoville's house and killed her. Finally, he knew where to find Ron Donovan fishing yesterday morning."

Bill scratched his chin and asked...

"So what kind of a profile are we getting of the killer?"

Riley thought for a moment, then said...

"He's fastidious, perhaps even fussy. He hates messes. That's why he likes using an ice pick in the particular way he does. One blow carefully placed. He's not really trying to make it look like his victims died of natural causes. He just likes the neatness of that kind of killing—just a trickle of blood, and that's it. It suits him."

"So we are learning something about this character," Jenn agreed.

Bill got up and started to pace.

He said, "All this makes good sense—but only to the three of us. I doubt that we'll persuade Agent Sturman to buy this theory, not while he's still sure he's got the real killer in custody. So the three of us are still on our own."

Jenn added, "What's worse, all the killings have been spread out geographically. He seems to travel around this part of the state. We have no idea where he might strike next. And in terms of a description, we've got nothing except his height and his hair and maybe an occasional limp. How the hell are we supposed to track somebody like that?"

Riley and her colleagues fell into silent thought. Riley got up and walked toward the window and looked outside, letting her mind wander in hopes of hitting upon an idea.

Three victims... three deformities.

It seemed too bad that they hadn't figured out about Vincent Cranston's cleft lip until now. For some reason, they'd assumed that Vincent hadn't had any such imperfections...

But why did we stick with that conclusion?

Now that she thought about it, that seemed odd to her.

Surely there had been some reason they had failed to think outside of that box...

Riley gasped aloud as a realization came to her.

She turned toward her colleagues and said, "Niles Cranston lied to us."

"What do you mean?" Jenn asked.

Riley said, "Do you remember what he said when I asked him if Vincent had any distinguishing mark or imperfections?"

Jenn squinted and replied, "He said his nephew was 'a perfect specimen.'"

"It wasn't true," Riley said. "It was a lie."

Bill's pacing grew more agitated.

"What are you trying to tell us, Riley?" he said. "That Niles killed his own nephew because he had a cleft lip? You're saying he found out he liked it or that it fulfilled him or something, so he went on to pick out two other victims?"

Riley bit her tongue to keep from saying...

"Yes, that's exactly what I'm saying."

She knew Bill had good reason to be skeptical.

But she remembered again Wesley's description of the killer...

"He had brown hair, slicked back, parted on the right."

Of course it was an innocuous description that could fit countless men.

Nevertheless, it *did* fit Niles Cranston.

Bill continued, "Not mentioning his nephew's cleft lip might not even have been intentional. Niles Cranston might barely have been aware of it himself. He said he hardly knew the kid, remember? Or maybe he didn't think it even counted as an 'imperfection.'"

Jenn shook her head and said, "I'm afraid I'm with Bill on this, Riley. I think you're seriously reaching now."

Riley stifled a discouraged sigh. She couldn't blame her colleagues for doubting her about this.

Still, she had a strong gut feeling about Niles Cranston now.

We've got to find some proof, she thought.

And she had a vague idea of how to do that.

She said to Jenn, "I need for you to go online. Find any pictures you can of Niles Cranston."

Jenn sat down at her computer again and clacked away at the keyboard while Bill and Riley stood looking over her shoulder.

After a few minutes, Jenn said, "Wow, this is tougher than expected. I'd always heard that Niles Cranston was reclusive. But it looks like he's gone to a lot of trouble not to be photographed in public at all."

Feeling a sense of urgency, Riley leaned on the table next to Jenn.

There had to be something.

"Go back in time, go back through his life," she said to Jenn. "Keep going until you find something. Anything."

Jenn soon found yearbook photos from Cranston's years at Yale and in prep school—nothing that showed them anything out of the ordinary. Finally she brought up a group picture that had been taken of Niles Cranston's class at an elite private kindergarten. Niles was sitting in the front row of children.

Riley heard her colleagues gasp at what they all saw.

As a little boy, Niles Cranston had had a brace on one of his legs.

Riley's hand shook with excitement as she pointed to the screen and said…

"It's him. Niles Cranston is the killer."

Chapter Thirty One

Riley couldn't stop staring at the photograph on Jenn's computer screen. She realized that both Bill and Jenn were fascinated by it too. The group picture of Niles Cranston and his kindergarten classmates suddenly brought everything into focus.

Cranston had suffered from some kind of disability as a child—something that had affected one of his legs.

Jenn remarked, "Cranston is the only kid in the picture not smiling."

"That's right," Riley said. "Whatever was wrong with his leg, it made him miserable. And he's carried that misery through his whole life. It's a permanent psychic scar."

Pointing at the screen, Riley asked, "So, does either of you have any doubts that he's the killer?"

"I don't think so," Jenn said.

"Me neither," Bill said. "But I've still got lots of questions. You mentioned that Wesley said that the killer walked with a limp. When we met Cranston at his mansion, he didn't limp at all."

"You're forgetting something, Bill," Riley said. "According to Wesley, the killer only limped when he was *approaching* his victim. He *stopped* limping after he killed her."

Jenn nodded and said, "Almost like the murder was some kind of—what? Therapy that made him feel better?"

"Something like that," Riley said. "Anyway, we know that the killer doesn't limp all the time. So it might make sense that Cranston didn't limp when we met him."

Jenn said, "The question is, what do we do now?"

"First things first," Bill said. "We need to let Rowan Sturman know about this. As the FBI agent-in-charge here in Connecticut, it'll be up to him to decide how to proceed. I'll give him a call."

As Bill took out his cell phone and called Sturman, Riley and Jenn huddled over the computer, hoping to find more information about Niles Cranston's childhood condition. A quick search found nothing, but Riley wasn't surprised. The rich and reclusive Niles Cranston had made sure that little about his life could ever be known to the public.

Meanwhile, Bill had been carrying on a contentious-sounding conversation with Agent Sturman.

As he ended the call, Bill grumbled, "That didn't go well. For one thing, Sturman had no idea we were still in Connecticut, and he didn't like being left out of the loop. Also, he thinks Wesley was either imagining things or making things up. He still believes that Bruno Young is the killer. And he sure as hell doesn't like the idea of us accusing the richest man in Connecticut of murder."

Jenn asked, "Should we give Meredith a call?"

Bill grunted and said, "Not a good idea. Believe me, he's in no mood to listen to any of our theories. He's already pissed with us."

Riley suppressed a discouraged sigh.

"The three of us will have to go it alone," she said, then added, "again."

Bill let out a bitter chuckle.

He said, "Well, I guess we ought to be used to going rogue by now. As mad as Meredith is, though, I doubt he'll fire us when all this is over. As long as his boss doesn't find out, we should be OK."

"Walder would definitely love to fire us," Jenn observed. "Especially you, Riley."

Riley nodded. She and Special Agent in Charge Carl Walder had been mutual enemies for a long time, and he'd suspended and even temporarily fired her in the past.

"We won't be fired if we can stop the killer," Riley said. "Meanwhile, I think we should pay Niles Cranston another visit—unannounced this time."

❖ ❖ ❖

A few minutes later, the three of them were driving south toward the Cranston estate. With Bill at the wheel, Riley and her two colleagues discussed lingering worries—including whether they'd even find Niles Cranston at home. If they did, why on earth would he be willing to talk to them? Worse still, what if they spooked him into fleeing?

Jenn got onto her laptop and brought up some satellite photos of the estate. Sure enough, they could readily see that the Cranston estate was fully equipped with a flight pad and what looked like a helicopter.

Riley shook her head worriedly.

She said, "We've got to be careful, or he'll slip out of the country before anyone can stop him. And it'll be our own damn fault."

"But if he is at home, how do we approach him?" Jenn asked. "What do we tell him?"

Riley shrugged and said, "We start off innocently enough—just assure him that we're confident that we've got the right man in custody, and we just need a little more information to help prove our case against him."

"And then?" Jenn said.

"We play it by ear," Riley said. "See if we can trip him up and get him to reveal himself."

Bill chuckled a little and added, "That means we let Riley do the talking, Jenn. Playing mind-games with killers is what she's good at, you know. There's a good chance that she'll get the truth out of him. If we're really lucky, we'll be able to make an arrest right then and there."

Riley appreciated the faith Bill had in her.

I just hope I don't let everybody down.

When they arrived at the edge of the Cranston estate, they found that the enormous front gate was closed. Riley remembered how easy it was to get through last time, when they'd been expected and Sturman had simply identified himself to the guard.

This time they had no choice but to show their badges again. When they did, the guard made a phone call—to the main house, Riley was sure. Then he opened the gate and waved the three agents on inside.

"This isn't good," Jenn said as they drove onto the vast, feudal-like estate with its many smaller structures scattered around the enormous wooded areas. "He's expecting us now."

Riley silently agreed.

So much for the element of surprise.

They pulled up to the castle-like main building, got out of the car, and rang the doorbell. They were greeted by the same elderly, stern-looking butler they had met the last time they were here.

"I just answered a call from the front gate," he remarked. "What business does the FBI have coming here again?"

Riley said, "We'd like to have a few more words with Niles Cranston. We'll try not to trouble him. We're just trying to wrap up a few loose ends."

A worried look crossed the butler's face.

"I'm afraid he's not at home," he said. "He left here early this morning."

"Did he say where he was going?" Jenn asked.

The butler hesitated, then said, "He said he was driving over to Holloway."

Riley and her colleagues exchanged uneasy glances.

"Did he say what his business was there?" Bill asked.

"No, I'm afraid he didn't," the butler said. "He's been coming and going rather a lot these last few days. I believe he sometimes just likes to... drive around and see things."

Riley could hear Bill curse under his breath.

Riley too winced inside at those words.

"I believe he sometimes just likes to... drive around and see things."

She was sure that she and Bill were thinking the same thing...

He's out stalking another victim.

Someone else might be dead already.

Bill muttered to Riley and Jenn, "We'd better drive over to Holloway. God knows how we'll find him there, though."

As Bill and Jenn started to turn away, Riley said to them in a hushed voice…

"Wait a minute. We're not going yet."

She turned and locked eyes with the butler. She sensed that he was deeply troubled.

This man knows something, she thought.

She had to find out what it was.

Chapter Thirty Two

The butler dropped his gaze for a moment, but then he looked up at Riley again. She was positive...

He not only knows something...

He wants to tell us about it.

The last time they'd been here, he'd treated them with icy efficiency. But something was different this time.

In a gentle voice, Riley said, "What's your name, sir?"

The butler bowed ever so slightly and said, "Edward, ma'am. I've been with the Cranston family since before Master Niles was born."

Riley's mind boggled at the thought of family secrets Edward surely knew.

The question was...

How deep is his loyalty?

What will he be willing to tell us?

Riley asked slowly, "Edward, have you noticed whether Mr. Cranston has been behaving... well, strangely lately?"

Edward fell silent, and his gaze seemed to turn inward.

Finally he said, "I believe the three of you should come inside."

Edward led them into an enormous living room and invited them to sit down. Still standing himself, he said, "You asked whether Master Niles has been behaving strangely. Indeed, he has. Something has been troubling him since his pains resumed several weeks ago."

"His pains?" Riley asked.

"Yes, he was born with a clubfoot. He had to wear a brace as a child, until surgery could be performed to correct his... debility.

Unfortunately, the pain recurs from time to time. He never says anything about it, but I can tell because he starts limping."

Riley felt a tingle of excitement.

Limping!

Edward shook his head slightly and said in a hushed voice...

"I fear that his pain...goes much deeper than the merely physical."

"What do you mean?" Riley asked.

"Other children teased and...shunned him. Worse still, his own father tormented him about it. 'A Cranston must be perfect,' the old Master Lew said. 'You're a hopeless addition to the family.' Even after the leg was corrected by surgery, his father wouldn't let the matter go. He kept railing against his son's 'imperfection'—especially whenever the pain returned and the poor boy couldn't help but limp."

When Edward fell silent again, a question crossed Riley's mind.

"Did anything happen to *trigger* his recent limping?"

"I believe so," Edward said. "About a month ago, his nephew Vincent came east to start college at Yale. Vincent comes from the West Coast branch of the family, and I can't remember that Master Niles had ever met him before. Once Vincent got here and Master Niles did meet him, he fell into a strange, brooding mood."

Riley asked, "Was it on account of Vincent's cleft lip?"

Edward looked surprised at the question.

"Why, yes, I'm sure that was the case. Master Niles took to limping again, and he wandered around the house muttering to himself...about his nephew's 'imperfection.'"

Edward took a long, slow breath, as if to gather up his resolve.

"Then Vincent died, so suddenly and strangely. Master Niles took it calmly—too calmly, I thought—and his limp disappeared for a short time. And yesterday I heard on the news that Vincent had been murdered—with an ice pick. Also that two other victims were then murdered in the same way. And all this while Master Niles has been coming and going, and limping and not limping, and he's always been such a troubled soul..."

The man shuddered deeply and added...

"I haven't known what to believe. But I'm glad you're here."

Bill asked, "Are you sure he didn't say anything at all about his business in Holloway? Anything about what he might do there or where he might go?"

"No, he said nothing about that," Edward said.

Then Jenn asked, "Edward, are you sure he's still in Holloway? Are you sure he hasn't come back to the estate?"

That's a good question, Riley realized.

Edward squinted and said, "I don't think he could have come back into the mansion without my knowing it, but...

He thought for a moment, then said, "Let me check."

Then he took a walkie-talkie out of his jacket and stepped aside and spoke into it for two or three minutes. Finally he came back toward his visitors and said...

"The gatekeeper says that Master Niles drove back here a little while ago. I also talked to the household staff, and he's definitely not in the mansion."

"Where might he be now?" Riley asked.

Edward said, "I'm afraid I have no idea. As you know, the estate is very large."

Riley stood up and said...

"Edward, you've got to help us find him. I think you understand how urgent this is."

Edward had gone pale now, almost as if he were in shock.

The truth is sinking in, Riley thought.

"Did you hear me?" she said.

"Y—yes," Edward stammered. "It—it should be possible, but it might take some time. In addition to the staff right here in the house, the estate as a whole employs over a hundred people. They're scattered all over the grounds. I'll gather the household staff together, and we'll all start making calls until we find out where he is."

Riley stifled a discouraged sigh.

This could take a long time.

Then something crucial dawned on her...

She said to Edward said, "Make your first call to the landing pad. Tell the staff to alert you if he turns up there. And talk to the helicopter pilot. Tell him not to take Niles off the grounds."

Edward's eyes were wide with alarm now.

He said, "But if Niles orders the pilot to fly him out—"

Riley interrupted sharply, "That can't happen. Make sure the pilot knows that."

Edward nodded mutely, then started making calls.

Wearing his bathrobe and slippers, Niles sat on the bed listening to Dawn singing in the bathroom.

He was worried now.

I should have planned this better.

This isn't like the other times.

After he and Dawn had finished their drinks, they had started to kiss passionately. Looking back now, Niles wasn't sure who had initiated it, although the woman had obviously been very eager.

Then Dawn had coyly suggested that they take turns in the bathroom to get undressed for bed. Niles had taken the first turn, and when he returned, Dawn went into the bathroom. She'd taken along a bathrobe and slippers that were kept in the house for visitors.

She was in there right now, singing cheerfully, apparently taking some time to get ready.

Meanwhile, Niles felt desperately unsure of what would happen next.

Was he really going to make love to this woman before he killed her?

Was he capable of doing such a thing?

Things seemed to be slipping out of his control.

And he hated feeling like he couldn't control things. The other three killings had been so swift and clean and efficient. When he'd met his nephew on the jogging path, the young man had naturally stopped to talk to him—and Niles had plunged the ice pick into his ear with one swift, decisive motion.

Before he'd planned and carried out that act so smoothly, he'd never given any thought to killing anyone. Such a scene had never seemed conceivable in his well-ordered life.

But he'd gotten immediate and deep satisfaction at the deed. He'd experienced a truly profound sense of righteousness.

He hadn't even been surprised when his foot stopped aching. That had seemed perfectly in keeping with the beauty of his deed.

How wonderful it had felt to rid the world of his nephew's imperfection!

Even his father might have been proud of him for that!

After that first ecstatic experience, how could he help wanting to do it again … and again …?

He had no regrets at all about the young woman and the fisherman. But he was starting to realize he should have known better than to take a different course with this young woman—to improvise, as it were, and see how events played out.

Now everything seemed vague and uncertain.

All he knew for sure was that, one way or the other, he was going to have to kill her.

Fortunately, the ice pick was ready and waiting in the nightstand drawer.

But then, after he'd done it, once she was dead …?

He shuddered to realize that he'd be faced with a problem he hadn't had to deal with the other three times…

How to get rid of the body.

At that moment, the singing stopped, and the woman came out of the bathroom wearing a bathrobe and slippers. She smiled as she began to walk toward him, but when she reached out to join him in an embrace, he said …

"Stop right there."

Her smile faded and she stood still.

His heart was pounding so loudly he could hear it, and he almost wondered if she could as well.

He said, "Take off your robe."

She looked startled for a moment, then smiled again, apparently taking pleasure in his command. She let the bathrobe fall to the ground, and she stood naked before him except for her slippers.

"Turn around," he said.

She obeyed, and he got up from the bed and knelt behind her.

She gasped sharply when he touched one of the scars in the bends of her knees and said...

"You've had surgery."

"Y-yes," she stammered.

"Here and elsewhere," he said. "Up on your back. Your stomach."

He stood up and stepped in front of her. "On your face too," he added.

She hastily reached down and picked up the bathrobe and put it back on, then stared back at him silently.

He asked her, "Do you feel better now? Less... imperfect?"

She said nothing, but she looked shocked and stricken and sad.

Why won't she reply? he wondered.

He had many more questions he wanted to ask her.

Was she teased as a child for chubbiness and plainness?

Was she shunned—not only in childhood, but in adulthood as well?

Most of all, he wanted to know...

Doesn't she understand she hasn't fixed anything?

Doesn't she know that she's nothing more than a living, breathing flaw who has no reason to exist?

Before he could utter any of these thoughts, the room phone rang. He walked over to the phone and picked up the receiver and heard Edward's voice.

"Master Niles? Are you there?"

With a jolt, he realized...

Edward mustn't know.

He hastily hung up the phone without saying a word and just stood there for a moment, shaken by the intrusion.

Then he heard a soft scurrying sound behind him.

He turned and saw Dawn darting out of the room.

"Stop!" he commanded.

But when he started to pursue her, his foot was seized with a fierce cramp of pain that almost brought him to his knees.

He heard Dawn's fluttering footsteps as she continued downstairs, then heard her opening the front door as she rushed outside.

Neither the woman nor his own body were obeying his orders.

He opened the night table drawer and took out the ice pick, then limped across the room, commanding himself…

Ignore the pain.

You've got to catch her.

But then his pain eased a little as something occurred to him.

He'd designed the gardens surrounding this house himself, and they were vast and mazelike…

And I know my way much better than she does.

Chapter Thirty Three

Riley and her colleagues waited as Edward went into action, calling his five-person household staff together and giving them orders, assigning calls for everyone to make as they tried to contact the personnel all over the estate. His energy, efficiency, and authority were impressive.

And I'm glad he's on our side, Riley thought.

She knew it couldn't be easy for a man who had served the Cranston family loyally for decades to suddenly turn against his current master. She didn't get the feeling that Edward hated Niles Cranston. But the butler had made it clear that he did pity Cranston for his childhood pain, and that he knew what kind of scars that pain had left behind...

And he understands what Cranston might be capable of.

As the room buzzed with servants talking on their cell phones, Riley fought back her rising impatience. She hoped Niles Cranston wouldn't realize that she and her colleagues were here on his estate—and that his own servants were trying to assist them in his apprehension.

He might try to escape by helicopter.

Of course, Edward had already called the landing-pad staff and the pilot, warning them not to let Cranston get away. But Edward couldn't make any promises about what they might actually do.

After all, Cranston himself wielded the ultimate authority here.

In the midst of all the chatter, Edward came hurrying toward Riley and her colleagues.

"I think I've found him," he blurted.

"Where?" Riley asked breathlessly.

Edward said, "I just called the main guest house. Someone picked up the phone and put it down again without saying a word. Nobody on our staff is supposed to be there—and besides, none of them would hang up like that."

Riley, Bill, and Jenn exchanged quick glances. Riley could see that her colleagues shared her surge of hope.

Bill said to Edward, "How do we get to this guest house?"

Edward says, "It's only a couple of minutes' drive from here..."

He rattled off some succinct, crystal clear directions.

The agents rushed out to their car.

With Bill driving, they soon arrived at an area where gardens divided by tall hedges spread out before them. The hedges blocked much of the view, but Edward had told them that the guesthouse lay at the very center of this complex network of gardens.

It's almost like a maze, she thought.

Finally they arrived at the house itself. A black SUV was parked outside—Cranston's own vehicle, Riley felt sure. The car appeared empty, but the front door of the house was standing wide open.

"I don't like the looks of this," Bill said.

"I don't either," Jenn said.

All three drew their weapons.

Riley called into the house...

"Niles Cranston, this is the FBI. We just want to talk with you, ask a few more questions. We think we may have a lead concerning your nephew's murder."

When no reply came, gave Bill and Jenn a silent signal to stick together as they searched the house.

In the living room, the first thing Riley noticed was a silver tray with a couple of empty glasses and a plate with leftover snack food.

He's not alone.

Was he here with another victim?

Was somebody dead already?

This whole scene didn't seem logical to her. So far, the killer had committed his murders in a much less complicated manner.

He'd simply approached and attacked. But what exactly had he been doing here? Had he been seducing his next victim?

It seems out of character, she thought.

But then, this monster had been changing his MO all along. He'd broken into Robin Scoville's house in the middle of the night, but he had approached his other two victims more casually. And after killing his nephew, he'd seemed to switch to killing strangers. His only consistency was in his choice of a weapon and how he'd used it.

Riley and her colleagues checked all the first-floor rooms, then crept quietly upstairs.

A single woman's bedroom slipper lay abandoned on one of the steps.

Riley's heart was pounding now.

This didn't look good at all.

She picked up the slipper, and Bill and Jenn followed her the rest of the way up the stairs.

When they went into the large bedroom, Riley saw that the covers on the bed were turned down, but it didn't look like anyone had actually been in that bed.

Bill checked the bathroom and called back...

"There are clothes in here—a man's and a woman's. It looks like they both got undressed."

And then what happened? Riley wondered.

She paused and tried to imagine how things might have unfolded. She reminded herself...

He's seeking out victims with imperfections.

That meant that the woman must surely have some distinguishing characteristic that had disturbed him.

Had that flaw been all the more apparent once she was naked?

For a moment she had a hazy sense of connection with the killer...

He couldn't resist talking to her about it.

He just had to point it out.

And that had been weird enough to frighten his intended victim.

Riley held out the abandoned slipper and said to her colleagues, "She ran away from him. She lost this slipper as she dashed down the stairs."

Another glimpse of the killer's mind revealed...

"He took off after her. Limping, but..."

Bill finished her thought. "In those intricate gardens, he's liable to catch up with her anyway."

Jenn added, "If he hasn't already. And killed her."

"We've got to spread out and search," Riley said.

The three agents dashed down the stairs and out of the house.

Weapons in hand, they headed off in different directions.

Riley followed a path that wound among small gardens that flowered with late-blooming roses and other blossoms. Hedges too tall to see over separated the gardens and blocked her view of anything ahead. As she turned one corner, she came upon an unoccupied bench. After another turn she saw an equally empty swing.

These well-tended grounds had been designed for private or companionable contemplation of nature's beauty. Now its twists and barriers were likely to be hiding a horror scene.

As she rounded another corner, Riley was startled to encounter a human form.

It was just a statue, a naked woman holding a jar.

With every step, she felt almost overwhelmed by the sheer difficulty of this hunt. How on earth were they going to find anyone in this maze?

Especially someone who doesn't want to be found?

She was afraid that one of the people she searched for might be already dead. At any turn, she might stumble across the woman's nearly naked corpse.

And Cranston might be already gone. He would easily find spare clothes. For all she knew, he had already gotten to the landing pad. Fortunately, she hadn't seen or heard a helicopter flying away.

Then she rounded a hedge and found herself facing them—

Cranston and a young woman, both of them wearing bathrobes.

And in that moment, a gleam of metal caught Riley's eye...

The ice pick.

He was holding it to the terrified woman's ear.

Cranston looked frightened himself—which Riley knew only made him all the more dangerous.

He barked at her, "Put down the gun, Agent Paige. If you don't, I'll stab her—and she'll be dead before she hits the ground."

Riley mentally calculated the risk of firing at him. But she didn't dare. He was holding the woman's body so that it shielded his own. And his arm was tense, ready to strike.

She stooped and put her gun on the ground.

Cautiously, she stood back up and said...

"This is hopeless. You know it. There are two more agents combing the area. You'll never get out of these gardens."

Cranston was shaking all over now.

"What makes you think I care?" he said. "You don't understand what this is all about, do you? You don't understand why I'm doing this."

Riley said, "Maybe you'd like to tell me."

Cranston let out a grim chuckle. "Oh, no. No mind games, Agent Paige. You can't manipulate me. I understand you better than you realize. You've got your own scars, don't you? You can't live the life you've lived without gathering your share of wounds—both inside and out."

Riley felt a strange, unexpected shiver.

He's absolutely right.

He was playing mind games with *her.*

And if she wasn't careful, he could win.

"Put down the ice pick, Niles," she said.

"Oh, I will, gladly," he said with a sneer. "But only after she's dead. And I'll have only one regret—that you won't be my final victim. I'd been hoping for that ever since we first met. But I'm afraid it's not to be. How sad."

Riley kept her eyes focused on his, afraid to divert her glance for even a second.

If she could keep his crazed mind focused on her...

But what could she do except postpone the inevitable?

Sooner or later, her gaze would weaken, and that would be the end of it.

Just then she heard a clatter of footsteps running on the trail behind her.

Bill, she thought. *Or Jenn.*

One or both of them must have heard their voices.

And at the sound, Niles Cranston glanced aside.

The ice pick in his clenched fist drifted a few inches away from the woman's ear.

Riley had no time to think…

Now!

She charged forward and threw herself bodily against both the man and his hostage.

All three of their bodies tumbled to the ground.

A fierce pain stabbed through her back.

The ice pick!

Riled writhed and rolled to one side, only to realize that she could no longer breathe.

The pain was overwhelming.

In another instant Niles Cranston had straddled her, the ice pick still clutched in his fist.

He was aiming it toward her ear.

Frantically, Riley twisted her head, trying to keep him from getting a clear thrust.

But she was weakening, and the world was losing focus…

It's hopeless.

Riley was certain she was going to die.

Then a shot rang out.

And everything went black.

Chapter Thirty Four

As Riley felt herself waking up, she strained for a moment to remember...

Where am I?

The nightmare she'd been through seemed as though it had happened just moments ago.

First there had been the mad tangle of bodies when she'd thrown herself at both Niles Cranston and his intended victim, then the terrible pain as the ice pick plunged between her ribs, then her certainty that she was going to die, and then the sound of a gunshot...

And then?

Now she heard the sound of a familiar voice...

"Mom..."

She opened her eyes and saw April standing in front of her, smiling.

Oh, yes, she realized.

I'm home again.

Now she remembered everything much more clearly.

The gunshot had been from Bill's pistol. He'd shot Niles Cranston a split second before he could plunge the ice pick into Riley's ear.

The next day, when she'd awakened in a hospital bed in D.C., Bill and Jenn had told Riley what all had happened after she'd lost consciousness.

Bill had aimed squarely at the center of Niles's chest, and Niles had died within seconds. Then Riley had been flown to the hospital by an emergency helicopter. Fortunately, the ice pick hadn't hit her heart or any arteries, so she was soon on the mend, and she was allowed to go home three days later.

And here she was right now, looking into her daughter's eyes…

Such a beautiful sight.

Life certainly did seem to be especially precious right now.

She was still bandaged, but was no longer restricted to her bed. In fact, she was comfortably propped up on the sofa in her family room, where she had dozed off for a little while. Her family had been seeing to her every need, and even spoiling her more than a little.

April stroked her cheek and said, "Mom, I'm sorry to wake you, but Blaine's here."

Riley almost laughed, but quickly remembered how much it still hurt to do that.

"Again?" she said hoarsely.

Actually, it still hurt to even talk.

"Again," April said, chuckling. "I figured you'd want to see him."

Riley smiled and nodded. Blaine had spent many hours at her bedside in the hospital. And since she'd been home, he'd stopped by every day.

April escorted Blaine into the family room. He pulled up a chair next to the sofa and sat down, then took her hand gently and said…

"Wow, you're looking better all the time. The color has returned to your face. You look more and more like your old self."

"Blaine, I'm doing fine," she said. "You don't have to keep coming around all the time."

"Yes, I do," Blaine said.

His smile faded, and a look of sadness crossed his face.

He said, "I guess I haven't told you—while you were in the hospital, I was desperately afraid of losing you."

Riley felt a twinge of sadness too.

She was sorry to have caused so much worry to the people she loved.

"Oh, I'm tough, Blaine. I've been through worse. It's just taking me a little longer this time to get back on my feet. I should be able to go back to work in another week."

Blaine's eyes widened, and his mouth dropped open a little.

"Back to work?" he said.

Riley was disturbed by his obvious disappointment. Hadn't he realized that she'd want to get back to work as soon as she possibly could?

Blaine lowered his eyes and said...

"Riley, I've got to be truthful. This has been..."

His voice faded away, but Riley had a feeling she understood at least some of what he wanted to say...

It's been hard.

Maybe too hard.

Blaine had been supportive of her career for quite some time. He had even acted courageously once when her job had put him and her family in terrible danger. But Riley knew that being in a relationship with a BAU agent wasn't easy for him. Had he finally reached his breaking point?

Riley felt a lump in her throat as she wondered...

Can we go on like this?

She squeezed his hand and said, "I guess we've got some things we need to talk about."

"Yeah," Blaine said, his own voice thick with emotion. "Not right now, though. Sometime soon."

Riley's cell phone rang. She saw that it was on the coffee table and picked it up to see who was calling.

"It's Bill," she told Blaine.

Blaine nodded and said, "I'll go and let you talk."

Riley wanted to protest and tell him she wouldn't talk long, and that he should stay awhile longer, but...

No, it's best this way.

Blaine got up and headed for the front door, and Riley answered the phone.

"I'm just checking in," Bill said.

"You've been doing that a lot," Riley said.

In fact, Bill had been spending almost as much time with her as Blaine.

Bill said, "Yeah, well. You're kind of stuck with me. It's a partner thing, you know."

Riley smiled. It was nice to have a man in her life who was simply a friend. And right now, "partner" sounded like a very nice word.

Riley said, "I'm doing great, but I'm tired of lying around. Tell me you've got a new case for us to work on."

Bill laughed.

"Riley, I hate to remind you, but you're on leave. You need some time to get better."

Riley sighed and said, "So people keep telling me."

"Anyway, I just got another call from Meredith. He keeps asking how you're doing."

Riley said, "I hope you told him I'm as ornery as ever."

"Oh, he knows that already," Bill said with a chuckle.

Riley was touched by Meredith's concern. He'd actually come to the hospital to visit her and congratulate her on a job well done. For once, he wasn't angry with how Riley and her team had conducted themselves. After all, despite testing his patience a good bit, they'd done things by the book this time—or very nearly so.

Then Bill added…

"Oh, and get this. I also got a call from Carl Walder. He sends you his best wishes. He says you did a great job and hopes you'll be back at work soon. I think maybe he's got a commendation in mind for you."

Riley was truly surprised now.

"I must be dreaming," she said.

"Weird, huh? Well, you sound tired, so I'll let you get some more rest."

Riley thanked him and ended the phone call.

She lay there alone in the family room thinking about that uncomfortable visit from Blaine. She wondered—what might it take to keep their relationship together? Should she pursue some other line of work—private investigation, maybe?

No, she thought. *I'm a BAU agent. I can't be anything else.*

And it came at a price.

Life had certainly not worked out the way she'd expected many years go.

She found herself remembering when she was young and had fallen so madly in love with Ryan Paige, and all the bright hopes she'd had for their relationship. It made her sad that it had ended so badly. While Ryan certainly deserved his share of the blame for the failure of her marriage, she had to wonder how much of a toll her work had taken on things between them.

And what was going to become of Ryan now?

She still cared about him enough to worry about him. He'd called her once when she'd been in the hospital, but he'd sounded terrible—worse even than she'd felt.

Is he going to be OK? she wondered.

She hoped he could find his way out of the mess he'd made out of his life.

Her musings were interrupted when Gabriela, Jilly, and April came into the family room with a plate full of treats. She spent a little while eating and chatting with them and trying not to hurt herself by laughing at their jokes. But she tired quickly and soon excused herself to go upstairs to her bedroom.

As she walked into the room, she saw a small square package sitting on her bed.

She remembered April telling her that something had arrived for her from Kevin Bayle, and she had told April to leave it in her room. Now she picked up the package and walked over to her desk, wondering what she'd find inside.

As soon as she'd gotten home, she'd called both Kevin and Wesley to thank them for all the help they'd given her. Those conversations had been predictably brief and laconic. Neither Kevin nor Wesley was much of a talker. But Kevin had mentioned sending her a get-well present.

When she unwrapped the package with eager fingers, she was surprised at what she found inside...

A gyroscope!

Seeing the little toy made her feel happy. She wasn't sure why.

She threaded the string into the hole in the gyroscope's axis, wound the string carefully, then pulled it to send the wheels spinning on the top of her desk.

She was surprised to feel a pleasant calmness settle over her.

A memory also came back of the gyroscope she'd played with as a little girl.

Now she realized—she'd used that fascinating toy to take her mind off of the miseries of her own troubled childhood, especially her father's emotional cruelty and verbal abuse. How would she have gotten through those times without that magical toy?

Might this new gyroscope offer her similar comfort in times to come?

If so, what did that say about her?

She remembered something Niles Cranston had said to her during their fatal confrontation.

"You can't live the life you've lived without gathering your share of wounds—both inside and out."

It was true, of course.

But what other life could she expect to live?

Normality just didn't seem to be in the cards for her.

She also remembered Kevin telling her that she was hardly "neurotypical," that her experience of the world was so different from everybody else's that she wasn't even aware of it, that she took it for granted.

She was like a swimming shark, Kevin had said…

"You never stand still, Riley Paige. You don't even think about standing still."

The gyroscope slowed and toppled over onto the desktop. She picked it up and threaded the string through its eye again, eager to watch it spin some more.

She wondered—what else did she still have to learn about herself?

Of all the mysteries she'd had to face and solve, it now occurred to her that perhaps the greatest mystery of all was her own mind.

Now Available for Pre-Order!

ONCE MISSED
(A Riley Paige Mystery—Book 16)

"A masterpiece of thriller and mystery! The author did a magnificent job developing characters with a psychological side that is so well described that we feel inside their minds, follow their fears and cheer for their success. The plot is very intelligent and will keep you entertained throughout the book. Full of twists, this book will keep you awake until the turn of the last page."
—Books and Movie Reviews, Roberto Mattos (re Once Gone)

ONCE MISSED is book #16 in the bestselling Riley Paige mystery series, which begins with the #1 bestseller ONCE GONE (Book #1)—a free download with over 1,000 five star reviews!

A serial killer is striking seemingly at random, first killing a man in his 50s, then a woman in her 50s. The only thing that links them is the lone souvenir he took: a dining chair.

What is the meaning? Are the murders random after all?

FBI Special Agent Riley Paige must fend off her own demons and her own dysfunctional family life as she races against time to enter the mind of a diabolical killer who is sure to strike again.

Will she stop him in time?

An action-packed psychological suspense thriller with heart-pounding suspense, ONCE MISSED is book #16 in a riveting series—with a beloved character—that will leave you turning pages late into the night.

ONCE MISSED
(A Riley Paige Mystery—Book 16)

Did you know that I've written multiple novels in the mystery genre? If you haven't read all my series, click the image below to download a series starter!

Made in the USA
San Bernardino, CA
28 March 2020